The Murdered Metatron

Book 1

By
Suzanne Madron

Copyright 2018 Suzanne Madron

No part of this work may be used without the author's express written permission.

Any and all character descriptions contained in this book are a work of fiction and not meant to resemble persons living or dead. Likewise places and events described herein are also a work of fiction.

The author is not liable for any misinterpretation nor misrepresentation of this work.

No angels or demons were harmed during the writing of this story.

Acknowledgements:

Thank you to the readers of the world.

Author page:

Suzi M:
https://www.facebook.com/SuziMOfficial.

Additional works by the author can be found on Amazon.com

Prologue

John Smith looked at his silent phone and tried to scratch his back. It had always itched for as long as he could remember–which was not a particularly long time–and his extensive collection of back-scratchers was no help. He had spent hundreds of dollars he didn't have on massage sessions where he asked only that the masseuse scratch him as hard as they could. Sometimes with a fork.

He took out his favorite tool, a serrated knife tied securely to a stick and began to run the teeth over his reddened flesh. He had been to countless dermatologists and doctors, and all seemed to say the same thing: potentially a result of the accident that had left him in a coma for two weeks. After the coma, he woke with no memory of who he was and with the only identifying marks being two long scars running the length of either side of his back. They itched like hell, dammit.

As a means of becoming a productive member of society and to support himself after his initial awakening and subsequent failure to draw family interest in his well-being despite thousands of media ads with his picture and description spread around Gettysburg, Pennsylvania and the surrounding cities of Baltimore, Harrisburg, York, Pittsburgh, and Philadelphia, John Smith worked to get his private investigator's license. His first cases were pity cases, a small town trying to help the underdog make a start. Gradually, those cases dried up and the money he had put into savings for a rainy day was now being eaten up paying the rent, electricity, and phone for his office space–an office space he'd recently begun using as an apartment, since the hospital told him it was time to leave the nest.

He glanced at the phone one more time then turned to the stack of newspapers that outlined his accident. It was referred to as an "accident" because he had come out of his coma with no memory and thus no way to confirm or deny the suspicion he saw in everyone's eyes. The details and those looks told him he had tried to commit suicide by jumping off a bridge and into a river.

The devil was in the details, as always. The only

snag in his theory was that there had been no note, and the bridge wasn't a very high bridge–certainly not high enough to kill him from the jump alone. The rocks beneath the surface of the water had done at least part of the job the fall hadn't accomplished; they'd left the two long scars down his back as a souvenir.

He scratched at the scars again as he read the specifics over one more time, cross-referencing with his notes. "Unidentified Man Falls From Bridge" and "Man Who Fell From Bridge Still in Coma". Not much coverage, he thought bleakly. But then if his life had been worthless to him at one point, how could he expect more from the media?

With a growl he threw the papers into the trash and stared up at the ceiling. He prayed someone would hire him soon.

Pazuzu was tired. He glanced up briefly from his ponderings as a man exited the shadows of the doorway across the street and splashed through puddles of streetlight.

"That is the one," Pazuzu's companion hissed.

With a sigh, Pazuzu snuffed out his cigarette in the palm of his hand. He had hoped they would be able to lurk a bit longer; opportunities for outings were few and far between in Hell.

"Are you sure?"

"Of course I am sure. He wears an overcoat."

"Very well," Pazuzu said.

He pushed away from the cool concrete of the building they had chosen several hours before as a perfect lurking spot and a charred outline was left on the wall in his wake. The smoke emanating from the outline smelled of fire and brimstone.

Pazuzu had his doubts about his companion's positive identification of their target based solely on the man's attire, but remained quiet. He had not been topside for many years, and who was he to argue that the man might not, in fact, wear an overcoat? They had watched all the movies from Hollywood to make sure they would fit in, and in the movies the detectives all wore overcoats. The demons followed the man in the overcoat for several blocks before the man stiffened and turned when Marduk stumbled over a large bit of trash. When the man saw them, they grinned at him from the darkness and ran toward him. With a cry of terror the man pulled a glinting metal object from beneath his overcoat and aimed it at them.

Pazuzu paused with a feeling that was more instinct than foreknowledge gripping his insides. His companion was less cautious and unused to the ways of humans. Pazuzu had learned during the Inquisition that humans were bold when they had a weapon, and from the way the man stood, the demon knew the metal object had to be a weapon. There was a loud bang and flash from the object and Pazuzu's companion flinched backward, clutching at his chest where a heart might have beaten.

"Hellfire and brimstone! That *hurts*!"

The human unleashed the weapon again, this time at Pazuzu, and the demon sidestepped the projectile.

He shook his head at the man in disapproval and the man ran. The demon turned his attention back to his companion, who was writhing on the ground. He glanced up at the fleeing man and decided to use the human's escape as an excuse to return to the waking world. As it was, he was not entirely sure that the human was the one they were seeking.

"Are you hurt, Marduk?" he asked.

His companion glared up at him, silver blood glinting over carnivorous teeth. "Of *course* I'm hurt! What *was* that thing?" the demon snarled as he climbed to his feet.

Pazuzu shrugged. "I am unsure. Possibly one of those "guns" we viewed in the films? Luckily, it was a small one."

"*Small*? I assure you, the pain is not small."

Again, Pazuzu shrugged. "You must be more careful when dealing with humans," he said. "They may seem incapable of harming our kind, but they are dangerous to both themselves and to us."

"Lesson learned," Marduk hissed and wiped silvery blood from the front of his shirt. "Damn it. I liked this shirt," he said with an angry pout.

Pazuzu shook his head and removed a soft pack of cigarettes, tapping a cigarette from the open portion of the pack and inserting it between his thin lips. He flicked the long fingernails of his right hand together and flames sprang up to meet the tip of the cigarette. He inhaled deeply and stared in fascination at the plumes of exhaled smoke.

"How long has it been since you were last topside?" Marduk asked him.

Pazuzu squinted up at the night sky, considering

the question. He took another drag on his cigarette, exhaled, and responded, "A century or more? Time is meaningless to me."

"So how did you know to avoid the weapon?"

The demon smiled and his wings twitched beneath his shirt.

"When a human aims something at one's person, one can safely assume it is a weapon. One should therefore make haste to avoid remaining in direct alignment with the dangerous end."

"Good advice," Marduk said as he lit his own cigarette. He gave a cough of anger as smoke swirled out of the hole in his back and chest where the bullet had pierced him.

"Damnation," he muttered, "When we catch that little prick I'm going to kill him."

"I believe we need to remember our mission, Marduk. And I do not think the human with the weapon was our target. We may need to try a different route to catch our man."

CHAPTER I

John Smith was not a run-of-the-mill P.I. At least *he* didn't think so. His exaggerated opinion of himself had not been paying the bills since he woke from his coma, however, and the ad that told the masses how good he was had only helped to get the electricity turned off in the end. Luckily, he kept office hours during the afternoon and his office had a southern exposure, so lighting was not a problem…but coffee was.

He glanced up from the magazine he kept in his desk drawer for occasions when he wanted to appear busy. "In case a client walks in," he told himself. The phone on his desk rang a second time and it took a moment longer for the sound to register in his brain. On the third ring, he picked it up and held it to his ear. He was too surprised to say anything.

"Mr. Smith?" the voice on the other end sounded tinny and far away.

"Yes."

"John Smith?" the voice had a strange accent, possibly European.

"Yeah, that's me. What can I do for you?"

"I am afraid I have some sad news…. You see, your cousin Virgil has recently died."

The voice paused and Smith wondered if he was supposed to recognize the name. He waited for some hint of memory, but none came. He scratched at his back absently. Dead relatives usually meant money, whether one could remember them or not.

"I'm sorry, but do you know me?"

"We certainly do, Mr. Smith, though it did take some effort on our part to find you."

"Oh…yeah. Sorry to hear about Virgil. When did it happen? How did he die?"

"His body was discovered last week…. Mr. Smith, his death was most gruesome. We would much prefer not to discuss details via telephone. When would be a good time to meet with you?"

Smith considered his empty calendar, pausing to flick the pages for effect. He even let out a convincing "ummmm" sound.

"I can squeeze you in tomorrow. Just need to re-arrange some appointments."

"Excellent. We will meet at your office at 2 o'clock tomorrow afternoon. Your electricity should be restored by the end of the day today."

Smith stared at the phone long after the click and dialtone. Whoever the caller might be, they had done their homework. He felt a flush rise to his cheeks and settled the phone gently into the cradle. Shit. The person (people?) had answers as to his identity, and he was creating a great first impression.

He looked around his office and gasped as if seeing it for the first time. When had it become such a godless shithole? He struggled to remember the last time he had had a client, then judged by the buildup of dust and fast food wrappers that it had been at least a month or more. He found himself wishing he had a girlfriend who might clean up his office out of pity.

He pushed back from his desk and began picking up crumpled documents and past-due bills that had missed the wastebasket during his many games of office hoops. Once the floor was cleared, he climbed onto his desk and tugged the pencils from the drop-ceiling. He really needed to find better ways to amuse himself.

While straightening knick-knacks that had been used as target practice or rebound casualties, he pondered his mysterious, deceased cousin. He realized with happy shock that the name was vaguely familiar. Every time he thought about it, there was a brief flash of memory from what must have been his later childhood or maybe early adulthood, but nothing that he could hold onto long enough to get a clear picture.

He remembered two people that he assumed were his parents arguing with some men who had visited his house once, long ago. Something about the memory said it was important, but for the life of him, he couldn't recall any more detail.

He remembered the expressions of rage on his parents' faces and the terror hiding behind the shouted words. The men–he blinked as the memory shattered like glass.

His expression tightened with his effort at concentration. He pulled up the memory again, remembered the shouts and his parents' faces. The men wore black clothing–black suits?–and the memory broke once more.

"Shit," he muttered.

He leaned against his desk and closed his eyes,

struggling to hold on to the images in his mind. One of the men had been taller than the other. They had been more than dressed in black; they had seemed covered in it.

"Cloaked," he breathed and opened his eyes.

The men had seemed cloaked in darkness; as cliché as that sounded to him, it was the only way to describe it. Beyond that one impression, his mind shut off and refused to remember further details, but it was progress! He finally had a memory of his past.

He must have asked his parents about the argument, he thought. Who could resist asking the existential "Why?" Whatever answer his parents had given him must have been convincing enough to both satisfy his curiosity and wipe the memory from his mind.

Smith jumped out of his thoughts and away from his desk when the lights flickered to life above him. As promised, his electricity was back on by the end of the day. With a nervous laugh that fell flat in the nearly empty room, he remembered he'd left the light switches in the on position, because it didn't matter if they were on or off when the electricity was shut off. Leaving his office in relative order, he flicked off the lights and left to walk around town and clear his head of the sudden misgivings he felt.

"Do you really think he will meet with us?" Pazuzu asked.

Marduk chuckled. "Of course. Humans love a good inheritance."

Pazuzu frowned skeptically. "And you are certain you called the correct human?"

His companion sighed and pointed to the entry in a beaten, dog-eared phonebook hanging like a dying man inside the even more beaten phone booth.

"For the third time, Zu, yes."

The demon scowled. He hated Marduk's habit of nicknaming everyone in Hell, and he hated the nickname that Marduk had given him even more. "Zu" made him sound less-than-hellish somehow. It took away the very essence of the terror he should be conjuring.

"You thought the human in the overcoat was the correct one, along with the three others before him," Pazuzu reminded his companion with a small thrill of told-you-so-ism.

Marduk growled and rubbed at his bandaged chest. The silver blood had stopped oozing from the wound, and silver coated Marduk's scowling lips in such a way as to suggest the demon had tried to eat a mercury thermometer.

"Agreed, the overcoat may have been the wrong means of identifying a detective. Damn Hollywood."

"What if he did not believe you? What if he suspects the communication was a trick and hides from us instead; or worse, comes armed to the meeting?"

"He will believe because we spoke embarrassing truths and gave him back his light."

Pazuzu's stare was doubtful. Marduk shrugged and dropped the electrical worker he had coerced into restoring power to John Smith's office to the ground.

The man's body lay still, his plastic hard hat rocking from side to side like an overturned yellow turtle on the sidewalk.

"Either way, we know where our man will be and when."

"How?"

Marduk smiled grimly. "We just made an appointment," he said and plucked a bullet from beneath the bandages with a wince. "I can only hope he will not have a weapon–nor the time to use it."

The demon folded the torn entry from the phonebook and stuffed it into his pocket. Then, adjusting their suits and ties, the pair side-stepped into a tear in the very essence of existence to meet with their caseworker in Manhattan.

The diner where they were to give their report was quiet. A bored cook and waitress chatted behind the counter as if the place was empty. It might as well have been. Only angels and demons occupied the booths lining the wall of windows.

It was a common misconception that angels and demons were constantly battling each other. The epic battle for heaven had fizzled out over the millennia and had evolved into the mere occasional skirmish between individuals with a grudge. It was largely agreed that humans were no longer worth the fight, and good riddance. Demonic possessions were now on a case-by-case basis, with angelic counter-attack making an appearance only if intervention was formally requested by a mortal. Heaven now had a process for such things.

Pazuzu and Marduk nodded to the angels they recognized as they moved past the tables to where Koth, their case manager, waited. He glanced up at them from his book and steaming cup of black coffee. His lips pressed into a thin line when he saw the blood on Marduk's shirt.

"Well?"

They slid into the bench seat across the table from Koth and the waitress appeared with two cups of black coffee. Without a word she set the cups down and walked away. Pazuzu wrapped his misshapen hands around the mug and enjoyed the agonizing heat emanating from the chipped porcelain for a moment.

"It was not our man," he finally told Koth.

Koth rolled his silver eyes skyward, folded the page of his book to mark his place before closing it, and settled his elbows onto the table. He heaved a sigh that suggested deep disappointment and stared at them.

"You two are 0 for 3 now. Fucking Hollywood. I keep telling management to update their training. Using films as instructional videos just doesn't work, especially when all they've got are the old black and whites."

Pazuzu nodded gravely and tried to appear as if he understood what Koth was saying, but the other demon had clearly spent too much time topside and had since gone native. Pazuzu also heard a light hint of a New York accent slipping into Koth's words. Marduk seemed equally lost, which was a small relief.

"Point is," Koth continued, "You guys suck at this, and it's not completely your fault."

The demon glared when a lone angel at a nearby booth laughed at his comment. Koth rose to his feet, readying himself for a fight.

"Yo, feathers! You got a problem? Mind yer damned business," he called out, emphasizing his words with a flung packet of sugar that hit the angel in the back of its head.

The angel turned slowly, disbelief and rage burning in the silver chrome of his eyes. Koth flinched, recognizing the angel as he raised an eyebrow at the demon. The angel straightened his neatly pressed white dress shirt and black slacks as he stood and approached their table. Black wings spread from behind the angel and disturbed the air around him with a cold gale.

"Shit shit shit," Koth muttered as he sank back into the booth. He seemed to hide behind his cup of coffee, which was now forming ice crystals on its black surface.

"Hello, *Koth*," the angel said, voice flat with suppressed anger.

"H-hey, Azrael. Sorry about that. Didn't realize it was you over there."

"Indeed?"

"It was an accident, won't happen again," Koth stammered.

Azrael leaned over the table, his fingertips barely pressing against the cold Formica, and said, "It is only because of your current mission that I accept your apology. Am I clear?"

"As window glass," Koth responded.

The demon visibly relaxed when Azrael moved away from them, black wings spread wide. Koth frowned when one of the wings caught his cup of coffee and knocked it into his lap, but said nothing.

"Dick," Koth muttered once the angel had exited the diner.

Pazuzu and Marduk exchanged awkward glances and shifted in their seat. No one liked to have to deal with Azrael, even on good terms. He was an angel devoted solely to his function, and his function was death for anything and everything. Neither demons nor angels were safe from him, and running was not an option. If he had to chase his target he got mean. He was kind of a prick about it, really. Or so the rumors said.

"I don't know what the hell He ever saw in that guy. He's got the personality of a headstone. Amiright?" Koth asked and held his hands out as if to catch their answer.

The demons nodded their agreement. Azrael always had been the death of a party, there was no doubt about that. The years had not improved his disposition, but no one would ever dare say that to his face. There were rumors that he had a friend, a vampire no less. Leave it to the angel of death to befriend a damned bloodsucker.

"Anyway, getting back to your issue," Koth said with a roll of his eyes, "What's your next move?"

"We made an appointment with a private investigator."

"Probably a good move," Koth said with a grim smile.

CHAPTER II

The next day, John Smith was on edge more than usual as he waited for his mysterious callers to arrive. He stared down at the street from his office window, watching the crowds of tourists move along the sidewalks.

He checked his clock one more time. It read five minutes past two o'clock. His lips pressed into a thin line as his eyes darted to the door of his office suite, then back out the window.

Two figures approached the building and Smith frowned. There was something not quite right about them, something *off* about the way they moved. Both men were ashen pale, with coal black hair styled into a slicked back hairdo that John remembered from old black and white detective films he had watched on late-night cable in the hospital. He frowned at the pair. They triggered the snippet of memory he had had the day before after talking to the person on the phone.

The pair entered the building, and Smith could hear the distant ding of the elevators descending a few moments later. His gut was suddenly seized with an unexplainable fear. He wasn't sure where it came from, but his every instinct was telling him to get the hell out of there. NOW.

He left his office unlocked, lights on, loading the gun he pulled from his desk drawer quickly as he slid along the wall in the corridor. He waited around the corner from the elevators where he could see his office door but not be readily noticed by anyone approaching from the elevators.

The pair of men he had seen in the street below exited the elevator and made their way toward his office door. He held his breath, watching them. At a closer distance they were even more odd. Again, the memory of people he assumed to be his parents fighting with a pair of black-clad figures surfaced in his mind.

The men stood outside his office door and one of them paused with his fingers mere inches from the doorknob. The man sniffed the air, a strange wind over PVC piping sound, and turned to face where Smith was hiding. His companion turned to face the spot a second later and Smith flinched. Caught. Smith would have felt embarrassed if the guys didn't give him the creepy crawlies.

"Hello," the taller of the pair said toward Smith's hiding spot, "Are you Mr. Smith?"

Smith tucked the loaded gun in the back of his pants and left his spot around the corner, cheeks burning slightly. He stared at the strange duo and said, "Who wants to know?"

"Our card," the shorter man said smoothly.

The light glinted off the men's matching, too-wide smiles and the detective felt a chill run up his spine. He glanced down at the offered card quickly as if taking his eyes off these two for even a second would be bad. The names on the card rang a distant bell.

"Look, I don't want any trouble," Smith blurted out and had no idea why he said it.

The two men looked surprised. The shorter man said, "We can assure you that we are not here to cause trouble."

"So why *are* you here, Mr. –?"

"Marduk," Marduk replied, extending a cool hand, "Lucien Marduk."

"Nice to meet you, Mr. Marduk. John Smith. Obviously." Smith turned to the taller of the men expectantly.

"This is my associate, Paul Azuzu," Marduk said, "There was a bit of a misunderstanding with the printer, so our cards have a few typographical errors," he added with a chuckle. "It would appear that American printers seem to have difficulty with foreign names."

Marduk paused as if expecting some sort of reaction, so Smith nodded sympathetically, as if he understood. Paul Azuzu, or 'Pazuzu' as his name read on the card, was staring at his companion as if it was the first time he had ever seen the man. That look sent more alarms ringing in Smith's head.

"Soooo…. What brings you gentlemen to my door?" Smith asked while letting them into his office. He waited for them to enter before joining them, maneuvering so they wouldn't see the gun in the waistband of his pants.

Smith moved to sit behind his desk and froze as Paul Azuzu closed the door behind them and locked it. The taller man looked back at Smith and gave an apologetic smile.

"We would prefer not to be interrupted…or

accidentally overheard," Marduk explained, "You see, we are here because this man has gone missing, but we think you may know where he is."

Smith stared emptily.

"Virgil?" Marduk tried helpfully.

Still Smith stared, completely drawing a blank.

"I suppose we will need to resort to 'the hard way' as your movies call it. Pity, I almost liked you."

"Whuh?" Smith began in confusion before he was silenced by a quick punch to his mouth.

"OW!! What the hell?!"

Marduk smiled at him and said, "The hard way. Tell us where Virgil Calahan is or you will suffer."

"Buddy, I don't even know who the hell *I* am much less know who you're talking about!!" Smith cried while rubbing his jaw.

"Do not lie," Pazuzu told him, "We tracked you to this area, and you seemed saddened by the news of his passing yesterday."

Smith let out a barking laugh and threw the old newspaper articles at them. "Shit, is that what this is about? As you can see from the articles, gentlemen, I don't remember much of anything before a couple of months ago. Did I seem sad when you told me of this guy's passing? Of course I seemed sad. I was hoping there would be some sort of inheritance and figured you'd be less likely to give it to me if I didn't seem like I at least *knew* the dead guy."

"You would mourn for profit?" Pazuzu asked incredulously.

Smith rolled his eyes. "*Yes*. Anyone would. Or don't they do that in Europe?"

Marduk and Pazuzu exchanged glances. Marduk

sighed.

"We have not been completely honest–"

"No kidding," Smith interrupted, crossing his arms.

Marduk glared then continued. "We are not from Europe, and Virgil is not deceased. We do need to find him immediately, however."

"Why?" Smith asked.

"He has information relevant to the case on which we are working. I suppose since you are not particularly busy at this time that we might be able to employ your services?"

Smith contemplated the offer.

"It may help you regain your memory," Pazuzu tried.

"OK, but no more punching. And I want half my fee up front and the other half paid in full upon completion. Do we have a deal?"

The demons nodded, smiling.

CHAPTER III

Having cash in his bank account, and a decent sum at that, made Smith's misgivings about the case melt away. He stared at the deposit slip from the bank again. It said he not only had money in his account, but five figures. He was glad his new clients didn't ask questions about his fees or try to haggle with him. He'd be able to live on the amount in his bank account for at least a year if he was careful. Maybe even get a small studio apartment in town somewhere.

He fired up his new laptop and wireless internet connection and felt nearly giddy as he got started on the case. He had let Marduk and Pazuzu name their price for his services and readied himself to argue the price, but their idea of his worth had come out to be ten times what Smith would have billed them.

He stared again at the five-figure bank statement on his desk, logged into his bank account online, and grinned at the pending payments to all of his bills. Finally he turned his gaze lovingly to the bottle of Dewar's blue label on his desk.

"Sweet Jesus, life is good," he breathed.

In the search box of his browser he typed in "Virgil Calahan"and hit Enter. Within seconds, a list of Virgil Calahan links filled the screen. Smith clicked the

Images search link then began scanning and comparing faces to the old black and white photo that Marduk and Pazuzu had left with him.

He found his man on the second page of search results. He almost laughed at how easy it had been to find the man—until he clicked the link.

Virgil was into some seriously weird shit. It wasn't S&M weird, it was more like Aleister Crowley weird. LaVey weird. His web page had been created by his "followers."

Smith read the About page with a growing sense of unease in the pit of his stomach. The pictures of this man dated back to World War I, *and the man hadn't aged since.* The photos and back-story had to have been faked, Smith decided.

He picked up the phone and punched numbers from the website into the keypad. On the third ring an older male voice came over a recording.

"Please leave a message," was all the voice said, followed by a prolonged beep.

"Hi. My name is John Smith and this message is for Virgil Calahan—"

There was a click and the voice from the recording came on the line.

"I see you have a new name now," the voice said.

"Is this...Virgil Calahan?" Smith asked.

"You know it is, *John*."

He could hear the smile in the voice, as if they were old friends.

"Do you know me, Mr. Calahan?"

"Don't be ridiculous. Of *course* I know you. What game are you playing at now, old man? Where are you calling from this time?"

"Gettysburg, Pennsylvania," Smith answered automatically, "I'm sorry, but I don't remember you, Mr. Calahan. The last thing I remember is waking up in a hospital from a coma several months ago."

"Then why, if you 'don't remember me,'" the man said with distinct sarcasm, "are you calling?" Virgil's voice suggested he thought it was a bad joke.

"Look, Mr. Calahan, I'm a private detective. I was hired by two men to find you. They say that you have information regarding a case they're working on."

"What were their names?" Virgil asked quietly.

Suddenly Smith recognized something in the tone of Virgil Calahan's voice. The man was scared, perhaps terrified. Smith paused, mouth open to speak, but he was interrupted.

"Did the two men claim to be European? One's shorter and the other's tall and they look like something out of an old Hollywood film?"

"How did you know—?"

"Don't talk to them!" Virgil yelled.

"I don't understand," Smith started to protest but Calahan interrupted him again.

"You're in Gettysburg, you said? Meet me at the castle monument on Little Roundtop at sunset. Tell no one where you're going or who you're meeting. Make sure you're not followed, do you understand me?"

Smith was about to ask what time sunset was when there was a click followed by a dialtone. He stared at the phone until it blurted a busy signal at him to let him know it was disconnected and left off the hook. He dropped it back in its cradle and continued to stare.

It was five o'clock; sunset would be in a little while. He jumped when his phone rang, shattering the silence.

"Mr. Smith, how are you?" asked Marduk.

"I'm okay. Hope you and your associate are well."

"Indeed we are. Have you made any progress on our case?"

"Mr. Marduk, I just started the case. These things take time."

"Please don't insult me by lying to me, Mr. Smith. We will come by your office tomorrow afternoon for a full progress report on the case."

The line cut out before Smith could respond and he frowned. Twice today he'd been hung up on, and it annoyed him. Glaring at the phone, he jabbed at his back and began to scratch.

Smith tried to appear casual as he left his office and wandered along Taneytown Road. It was a hike from his office, which was located in the center of town, to the monument at Little Roundtop, but he figured if armies could do it while laden with ammunition and supplies, he could surely do it wearing a shirt, slacks, and comfortable shoes.

He was out of breath and sweating when he reached Wheatfield Road. By the time he got to Sykes Avenue, he could see the monument and his own imminent demise.

"Hell with exercise. I'm staying the night up there," he gasped.

He leaned on his thighs for a few minutes, staring

up the hill at the small castle dedicated to the 44th New York Infantry Regiment and the smaller castle-esque monument that always reminded him of a chess piece that was dedicated to the 91st Pennsylvania Infantry Regiment. Why couldn't Calahan have chosen the larger State of Pennsylvania monument which was on much flatter ground?

With a sigh, he climbed the hill until he reached the monument. Standing at the foot of the miniature castle, he could see clearly down to Devil's Den and the few tourists milling about among the large stones. None of the tourists seemed particularly interested in his movements, nor were there any tourists who looked like a throwback from a 1940's Noir film.

A short "psst!" from above caught Smith's attention and he looked up to see Virgil Calahan motioning for Smith to join him on the little observation deck of the monument. Smith let out a weary sigh and all but crawled up the stone steps of the tiny spiral staircase.

Virgil Calahan looked suspiciously like a tourist. Khakis, hiking boots, a Gettysburg t-shirt, and a lightweight windbreaker were all topped off by a dark-blue baseball cap with the word 'NAVY' embroidered in gold across the front. Calahan held a camera up to his face as if he was recording every stone of the monument for posterity.

"Were you followed at all?" he asked Smith casually from behind the camera without acknowledging Smith's presence in any way, his voice low so no one else would overhear.

"I don't think so," Smith replied with another quick check of the tourists below.

"Good," Calahan said, dropping the camera from his face and motioning to the stone floor, "Sit."

The old man dropped below the edge of the wall with the agility of a thirty year old. He leaned his back against the stones of the wall, the Valley of Death and Devil's Den behind and below them. The man was impossibly spry for someone who had seen World War I. His eyes met Smith's and he stared for a long moment. Without a word, he took out a pack of cigarettes and tapped out two.

"I don't smoke," Smith said at the offered cigarette.

"Of course you do. Always have. Smoke it," the old man scolded.

Smith took the cigarette and automatically leaned in toward the offered light, protecting the flame from the wind. It was as if he was on autopilot, his body taking a deep drag and his hand working independently of his mind as the fingers flicked ashes from the glowing tip. He was surprised he didn't cough.

"See?" Calahan said with a smirk, "You smoke."

The old man took a deep drag on his own cigarette, and with his free hand, removed a flask from inside his jacket. He opened it, took a swig, offered it to Smith.

The younger man paused, staring at the engravings on the flask. Memories flickered in the recesses of his mind, but none stayed long enough to grasp. He took a sniff at the mouth of the flask, smelled bourbon, and drank.

"You really did get a knock on the noggin, didn't you, old boy?" Calahan asked with a disbelieving shake of his snowy white head.

Smith shrugged. It felt weird to be talking to the man he was supposed to be bringing to his clients, but nothing about the case had been normal thus far.

"So which ones did they send this time?" Calahan asked.

"How do you mean?"

"Names, man! What are your 'clients' names?"

Smith frowned. "I can't give you that information, it's confidential."

Calahan smirked and took a drink from the flask.

"Do you want to know who you are?"

The ice of Calahan's eyes was so blue and piercing that Smith flinched when the old man looked at him. Quickly the detective looked away and took the offered flask.

"You don't know who I am...."

"Bullshit. Of course I know who you are. We've known each other your entire life."

Smith was doubtful. "If you know who I am, why didn't you come forward to identify me?"

"You were safer that way," the old man told him gravely. He paused to light a new cigarette off the glowing tip of the old one, snuffed out the spent cancer stick and pocketed the filter. He took a long drag, then continued. "We got ourselves into a real mess this time, and the way I figured, if you had no idea who you were, then no one else knew you either. I hoped by the time the dust settled you'd be back to your old self. Obviously not. Which brings me back to my original question: Which two did they send this time?"

He stared at Smith, and Smith had all he could do not to speak the names. Calahan sighed.

"Tell me their names, and I'll tell you your name. Fair trade?"

It was Smith's turn to sigh. He really wasn't a good

detective, anyway.

"Paul Azuzu and Lucien Marduk."

Calahan let out a laugh and rolled his eyes. "They really didn't try very hard, did they?"

"Who?"

"The two demons that hired you. Don't say their real names aloud. They might be in earshot and get summoned. That would be the end of the game, I suspect."

"All right, if I knew their real names, I wouldn't say them. Now what about *my* real name?"

"You open up a Pandora's Box by having me tell you this, you know," Calahan said in the tone of a man who has said the same thing numerous times.

"I have to know my name," Smith pleaded.

Calahan smirked. "Your name's Calahan. Virgil Calahan."

Smith stared at the old man. The old man stared back, then his face broke into a grin. He wasn't lying.

"*You* are Virgil Calahan, not me," Smith protested.

Calahan's smile widened. "We are *both* Virgil Calahan. You're my son."

Smith felt like the world was sliding out from under him.

"The pictures," he said weakly.

Calahan laughed. "They're real. You're even in some of them, but I had you edited out of the ones on the website."

"How...?"

"There's a kid who's a genius with photo editing–"

"No," Smith interrupted, "I meant how is any of this possible?"

The old man considered the question for a moment. He took a swig from the flask and stared off at the horizon.

"It was around 1900 or so, and we fell in with Crowley and his lot. Looking back it was just games, or so we thought. All a game–until we killed someone. As it turned out, that someone was very important."

"We killed someone?" Smith asked incredulously.

Calahan nodded and took a longer swig from the flask.

"Around 1900?"

Another nod from Calahan. "If it's any consolation, it was an accident," he tried.

"Old man, you are batshit crazy."

"I had a feeling you might think that, so I brought this along to show you," he paused as he started to remove something from one of his jacket pockets then gave Smith a hard look, "I recommend you tell no one about this. Especially those two demons."

In his hand Calahan held a grainy black and white photograph. The paper was sepia-toned with age, the edges worn and dog-eared at the corners. It was a picture of two men standing on either side of something they held between them. Their poses suggested it was a hunting trophy photo, but the creature between them was nothing Smith had ever seen.

At first glance, he thought it was a naked man, but realized there were wings coming from his back. The wings were spread and held wide between the men in the picture. The man portion of the creature was slumped so its head hung forward, arms limp. Dead. The two men in the photo were clearly the Virgils

Calahan.

"Photoshopped," Smith said, his voice hoarse.

"Afraid not, son," Calahan told him quietly, "I wish now that it was."

Smith wiped away the cold sweat that had seeped into the regular sweat on his forehead. Deep down, he believed the old man and knew the picture was no fake.

"What the hell is that thing?" Smith finally asked, unable to bring his voice above a whisper.

The old man looked at him gravely and raised an eyebrow as if to say "what does it look like?" He put the photo back in his jacket and the two men sat in silence as a pair of tourists wandered onto the small observation deck. They glanced at Smith and Calahan with uncertain smiles, snapped a few quick pictures of the view, then left.

Calahan released a bone-weary sigh and let his head fall back against the stone wall with a crack. Smith flicked at the ash and lit the offered fresh cigarette with the old one and took a deep drag.

"So what do we do?" Smith asked after a long pause.

"Nothing, you idiot! Do you know what they'd do to us if they caught us?"

"No. What?"

The old man stared at him as if his brain had dropped out of his nose while they talked. "Well...I don't know *exactly*, but it would be bad, rest assured. It would be *very* bad."

Smith remained at the monument long after sunset, and long after Virgil Calahan had left him with a head full of questions. Eventually one of the park patrols found him and he claimed that he had wanted to watch the sunset and get a bit of exercise, but then his leg had cramped. The ranger gave him a doubtful look, but since he was alone and carried no obvious tools of vandalism, the ranger let him slide. Just this once. The man was even nice enough to drop him off at Taneytown Road, saving Smith an extra hike.

He pulled out a cigarette from the pack of smokes Calahan had left with him along with an old Zippo. Pausing briefly, he lit the end and took a long inhale before continuing on his way. It was odd how easy it was to pick up where he left off with his smoking habit.

When he reached his office, Pazuzu and Marduk were waiting for him. They did not look happy.

"Gentlemen...?" Smith asked by way of a wary greeting.

The demons glared at him and he felt his testicles climbing up to hide inside his abdomen. The air around him crackled with electricity and he could swear he smelled a hint of sulfur.

"Mr. *Smith*," Marduk hissed.

"Yeah.... It's late, guys. We were going to meet tomorrow, I thought? What's up?"

"We would like an update on our case," Pazuzu said, his words calmer than his companion's.

"I have some leads, but...."

"But WHAT?" asked Marduk, "Our superiors want this resolved."

"How about more details?" Smith stalled, "Like why is this guy so important? What's your case about? All you've given me is a name and an old picture that could be Bigfoot, and it's not a whole hell of a lot to go on, honestly."

"Fair enough," Pazuzu said before Marduk could give vent to what were obviously curses, "our case is a murder investigation, and we do not want Virgil Calahan simply for questioning. We believe he is the murderer."

Smith tried not to think about the photograph of the dead, winged man as he poured himself a healthy dose of Dewar's. He tried to hide the tremble in both his voice and his hands when he sat down and asked, "Does this Virgil Calahan have any relatives? Any family?"

Pazuzu sighed. "We are unsure. The murder is an old one, and it is possible that the man's family are all dead."

"How long ago did this murder happen?"

"Around the time of the first World War," the demon replied somewhat sheepishly.

Smith's reflexive laugh was more a bark than a sign of humor.

"Guys, your *murderer* is probably long dead."

"He is alive!" Marduk finally erupted, "Don't you think we would know if he was dead?!"

"How the hell could you possibly know that he wasn't dead?" Smith asked nervously.

"Just *find him*," Marduk growled, "And bring him to us."

CHAPTER IV

The last thing Smith expected was to find himself trying to talk Virgil Calahan into turning himself in the next day. The two men sat in a dimly lit pub on the square in Gettysburg, hunched over stiff drinks and voices lowered to just barely above a whisper.

"I don't think you understand just how bad it is, old boy," Calahan said, frustration creeping into his tone.

"Then show me. Whatever we did must have been pretty damned bad for me to attempt suicide."

The old man nodded and took a sip of whiskey.

"You took it harder than I thought you would, I admit. This last time.... Well, it was even worse than the others."

"Last time?" Smith asked.

He felt his stomach rising up in his throat to meet the swig of Jack Daniel's still burning in his mouth.

The old man gave a nod and his hands shook around the rocks glass as he raised it to his lips. The thick bottom of the glass rattled on the tabletop when he put it down, slicing into the quiet hum of the lull before the afternoon rush.

"This isn't the first time you've attempted…something like what you did on that bridge," Calahan began.

He smiled and offered up his glass to the waitress when he caught her staring over at them. They sat, silent as she swiped away their glasses and went to the bar to refill their drinks, and they remained silent until she placed their refilled glasses back in front of them.

Calahan took a long sip from his drink and stared hard at Smith. He seemed to study Smith's eyes for a moment or two as he had during their conversation at the monument. After a long pause, he let out a sigh.

"Are you sure you want to know your story, son?" he finally asked, "You seem much happier this way. Not knowing."

"Of course I want to know!"

Calahan sighed again. "I was afraid you would say that…. Well, old boy, you asked for it. Don't say I didn't warn you."

The old man took another sip from his drink, smacked his lips, and raised his glass. His grin was forlorn.

"To the beautiful embrace of ignorance and the sweet perfume of amnesia," he toasted and downed the rest of his whiskey. "In order to know what brought you to the end, it's important to know the beginning. You were born July 4th, 1875. Your childhood was relatively uneventful. You studied law at university and fell in with my old crowd–well, their sons, rather.

"We'd all meet up once in a while for cards and drinks, and we'd talk a lot of bullshit. The occult was very in vogue at the time, and we dabbled in what we thought of as 'magic'. During one of our gatherings, we hosted Aleister Crowley himself. To be honest, the man was a bit of a prick, but his ideas had so much allure to them. More allure than we could ever muster with our reputation. After Crowley left, one of the kids asked why we didn't do any rituals. We always kept our group shrouded in mystery, and rituals were part of the rumored initiation and daily practices. Sure, we had collected plenty of books on the occult. Many of them were very impressive first and in some cases only editions, and we flaunted them to our fledglings. The sad truth of it all was that we had never used any of them for anything other than hazing props.

"We laughed the kid's comments off, not realizing just how serious he was about it until he came to our gathering one night laden with notes and supplies. He was feverish and claimed that he had successfully summoned a demon. We humored him, God help us. We let him show us his 'parlor trick'. I wish now we had taken him more seriously instead of what we did," Calahan paused while his glass was refilled. He stared into the amber liquid and seemed to suddenly be every minute of his age.

"What did you do?" Smith asked quietly, his own drink now forgotten.

"Not 'you,' *we*. You were there."

"Who was the kid? Me?" Smith asked, but decided he really didn't want to hear any more.

Calahan shook his head. "No, it wasn't you. Perhaps if it had been you, we never would have gone as far as we did. We'd have just gotten enough of a taste to laugh it off. Your younger brother was a different sort, though, and his head never sat quite straight on his shoulders."

"My brother? I have a brother?"

Calahan motioned for him to calm down, then

continued, "I'm getting to it…."

The old man toyed with his pack of cigarettes and glared at the discreet "No Smoking" plaques around the bar that forbade him to light one up. As if sensing his nicotine angst, the waitress made a beeline to their table.

"Any of your drinks need refilled?" she asked with a smile that didn't reach her eyes.

Calahan shook his head and Smith covered his glass in the universal sign for "no more." She considered the drink levels and the open pack of cigarettes, gave a nod then walked back to the bar.

"She talks funny," Calahan muttered.

"Everyone around here talks like that. Unless they're not from around here, of course," Smith said, "It's a throwback to PA Dutch. At least that's what the nurses told me when I asked about it."

"Still sounds damned odd. Like there's words missing," Calahan grumbled.

His own words were tinged by the liquor and were beginning to spread together like a slow puddle. He fondled a cigarette out of the crumpled pack and stroked it lovingly. He sighed when he felt the waitress come to attention, staring over at them and at the cigarette in particular.

"I remember when the damned government stayed out of your damned business so long as you didn't kill anyone," the old man growled. "Now a man can't even kill himself without retribution. Uncle Sam's a damned funny uncle."

Smith grimaced in place of a smile.

"My brother?" he prodded.

Calahan seemed to deflate. His eyes swam in

sadness and whiskey, and Smith wondered if he should book the man a hotel room for the night. He had no idea how he'd gotten there or even from where he'd come. The only certain thing was that the old man wasn't driving back that night.

"We were just humoring him. We said the words, did the ritual, every one of us referring to it as the dog and pony show behind your brother's back up to that point. We never thought it would actually *work*," Calahan paused to place the cigarette in his mouth in a movement that was more than habit before angrily pulling it out with a glare toward the waitress. He continued, "We didn't summon a demon or even a ghost. We summoned something we never would have even thought possible…."

"What was it?"

Calahan gave the universal sign for "hold on a minute" and toyed with the cigarette. After a long pause he motioned to the waitress for a refill. When she came over she raised an eyebrow, glanced at Smith's glass and then at Smith himself in the universal bar question.

"Get one," Calahan said, "You're going to need it."

Smith shrugged and nodded at the waitress. "Yes, please."

The two men waited in silence for their fresh drinks. When the waitress set the new glasses down and turned to leave, Calahan placed a gentle, but firm hand on hers. Smith braced himself for the verbal flaying the old man was about to receive from their server.

"Please, miss, if it's not too much trouble, I'd like to order another one and a glass of water or two," he said politely, "My friend and I are discussing some private business and would appreciate not being disturbed."

With the last sentence he handed the girl a hundred dollar bill. She stared at Ben Franklin's smug face smirking up at her off the note, then held it up to the light to ensure it wasn't counterfeit.

When she returned with not only a second but a third drink for each of them and two waters each, her smile was more genuine. She quickly set up the glasses in front of them and took a step back from the table.

"I'll stay out of your hair and sit people away from you both," she told them, "You just yell if your drinks need refilled."

Both men nodded and as she walked away Calahan muttered, "She still talks funny."

"Who gives a shit!" Smith hissed. "What did you summon??"

"An angel."

Smith stared in shock while Calahan drank.

"So.... An angel? Holy shit. Really?"

Calahan gave a slow nod, as if he couldn't believe it himself.

"What happened after you summoned the angel?"

The old man slumped forward over his drink and it took Smith a moment to realize that Calahan was sobbing. His tone instantly became more gentle.

"Hey, I'm sorry, I didn't mean–"

Calahan waved off the apology. He mopped at his eyes with a napkin and took a deep shaking breath.

"What happened after we summoned the angel?" he repeated, his watery eyes far away and staring at a time and place that Smith couldn't reach. "All hell broke loose. The thing went insane, furious that mere men had not only been able to summon it, but to *capture* it. We couldn't control the damned thing, that's for sure. And when it saw your brother Billy wearing the ceremonial robes, well...."

Calahan paused and took a long sip off his drink.

"By the time we got to him, the thing had torn Billy's head clean off his body, along with his arms and legs. What you did was more self-defense than anything else."

"What did I do?" Smith asked and his stomach churned.

"You killed it. Grabbed the dagger we had been using for the ceremony and stuck it into the thing up to the hilt. It may have gotten your brother, but it didn't get the rest of us, thanks to you."

"Why don't I feel like that was a good thing?" Smith asked no one in particular.

He wrapped his hands around his drink glass and held on to the reality shining in the melting ice cubes. The bar was suddenly stifling and he tugged at his collar to loosen it.

"In the end, it really was a good thing," Calahan told him.

He downed the rest of his whiskey and his face registering only a hint of a wince at the alcohol burn now.

"Damned thing wuduv killed us all if you hadn't done something."

The old man's words ran together and he pointed at Smith with his unlit cigarette for emphasis. His eyes closed to a squint in order to better focus.

"That thing was a nasty piece of work. Never let

anyone make you believe angels look like fat flying babies. 'S'not true 't'all. Tooka chunk outta you before it went, too."

Smith felt queasy. He tried to focus on the old man while the bar swam around him.

"Chunk out of…me?"

Calahan nodded and his head dipped a little lower each time until Smith expected him to start snoring. The old man made a motion toward his own back, slashing the air with two fingers, and Smith's blood ran cold.

"It tore two holes in your back. You got the scars to prove it, too."

"How did you know about those?" Smith asked, forcing his voice to rise above a choked whisper.

Calahan slammed a fist on the table and people in the pub cast curious looks their way.

"Dammit, boy, I just *told* you how you got them! Pay attention!"

Smith grimaced and hid behind the rim of his drink glass. After a moment he glanced around the bar to see if any of their fellow patrons were still staring their way.

"All right, just keep your voice down!" Smith hissed.

Calahan shook himself and slid off his barstool. Smith stared but said nothing as the old man faced the door.

"Smoke," he muttered, and stopped up any extraneous words with the unlit cigarette.

Smith was tempted to follow him but decided there were still too many questions to answer and if the demons saw him with Calahan it would all be over.

Instead he sat at their table and sucked down another drink before the old man returned. Calahan's gait was steadier than it had been when he stepped out to smoke his cigarette.

"So," said Calahan as he slid back onto his barstool.

"So," Smith answered.

The two men sat in silence for a moment with Smith still digesting the details of the story while Calahan stared into his drink, his face grave. The next questions stuck in Smith's throat and he was unsure if he wanted to know the answers.

"What happened after?" he finally managed.

Calahan let out a shaking sigh as if he had been preparing himself for it. He drew himself up from his slouch and met Smith's nervous gaze.

"At first, nothing," he began. "We took Billy to a hospital saying a bear had mauled him. They told us he was dead, closed casket, the end."

"What about the angel?" Smith asked.

Calahan let out a short cough that might have been laughter. "The night before your brother was to be buried, we dumped the body in the fresh grave and threw in enough dirt to cover it. No one noticed."

"No one noticed?"

"Not even God," the old man said and his voice was bitter, "At least, not at first."

Smith opened his mouth and closed it again as the old man wept quietly. He told himself once more that Calahan was crazy, but the lie felt like a lie and he washed it down with a swig of his drink.

"You think I'm crazy," the old man said, his voice quiet.

Red eyes met Smith's and the younger man flinched back from the intensity of the stare. Smith dropped his glance to the surface of the table, needing to look anywhere but into the raw chaos of Calahan's very soul.

"I've done things I'm not proud of, I'll admit it. Some things I'm even ashamed of. It's not excuse, but you don't see what I've seen–what *we've* seen–without losing your mind at least a little," Calahan sighed.

Smith cleared his throat and after a pause asked, "So how did you know God noticed he was missing an angel?"

"By the silence."

"Silence?"

Calahan nodded and pointed to his chest. "Here. It was silent, like I'd been disconnected from everyone and everything else on Earth. Like I didn't belong here anymore. As the days went on I started to see that same look of being disconnected in the faces on the street, too. We had been set adrift.

"Then one night you came to see me and told me about a dream you'd been having. You said there was a voice in the darkness and that it was loud, all-consuming, and that the desire to become part of that voice was so strong you had difficulty waking up. You said when you did wake up from the dreams you knew the only way to achieve becoming one with the voice was to die.

"We watched the world fall to shit around us in the months and years after we'd killed the angel. Humanity seemed to go crazy in just a few years. No one gave a damn about each other or anything else, and it just kept getting worse."

Calahan trailed off and stared into his drink. When next he spoke his voice was so quiet Smith had to ask him to repeat himself.

"Five years after it all went to hell, you tried to kill yourself."

Smith blinked at the old man but said nothing.

"You came to me and claimed the dreams were occurring every night. Then you said two demons were following you around," Calahan went on, "I tried to get you some help, but you said you knew what you had to do."

The old man's voice hitched and Smith realized he was crying again. He slid a bar napkin across the table in what he hoped was a discreet fashion and waited in patient silence for Calahan to pull himself together. After a few minutes, Calahan mopped at his eyes and blew his nose, then continued his story.

"The next time I saw you was on a street in New York. You had no idea who I was and claimed you had been released from the hospital after being found unconscious and half-drowned on the banks of the Hudson. We went to the library and I looked up the newspaper articles from the time period. Sure enough it was all there in newsprint. I told you who I was and we spent days and weeks trying to trigger your memory. Finally we went to your apartment and discovered the note you'd left. It broke my heart to know your solution was to end your life.

"Each time the notes get more and more cryptic, and each time there always seem to be two demons lurking somewhere nearby."

"'Each time'?" Smith asked, "How many times have I done this?"

Calahan stared up at the molded tin ceiling and his head nodded slightly as his lips counted. After a pause he said, "To date, two hundred times."

"Two *hundred*?"

"It would have been more, but I had you committed for a decade after the second time."

"Jesus Christ," Smith whispered.

"So far he's had nothing to do with this," said Calahan.

The pair sat in silence and finished their drinks just as the waitress came over to see if they were all right. They ordered another round and waited while she went to get them their liquor.

"We're drunk," Smith said to no one in particular.

"I'd like to be drunk more often, but doing it every day is already seen as excessive," the old man replied with a wry smile, "At least you get to forget all this with the next go round. I don't have that luxury. I suppose that's my punishment for the part I played in the whole damned mess."

The waitress returned with their fresh drinks and Calahan asked for the check. Smith fished in his pocket for his wallet and the old man stopped him.

"I got this one."

"Thanks," Smith said and let out a long breath. "You said there were others…what happened to them?"

Calahan shrugged. "All dead within ten years of the summoning. Some were suicides, others were 'accidents'. They all died violently. I have my suspicions."

"Suspicions?"

"As to what really happened to them all."

Smith stared, waiting.

"The demons got them. Might have been looking for information on how to locate the guy who killed the angel. I suspect it's how they got our name, at least. Could be why I'm still around to tell the tale, too. We're the only two who know where the body's buried, after all."

"Oh," said Smith and felt his stomach turn over, "So what do we do now?"

In spite of all he'd had to drink, the old man's eyes were sharp.

"No idea. This is usually the point where you go and try to off yourself. At least with the internet it makes it easier to find you when you pop up again. And the website made it easy for you to find me this time."

"Do your…followers…know about…?"

"Sweet Jesus, boy. Do I look like I advertise that kind of thing?" the old man hissed. "No, they don't know anything other than that I have the uncanny ability to not age. The rest I make up as I go along."

Smith heaved a sigh and wobbled as he climbed off his barstool. He saw that the old man was wobbly again and stopped him.

"You're not driving, right? To wherever it is you came from. I don't want to know where you live," he spoke quickly when Calahan looked suspicious, "I just want to know you're going to be safe tonight. Maybe get a room at the hotel?"

The old man seemed about to protest, then gave a resigned nod.

"Might not be a bad idea at that…. Guess I'll see you when I see you. Until next time," he said and gave a brief salute. "I love you, son."

"I wish I could remember you," Smith said quietly.

"Someday, maybe," the old man told him as he hugged him tight.

They left the pub separately so as not to draw attention to themselves. Smith emerged from the cool dimness just as the sun was low on the horizon. The bar was now packed with tourists along with a few re-enactors and he was glad to be out of the growing volume of multiple conversations.

He stumbled over the sidewalk and considered all he and Calahan had discussed. There was a pattern, he knew, but damned if he could see it at that moment. Each time he offed himself, there were two demons lurking. He didn't feel particularly suicidal and wondered if the demons killed him each time and made it look like suicide or an accident. If that were the case, Marduk and Pazuzu could have killed him at the very first meeting.

No, there was something else. The answer was on the edges of his consciousness and he strained to catch hold of it without success. He rubbed at his temples, already feeling the hangover that was waiting in the wings.

Smith made his way to his office and dropped the keys several times before he was able to unlock the door. As he fell forward into the darkness, he at last knew what he had to do.

CHAPTER V

When Smith woke the next morning he found a hand-written sticky note on a letter. It was his own handwriting, but he didn't remember writing it. He unfolded the letter the sticky note had been attached to then read it and groaned. He couldn't argue with it because it made so much sense. He wondered why it had taken him so long to figure it out.

He picked up the phone and dialed Calahan's number, popping two aspirin while he waited for the old man to answer. When the other end of the line went to voicemail he was tempted to hang up, but instead left a message.

"It's Smith. Could you drop by my office today? Thanks for the drinks and the hangover."

He hung up and let his head fall back against his chair as he stared at the ceiling. A minute later the phone rang and Smith expected to hear a hungover Calahan's voice on the other end. Instead there was an eerie pause and the line crackled.

"Hello?"

"Well, Mr. Smith?" came Marduk's faraway voice.

"Ahh, good, I was hoping you'd get in touch with me today. I have an update."

"You do," the demon said, voice skeptical.

"Meet me at the pub in the Gettysburg Hotel in fifteen minutes. I'll see you there."

Smith hung up without waiting for a reply and got to his feet. He left the letter propped on the desk, making sure the side with Calahan's name printed in large letters was easily visible from the door. He left the lights on and the door unlocked when he exited his office for the last time. It was a bittersweet event leaving this brief life behind, but it was time to move on.

Pazuzu and Marduk found him five shots deep at the bar in the Gettysburg Hotel. He finished the sixth shot as they drew up next to him and he slammed the glass on the bar top. When the bartender looked up Smith motioned for him and the man walked over to the trio.

"Already told you, you got to hold off for a few minutes, Mr. Smith."

"Not for me," Smith said, "For my friends here. I'd just like a Coke."

The bartender eyed the two demons, raised an eyebrow, then went about pouring a glass of Coke and two shots of Jack Daniel's. Smith slid the man a twenty dollar bill along with the other cash and change left on the bar in front of him.

"All yours, Dan. Thanks."

The bartender gave a nod and slid the notes and change off the bar into his hand. "Thanks, John. You have a safe night."

He gave the demons another glance, this one filled with hate, before moving back to the cash register. The demons watched him in silence, their expressions forced to neutrality.

"You know Dan?" Smith asked.

Marduk sneered, his eyes never leaving the bartender's back. "We know Dan."

Sensing his companion's growing rage, Pazuzu interjected quickly, "You said you have information for us, Mr. Smith?"

Smith nodded and raised his glass in a toast. When the demons stared blankly at him he indicated that they should raise their shot glasses.

"Gentlemen, I found Virgil Calahan," he told them and took a drink from his Coke.

At first neither Marduk nor Pazuzu moved. They sat facing him, glasses still raised and eyes indicating that they had not yet registered the meaning of his words.

Pazuzu blinked and his silver eyes seemed ghostly in the dim light and dark woodwork of the hotel bar. He set his shot glass down with a heavy clink and continued to stare at Smith.

"Drink up, boys!" Smith told them. "We're celebrating!"

Automatically both demons downed their shots and all at once began to cough as the alcohol stung their throats.

"What did we just drink?" Marduk asked with an annoyed cough.

"Whiskey."

Marduk wore the expression of someone who had been tied to a stake and assured there would be no fire. Pazuzu struggled to appear unfazed.

"Where is Virgil Calahan?" Pazuzu asked and his voice was raspier than usual.

"One more drink before I tell you."

Marduk rolled his eyes. "Fine."

Another round was ordered and the demons seemed to enjoy the burn of the alcohol the second time around. Smith watched closely as the silver eyes dimmed and the pair leaned into their seats, Marduk leaning a little more than Pazuzu. Lightweights. Smith wondered if they served alcohol in Hell. Probably not.

"Misssterr Smith," Marduk said, his finger pointing at Smith as if to keep him in focus.

Pazuzu stared at the ceiling, head lolling from side to side. Smith struggled to keep a straight face as he watched his two visibly drunk companions.

"He has made us drunk because he fears our reaction to his having no update," Pazuzu mumbled, then let out an unexpected bark of laughter. "Does he know we plan to kill him once he has given us the information?"

"Really?" Smith asked, unable to hide his surprise. The thought that they meant to kill him had not entered his head since the first meeting, and now fear bubbled in his gut with the alcohol.

"We cannot have humans running about telling each other of our existence, Mr. Smith. So yes, I am afraid you will need to die."

"What if I refuse to tell you what you want to know?"

The demons blinked as realization hit them. They had not thought of that aspect, clearly. Worse, they had made their potential prey aware of their plans before they had had a chance to find out what they needed to know. Pazuzu heaved a sigh.

"Very well, I give you my word that we will not harm you."

"Riiiight," Smith countered, "How about promising I'll die of natural causes and no demonically-laden mishaps?"

Marduk growled, but the pair nodded.

"Enough games, Mr. Smith. You have our word we will neither hurt nor kill you, now tell us where Virgil Calahan is."

Smith raised his glass and smiled grimly. "You're looking at him."

"What did you say?" Marduk asked.

Smith felt the shots coursing through his veins and the feeling gave him bravery he would not have otherwise had. He took another sip of Coke and shrugged.

"Look, I'm as surprised as you are, guys. Trust me."

"But your name is Smith," Marduk growled.

"That was the name they gave me at the hospital because I couldn't remember *who* I was. Turns out, my real name is Virgil Calahan."

Pazuzu smirked and shook his head. He finally understood irony. Marduk slammed a clawed fist onto the table and looked about ready to tear flesh from bone.

"Let's talk about it over another drink," Smith told them while motioning for two more drinks for the demons.

The pair were less averse to the next round of shots. And the round after that. While they drank, Smith explained what he had found out from Calahan. By the time he finished, both Pazuzu and Marduk were visibly drunk and Smith was mostly sober. He stared into the depths of his Coke and let out a shaking breath.

"So I guess now's the point where you guys decide you're going to kill me anyway, right?"

Pazuzu blinked in surprise and his mouth fell open. Marduk glared into his empty shot glass and seemed not to hear.

"*Kill* you?" asked Pazuzu with a laugh, "You misunderstand, Mr. Sm–Calahan. We were never here to kill *you*."

Smith dared to feel a wary sense of relief at the demon's words. When Dan looked their way he motioned for three shots.

"You're not here to kill me," Smith repeated, musing. "So you are here to…punish me?"

Pazuzu laughed, exposing large, carnivorous teeth. When he had finished, he dabbed at his eyes and nudged Marduk, who was busy sucking down the latest shot.

"This man thinks we are here to hurt him, Marduk. Is that not delightfully ignorant?"

The demon's companion gave a short bark of laughter and fell face-first onto the table. Pazuzu stared at his fallen comrade for a moment then burst into fresh laughter.

"He has never had worshippers leave alcohol to him as an offering," Pazuzu explained.

"Oh. Okay."

The demon leaned across the table and closed the distance between them. His teeth glinted razor-like in the dim light when he smiled, and Smith noticed some of the demon's appearance was slipping. It was as if he could no longer hold the image of a human being on his skin.

"Be honest with me, Mr. Calahan," Pazuzu said in

a conspiratorial way, "Did you really believe we were here to kill you?"

"Well, yeah. Why else would two demons be chasing me for decades?"

Pazuzu flinched at the word "demons" but gave a grudging nod. He leaned back in his seat and reached up a claw to flick the top button off of his shirt. As the collar fell open he released a sigh of near ecstasy.

"Perhaps the previous search teams–ourselves included, I am ashamed to say–did not make it entirely clear why we were searching for you. Perhaps if they had, we would have located you much sooner. Allow me to clarify."

The demon surprised Smith by motioning for the bartender to approach. Dan came over to them, his face neutral now, but wary. He glanced at Marduk, who had started to snore.

"May we have two drinks, please?"

"Sure," Dan said and relaxed slightly at not having to tell Pazuzu that Marduk was cut off. "What can I get for you?"

"Something strong."

Once Dan had returned with two Long Island iced teas and left again, Pazuzu took a sip of his drink and frowned. He stared at the drink and took a longer sip, his frown deepening to a scowl.

"This is not a strong drink," he scoffed.

Smith laughed. "It is, actually. It's kind of undercover, if you follow me. It is deceptively strong, in fact."

"Truly?"

"Oh yeah. It'll knock you on your ass and you'll look like our buddy there," Smith said with a nod toward Marduk.

"Very well. Let us drink and I will explain exactly why we are here."

Smith sipped his drink and kept one eye always on the demon. Pazuzu seemed to relax more and more with every sip of his drink until he was practically slumped in his chair.

"We are on a special mission. A type of cooperative effort between Heaven and Hell," Pazuzu began.

"Like a taskforce?"

"If you like," the demon responded, "We were initially sent here to retrieve the body of the angel Metatron."

"I'm not familiar with that angel," Smith interrupted, the effects of the Long Island iced tea beginning to settle upon him.

The demon looked aghast, as if Smith had just claimed he had no idea who God was. The silver eyes remained wide and locked with Smith's as the demon took a gulp of the drink, as if Smith might do something even more shocking at any moment if the demon looked away.

"Voice of God," Pazuzu said after swallowing, "You did not kill just any angel. You killed the Voice of God."

Smith heard the glass breaking when he dropped it and distantly felt the cold sticky wetness seeping into his pants, but he was too numb from what the demon had just told him to fully register anything outside of that one sentence. His hands dropped into the spilled drink spreading across the table and broken glass cut into his palms, mingling blood with liquor. His own life felt suddenly very insignificant in comparison to the bigger picture. When he was able to form a coherent thought again, he spoke in a strained and squeaky voice.

"How the hell am I supposed to make amends for something like that?!"

The demon shrugged and took another swig of the Long Island.

"If you are asking how to say you are sorry for such a heinous act, I am unsure."

"Then why are you here, exactly?" Smith asked, exasperation seeping into his voice as sobriety left it.

"You are a terrible detective, Mr. Calahan."

"No shit."

"We are here to ensure that the Voice is restored. Since you used a very specific dagger to kill Metatron, only you can repair the damage. Otherwise, the angel would simply have regenerated or been replaced by another angel."

"And what would have happened to me in that other instance, where the angel regenerated or got replaced?"

"You would be sent to Hell, naturally. Unless it was an accident."

Pazuzu contemplated the nearly empty glass in his clawed hand. He had slumped further down in the seat and was now leaning on Marduk's back.

"But it *was* an accident!" Smith exclaimed, "I only killed it because it had just killed my brother and was about to kill everyone else in the room!"

"Ahhhh. The loophole, I believe you call it? Where did you hide the body?"

"In my brother's grave. Under the casket. At least

that's what my father told me."

Pazuzu nodded thoughtfully then straightened up. He nudged Marduk, and his companion gave a loud snore and lay still.

"Help me move him," the demon told Smith, "We cannot stay here, and I fear Dan will no longer serve us these delightful drinks."

Indeed, Dan the bartender glared as Pazuzu and Smith dragged the unconscious Marduk out of the bar. Pazuzu paused when they emerged on the sidewalk, considering their options.

"We can't leave him on the sidewalk," Smith told the demon.

Pazuzu frowned and glanced over at Smith. His expression said that leaving Marduk's unconscious body on the sidewalk had been exactly what he had been planning to do.

"We can put him in one of the hotel rooms?" Smith tried.

Pazuzu gave a nod and they dragged Marduk back into the hotel. The unconscious demon's feet made a thunking noise as the trio made their way up the short flight of stairs between the hotel bar entrance and front desk. The woman at the desk's smile froze as she watched them approach.

"One room for the night, please," Smith said, without waiting for the woman to greet them.

She punched information into the computer and looked back up at them. "We only have the honeymoon suite available."

"Isn't that just one bed?" Smith asked, "Don't you have any with two beds?"

The woman's smile was professionally apologetic.

"Sorry, sir, it's coming up on the anniversary of the Battle and we book up pretty quick."

"Very well," Pazuzu said wearily.

They dragged Marduk to the elevator and rode in drunken silence to their floor. After they opened the door to the room they deposited Marduk in the jacuzzi. While the basin was large enough for two people, the demon still appeared crunched into the space.

Pazuzu and Smith moved out to the bedroom area and Smith climbed onto the bed while the demon took a chair. They stared at each other in silence for a moment and then the demon started to laugh. The sound sent chills down Smith's spine.

"What's so funny?" he asked.

"There is a demon in the bathtub of the honeymoon suite," Pazuzu said and laughed harder.

Smith snorted then joined in laughing. For a few minutes, it felt almost as if they were old friends sharing a prank they had played on a drunk buddy. When their mirth finally faded out, the silence between them was almost tangible.

"How can I make things right?" Smith asked at last.

Pazuzu said quietly, "You need to use the ceremonial dagger upon yourself."

Smith considered this for a moment. "You'll forgive me if I think there has to be a better way to fix this mess. Maybe one without me dying?"

The demon shook his head.

"I wonder if I found out the same information all the other times," Smith mused, "And decided to put it to the test by killing myself in different ways."

"It is possible, I suppose, but the fact of the matter remains and we have wasted far too much time to delay any longer. The Voice of God has been silent for a century, and I believe there may be topics which the Creator would like to discuss. Where is the dagger?"

"I don't know," Smith admitted, "But I know someone who should know."

Smith left a message for Calahan asking him where they could find the dagger then collapsed into the hotel bed. Within seconds he was asleep.

The demon contemplated sleeping, but decided to stay up in case Marduk regained consciousness during the night. Marduk was not a morning person, and tended to be punchy when disoriented. It wouldn't do to be this close to success in their mission only to have Marduk kill the one man who could solve the case once and for all.

CHAPTER VI

The next morning Smith woke before the demon in the tub. His groan echoed around the room before circling back around to stab him in the eye sockets. He fumbled across the nightstand for the thing that had pulled him from unconsciousness and stared in confusion at the cell phone in his hand. When the hell had he gotten a cell phone?

"Hello?"

Sweet Jesus, he was hungover.

"Meet me at the Old Bergen Church Cemetery in Jersey City at ten o'clock tonight."

Smith blinked at his cell phone as it clicked off, indicating Calahan had already hung up. He struggled to remember when he had given the old man his cell phone number, then recalled the voicemail he had left for him the night before.

He looked around the room and pieced together the previous night. It all seemed like an odd dream, especially in the empty silence of the hotel suite. He jumped in surprise when Pazuzu appeared by his side with a glass of water in one hand and two aspirin in the other.

"Marry me," Smith whispered hoarsely as he took the offered pills and drink.

"Neither demons nor angels marry," Pazuzu began then realized it was not an actual proposal.

The skin around the demon's eyes was dark as he watched Smith take the pills and struggle into a sitting position. The silence spread between them to the point of awkwardness until finally Pazuzu spoke again.

"Good morning, Mr. Calahan." The demon's voice was hoarse and quiet, as if his head might shatter if he spoke too loudly.

"Morning."

They heard a fumbling clunk from the bathroom followed by curses. Moments later Marduk emerged. He looked worse than Smith and Pazuzu combined. The demon clutched the sides of his head and growled at them.

"Where the hell are we?" Marduk hissed.

"We are presently in the honeymoon suite of a hotel," Pazuzu replied.

"How–?"

"We dragged you from the bar to here," his companion said helpfully. "Mr. Calahan said it was improper for me to leave you on the sidewalk with your pants around your ankles, so I took my pleasure with you here instead. After I finished with you I let Mr. Calahan have a turn as well."

Marduk stared in shock first at Pazuzu, then to Smith. Smith's mouth opened and closed, but he was too surprised to speak. They both looked back to Pazuzu and the demon laughed loudly.

"I am attempting to repair my sense of humor," he explained, still laughing. "I assure you nothing of what I described took place last night."

"Thank goodness, because that would have been a

little awkward," Smith said with a small sigh of relief.

Marduk shook his head incredulously. "You got me, 'Zu. You got me good."

Pazuzu smiled, but it was thinned by Marduk's use of the nickname.

"So what are we doing today?" Marduk asked.

"Today we are taking a trip, correct?" Pazuzu asked, aiming the question at Smith, who nodded.

"Trip? To where?"

"Jersey City. But first, gentlemen, I need some coffee…and maybe breakfast. We'll see how the coffee settles first."

"You can get some on the way," Marduk growled.

He grabbed hold of Smith's arm in a grip like a vice and Smith stared in horrified fascination as the air shimmered, then split to reveal a city street beyond. Marduk pulled him into the tear and Pazuzu followed. They arrived in front of an old beat-up diner in what appeared to be New York City.

The demons motioned for Smith to follow them and they entered. Smith looked around them at the old booths and kitschy décor and wondered if they had stepped back in time or if the place had just never updated after 1957.

They moved toward a booth at the back, passing patrons and nodding here and there. Smith glanced at the people in the diner and felt a strange tingle run down his spine. They looked human enough, but there was something off about all of them. As they looked at him, he realized it was their eyes. Every single one of them had silver eyes similar to his companions'. Were all of these "people" actually demons in human form? The thought chilled him to the core.

"Angels and demons," Pazuzu whispered as he slid into the booth next to Smith.

"Ahh."

The waitress walked over to their table as if in a daze, then seemed to wake up when she saw Smith. A slow lewd smile crossed her lips.

"Hey there, Calahan," she said with a wink, "What are you doing hanging out with this crew?"

Smith blinked and wished he could remember the pinup posing as a waitress. He smiled weakly and shrugged for an answer.

"Business," Marduk said, glaring.

The waitress rolled her eyes at the demon and sighed. "What can I get you, fellas?"

"Coffee, please, and..." Smith said and looked around for a menu.

"Eggs Benedict," the waitress told him, "They're your favorite. Especially after a night out on the town."

Her smile was like sunshine, perfect white teeth flashing at him from lips so red they could have been fresh-picked cherries. He nodded, speechless. Eggs Benedict sounded heavenly.

She turned to the demons. "Coffee, black, right?"

They nodded and she sauntered off. Halfway across the diner she glanced back over her shoulder to blow a kiss to Smith.

"Looks like you two knew each other," said Koth as he slid into the booth next to Marduk.

Smith nearly jumped out of his skin at the sudden appearance of another demon. Where the hell had the guy come from? He hadn't seen anyone enter the diner. Then again, he hadn't exactly been watching the door, he reminded himself.

Pazuzu nodded to Koth and made the introductions. "Koth, this is Virgil Calahan. We found him."

The third demon clapped his hands and smiled with satisfaction. "Great job, guys. So, we can go ahead with the ritual?"

"Not…yet," Marduk mumbled, "We don't have the dagger. Or the body."

"Shit shit shit," Koth groaned. "Why the hell do these things always get so complicated?"

"Because Prometheus let the soil-dwellers know our secrets," Marduk said, "Then he helped them make weapons that could kill us. Remind me again why we thought it was a good idea to let him know *everything* about us?"

Koth shrugged, clearly embarrassed. "Best laid plans, blah blah blah," he said, then asked, "So what's the next move?"

"We are traveling to Jersey City to find both the dagger and the body," Pazuzu told him.

Koth nodded his approval. His eyes wandered upward as the waitress approached the table and a slow grin spread over his mouth.

"Hi, Cherry," he said.

"Get soaked, Koth," she replied, her tone filled with sweet venom as she set the coffees in front of Smith, Pazuzu, and Marduk.

The demon clutched at his chest in feigned injury. "Oh, gentlemen, the lady doth reject me yet again!" he cried.

She rolled her eyes and walked away. The rest of the table looked embarrassed for Koth, though the demon seemed unfazed by their waitress' reaction to his behavior.

"She doesn't know it yet, but I'm her personal Hell," Koth told them in a conspiratorial whisper, "You know, when she gets out of Limbo."

Smith didn't know why, but he felt protective of the waitress. He cleared his throat and took a sip of his coffee in hopes it would set Koth in a different conversational direction. The demon looked at Smith and seemed to remember why they were gathered there.

"So, Jersey City. When are you guys heading over there?"

"As soon as we finish here," replied Pazuzu and took a sip of his coffee.

Koth contemplated the trio and nodded. "Yeah, you guys look a little rough around the edges this morning," he said with a laugh. "You drink too much last night?"

Marduk sneered at the case manager and sipped his coffee. Koth laughed even harder and shook his head.

"Try some Gatorade and a slice of pizza," he said, "Or if you're not into Gatorade, get some hair of the dog."

Marduk looked disgusted. "Why the hell would I want to eat dog hair to cure a hangover?"

Smith felt the hot coffee shoot from his nose even before he realized he was laughing. Koth's laughter was equally loud, and Marduk glared at them both in confusion.

"He means you drink more of what got you drunk," Smith explained, still chuckling.

Marduk stared at Smith as if he had sprouted a second head. "I assure you, I will *not* be drinking again for a very long time."

"Be that as it may," Pazuzu interrupted quickly before Marduk could go on about the ills of drinking, "We should go soon. We have things to accomplish today."

Smith nodded grimly and downed the rest of his coffee. As they got up to leave, the waitress came back over to them. She ran a hand up Smith's arm and squeezed as she slid a plate of Eggs Benedict in front of him.

Smith slid the plate back toward her with an embarrassed grin. He gave a small shake of his head, and held his stomach for emphasis.

"I'm sorry, but my eyes felt better than my stomach. I think I'll skip breakfast, but thanks."

"You come back and visit real soon, Cal. I missed you. Don't let these guys rub off on you, okay?"

He nodded, then on a whim he leaned down and kissed her full on the mouth. If he was going to head into uncharted waters and possibly die in the process, by God he was going to at least get a kiss before he went.

Instead of slapping him she let out a small gasp and threw her arms around his neck. Their kiss deepened and Smith could taste a sweetness like fresh ripe cherries on her lips. With an extreme effort of will he pulled himself away from their embrace and took a deep breath.

"I'll see you around."

"I know you will," she said. "You always come back."

Smith and his demon companions exited the diner and Smith could feel the waitress watching them the whole way. When the door had closed behind them, the demons turned to stare at him. Koth went so far as to clap him on the back and shake his hand.

"Congratulations, Mr. Calahan. You have accomplished what all of the minions of Hell have only dreamed about."

"What is that, exactly?"

"You got Cherry to flirt with you, for one," Koth said with a grin, "and then you actually *kissed* her. That's a big deal. Wait'll I tell the guys."

"I...don't get it. Why is that such a big deal?"

"She generally doesn't even acknowledge us. We have to practically beg her for coffee. And it's not just with demons. She's like that with *everyone*. Except you," Koth finished with a wink.

"I guess I must have known her before," Smith replied lamely.

"Yeah, in the biblical sense," Koth said with a laugh.

Smith rolled his eyes and shoved his hands in his pockets. He could feel a blush creeping into his cheeks and he had no idea why.

"So how do we get to the Old Bergen Church in Jersey City?" he asked, his voice gruff.

"Follow me," Koth said and nodded his head toward 6th Avenue.

"Aren't we just going to get there the same way we got here?" Smith asked, confused.

"We've got to pick up a few people first," Koth told him.

They walked through the turnstyles at the 23rd street PATH station minutes later and boarded a train bound for Journal Square. As the train clacked and clattered, lurching left then right, they stared everywhere but at each other. The demons seemed not to be noticed by anyone else on the train, and Smith wondered if it was intentional or if he really was the only one who could see them.

So as not to seem conspicuous, he stared out of the plexiglass train windows into the darkness of the tunnels. As the train screeched through a section of tunnel, he could make out what appeared to be an old subway station. The ornate walls and tiling were partly covered in graffiti, visible only in the strobed flashes from the sparks coming off the wheels and tracks as the cars rattled through. What caught his attention more than the abandoned station itself were the people standing on the platform as if waiting to board. He stared in surprise as the train screamed to a sudden halt then looked to his companions.

Grim-faced, Koth stepped off the train and moved to where a small group of men waited on one of the dust-coated benches. He motioned for them to follow him, and they fearfully obeyed.

The group stepped into the car, squinting in the sudden glare of the fluorescent lights. Smith noted with alarm that they seemed somehow translucent. Dust billowed off of them when they moved and he wondered who, or what the men were.

He turned to ask why the train had stopped for the people at an obviously abandoned station and the words died in his throat. Koth's expression was filled with sadness and the demon averted his eyes, but not before Smith had seen.

"It's best not to ask questions about it," Koth warned.

Smith gave a short nod, but still felt uneasy when he looked at the ten men gathered in a corner of the train car. They whispered amongst themselves and cast an occasional glance his way, quickly averting their eyes when he caught them in the act.

When the conductor finally announced their stop at Journal Square, Smith breathed a sigh of relief. The rest of the ride had been awkward and his demonic companions unusually silent. Their expanded group exited the upper portion of the train station and made their way toward Pavonia Avenue.

When they reached Tonnele Avenue they turned, following the street to Kennedy Boulevard, then to Bergen Avenue. Just after Vroom Street, one of the men in the dusty group spoke.

"We're here," he said simply.

Dust seemed to emanate from his mouth, as if he had spent years in the old subway station breathing in the grit and concrete of the city above. For all Smith knew, he might very well have done just that.

The group wandered into the cemetery, following the lead of the man who had spoken. He brought them to a worn grave marker toward the back of the cemetery and they stopped.

Smith looked at the marker and read aloud, "William Calahan."

"Your younger brother," said another member of the subway group.

"Did you know him?" Smith asked.

The group gave a collective nod. Smith had so many more questions to ask, but was interrupted when Koth stepped up to the group.

"*Dig*," commanded the demon.

Smith stared in shock, first at the sudden authoritativeness of the demon, and then at the group as they fell to their knees and began clawing at the earth. Pazuzu and Marduk seemed to fade into the shadows cast by the trees, each of them leaning on a grave marker. Smith moved over to them while Koth continued to oversee the digging operation. He felt like it would be a good idea to distance himself from the group in case the police noticed a bunch of crazy-looking dust people digging up a grave in broad daylight.

"Who are those guys?" he asked the demons.

Marduk growled in response, one hand held up to the side of his head. He squinted against the daylight and inclined his head toward Pazuzu. Smith looked to the other demon, eyebrows raised in question.

"You do not recognize them?"

"No. Should I?"

Pazuzu nodded. "They are the other members of the group you were with that night."

Smith leaned against a grave marker and let out a breath. He looked over his shoulder at the digging men. Their fingers had started to bleed, but the hole was a sizable one and was at least two feet deep. *Only four more feet to go before ten o'clock tonight*, Smith thought, morbidly.

"So...?"

"So how did they come to be in an abandoned subway tunnel?" Pazuzu asked.

Smith nodded. Suddenly he craved a cigarette.

"When the...event occurred, we were unsure of exactly what had happened. By the time we were informed, many of the original group had either scattered, or in your brother's instance, had been killed. We have managed to locate ten of the original thirteen over the last century.

"In order to keep them safe and contained, we held them in the subway station until the time was right. Many others are awaiting their time in those stations," Pazuzu said with a hint of sadness in his voice.

"So how did my father and I not end up in the subway?"

"You and your father gave us some difficulty. It seemed every time we located you, you would mysteriously die. When that happened, we would lose both you and your father. This is the only time we managed to locate you before he did."

"Wait, what?" Smith asked.

He could feel something itching down his back and at the back of his mind, as if locks were being thrown open. Something important, but what? He scratched at his back and was suddenly aware that his back had not really itched since he had met the demons.

Pazuzu said simply, "Varying teams have managed to locate you over the years, but as soon as we made contact, you inevitably made a suicide attempt shortly afterwards. Several times your father was present shortly before the attempt occurred," the demon finished and took a cigarette pack out of his pocket.

Smith eyed up the cigarettes and took one when the demon offered it. As he placed the cigarette between his lips, Pazuzu flicked his fingernails and a small blue flame appeared at the end of his fingertips. He held the light to both cigarettes and the flame disappeared.

"How do you know my father was there at the time I committed suicide?"

"We have been following you. On the occasions we witnessed your suicide, we saw your father a short distance behind you and we saw him leave without you. When we searched for you, you were gone. Often we would read of a suicide attempt in the next day or week's newspapers."

"Holy shit," Smith breathed as one more tumbler in the lock clicked open. He looked at his cell phone's clock, then back at the digging men, then at the demons. "You guys have to hide. Quick."

Both Marduk and Pazuzu looked at him in confusion. He pointed to the time on the phone. Where the hell had the time gone? It was already seven o'clock and only minutes before the day seemed to have just started. He ran over to Koth and tugged his jacket.

"Look, my father is on his way here right now. We're meeting at ten o'clock, but I think he'll show up early. He'll be here any minute and I think he'll make a run for it if he sees all this going on," Smith told the demon.

Koth's expression shifted from annoyance to sudden realization. He turned back to the digging men and cleared his throat.

"Get up, gentlemen. We need to move and quick."

Smith turned back to Pazuzu and Marduk. "You guys, too. I need to look like I'm alone when my father gets here."

The demons faded into the shadows of the trees and Smith dove into the hole that had been started by the group of subway dwellers. He clawed at the earth, throwing out handfuls over his shoulder and letting it fall over him in an attempt to appear as if he had been digging for hours.

After an hour or more of digging, the sound of footsteps at the rim of the hole caught his attention and he prayed it wasn't a cop. He looked up to see Virgil Calahan, Sr. standing at the edge of the grave.

"You're early," he said with a forced grin.

"Son, what the hell do you think you're doing?" asked the old man.

There was a note of caution in his tone, and Smith shuddered as another piece clicked into place. He motioned for the old man to join him in the hole.

"Help me out," he said, "We have to get the dagger."

"Why on earth would you need that old piece of junk?" asked Calahan.

"I had hoped to get the dagger before you got here and then we could hit up some bars afterwards to celebrate. I just need to get it to the demons and they'll leave me alone."

"Is that what they told you?" the old man asked.

"Yeah," Smith said as he continued to throw out clumps of earth from the grave.

Calahan watched him for a few moments then held out two shovels. "Will these help?"

Smith nodded gratefully and Calahan dropped into the grave with him. The pair dug in silence for a few minutes, both men removing jackets and rolling up sleeves as the work became more arduous.

When at last they hit the coffin, the wood splintered beneath their shovels. Smith let out a cry of surprise when his feet were next to drop through the casket's rotten lid. His feet hit something soft yet solid and he groaned.

Calahan stared in horror at the broken casket lid then jumped out of the grave. Smith could hear him retching, and then the sound abruptly stopped.

"Calahan?" he called, trying to see over the rim of the hole they had dug. "Dad?"

There was no answer, and Smith pulled his feet clear of the coffin without looking down. He struggled to climb out of the grave, expecting to see police gathered around Calahan, but that was not the case.

The old man stood over the grave, shovel raised. His eyes were red and tears coursed down his leathery cheeks as his chest heaved with barely suppressed sobs.

"Dammit, boy! Why did you have to go and dig up Billy?" Calahan asked quietly.

"It's the only way to end it," Smith said gently.

"I don't *want* to end it," the old man seethed, "I *like* being alive. Killing that angel was the best thing we could have done. Don't you see that?"

Smith was about to ask what the old man meant when the last piece fell into the puzzle. He stared in horror at the raised shovel in his father's hands.

"I didn't try to kill myself," he said quietly, "*You* tried to kill me. That's why none of my attempts were officially looked at as attempted suicides. There was never a note because I was murdered each time. Wasn't I?"

Calahan's face hardened. He planted his feet in a batter's stance and hoisted the shovel higher over his shoulder.

"That's right," he said, voice quiet, "Every damned time you came back, you wanted us to turn ourselves in to the demons. *Pay our dues*, you said. I knew better, though. I knew we'd be up shit's creek if we turned ourselves in. I knew at least *I* would be up shit's creek."

"Why?"

The old man's face contorted with effort as he brought the shovel down, aiming for Smith's head. The clang as it hit a heavy-looking ring on Koth's outstretched hand sent a wave of relief through Smith as he cringed and braced for the impact of the shovel with his head.

Pazuzu helped Smith out of the grave and he stared at Calahan. The old man looked to each face of the gathered former members of his group and began to cry.

"Virgil Calahan, please retrieve the dagger of Kryth," Koth said.

The old man shook his head and looked defiant. The demon stepped closer and without a word shoved Calahan into the open grave. He stood staring down at Calahan, his expression stony.

"*Now*," Koth said.

One of the members of the subway station group stepped to the edge of the grave and stared down at his former friend. The man's face was middle-aged, but haggard. Even in the evening night light his skin still held a gray pallor.

"You knew where it was the whole time?" he asked.

The old man in the grave was silent as he looked up at the speaker.

"We spent a century in an abandoned limbo because none of us knew where you had hidden the body or the dagger. You told us it had disappeared; yet this whole damned time you *knew*. We suffered while you hid like a coward!"

"Correction, Jensen, I *lived*," Calahan spat, "I saw what happened to you after the demons got to you, and I decided it wasn't for me. And if you had had the chance, you would have done the same. When Junior had an attack of conscience and wanted to surrender, well…it was him or me."

"Shut up and retrieve the dagger, Mr. Calahan," Koth cut in. "If I have to join you in that grave, only one of us will be emerging. I assure you, it will not be you."

Calahan growled as he turned his attention to the coffin and began to pick pieces of the broken lid out of the way. When he saw the body within he paused and let out a small sob before steeling himself and reaching into the casket.

He withdrew an object wrapped in stained oilcloth. It was oblong and narrow, and there was a gleaming edge stabbing through one end. Smith watched Calahan struggle to climb from the grave and felt a pang of guilt. Without a word, he moved to the edge of the grave and held out a hand to Calahan.

The old man looked up at him in surprise, but appeared thankful for the assistance. Smith hoisted him to his feet and they faced each other.

"I'm sorry," Calahan said quietly.

"Hey, it's okay. I don't really remember it anyway and–"

Smith's words died in his throat as something cold slithered into his chest and the air went out of his lungs. He looked down to see an ornate handle jutting from his shirt; he was unable to process what had happened.

"I truly am sorry, son," Calahan told him.

Blood covered the old man's hand as he withdrew the dagger from Smith's chest. When he tried to protest, blood bubbled from Smith's lips but no words came out as the old man plunged the dagger into his chest again.

The shock that had frozen the others lifted and the demons rushed to rescue Smith from the attack. Koth cried out in anger as the dagger severed one of his fingers and Pazuzu and Marduk sidestepped multiple swipes from the shimmering blade.

"Enough of this," Koth muttered.

The demon dropped his skin and clothing to the ground and spread large bat-like wings out behind him. His face contorted in rage and Calahan screamed at the sight of the demon in his true form.

"Drop. The. Knife."

Calahan dropped the dagger to the ground and tried to run. When at last the group managed to subdue him, the old man hurled curses at them. Koth shrank back into his human form and adjusted his tie.

As soon as the demons were sure Calahan was no longer a threat, they turned their attention to Smith as he lay dying upon the ground at the edge of his brother's grave. His blood ran into the open hole, spilling from between his grasping fingers as he attempted to apply pressure to the wound, but already his strength was waning.

Pazuzu crouched down next to him, studying him with intense, silver eyes. The demon moved the remnants of Smith's torn shirt aside and winced at the wound.

"I do not believe you will recover from this," the

demon told him quietly.

Koth joined them and frowned at the implications of the blood. He dropped to the ground and glanced at Pazuzu, who gave a brief shake of the head.

"Well, Mr. Smith," Koth said at last, "You're fucked."

Smith extended his middle finger at the demon and let his head fall back onto the ground.

"At least he hasn't lost his sense of humor," Marduk said from behind them.

Smith stared up into the canopy of trees and decided it was a fitting place to die as well as a fitting end. Defending his brother, he had killed an angel with the dagger that had ultimately killed him. Now he lay dying next to his brother's grave, which had covered the body of the angel. No wonder God was silent. If there was a better display of justice, he had never seen it.

"This is not right," Pazuzu said.

Koth cleared his throat.

"You know it to be true, Koth. He is not the one who committed the crime!"

CHAPTER VII

Koth heaved a sigh and nodded. Smith looked up at the demons, his eyes questioning.

"Virgil Calahan killed Metatron," Pazuzu said, "*You,* Mr. Smith, are not the Virgil Calahan we sought. After discussing the murder with you last evening, it became clear that you were not the man we had been searching for; it was your father."

Smith stared in shock, then whispered, "I didn't kill Metatron? He…my father was going to let me pay for it?"

"Unfortunately your dad threw a monkey wrench into what should have been a cut and dried procedure," Koth growled.

The sound of large wings came to them over the gravestones and seconds later, a man in a white dress shirt and black pants sailed from thin air to land next to them. Black wings folded and disappeared behind him and he gave a small bow to all assembled.

"Gentlemen," said Azrael, "You have found Metatron's body?"

Koth gave a nod toward the open grave. "In there."

Azrael contemplated the hole in the ground with its broken casket for a moment, then turned silver eyes toward Smith. The angel of death approached the dying man and dropped to one knee.

"You are a victim of circumstance, I am sad to say," said the angel, "And you have paid the price for the sin of your father. So I give you a choice. You may die a peaceful death, or you may become one with Metatron and allow the Voice to speak once more."

Smith choked on his own words, asking, "Will Metatron live if I die?"

Azrael shook his head. "There needs to be a mortal sacrifice to lend corporeal energy to the angel."

"Like jumpstarting a car?" Koth asked incredulously.

"Somewhat like that, yes," said the angel and turned to Smith, "I understand it is a big decision, but I am afraid you must decide sooner rather than later. What is your choice? You do not have much time."

Smith spoke one last word, and that with great effort.

"Metatron."

The demons and angel prepared a makeshift circle from the gathered subway group and Smith himself. They encircled the scene, holding a struggling Calahan in place. The demons and angel spoke in unison and a glow came from the open grave. They motioned for the others to join in the chant and the glow brightened as darkness stretched over the cemetery. One by one each of the streetlamps around the gathering burst in a shower of sparks until the only light left came from the open grave.

After a few moments, the glow subsided and the sound of tearing boards could be heard within the earth. The stench of death and wet dirt filled the air as a filthy hand reached over the edge of the hole.

The angel hoisted itself onto the grass, scanning its surroundings with golden eyes. When it caught sight of Smith it crawled to him and gathered the now lifeless body in its arms. Gently, it kissed him, and a glowing orb passed from Smith's lips, floating into the angel's mouth. Moments later, Smith's body was also absorbed into the angel. Metatron straightened up.

Without a word, it stood there and attempted to clean itself off as the others watched. Finally it turned to face them all and gave a wry smile that was reminiscent of Smith's own smile.

"Metatron, welcome back," Azrael said.

"Yeah, sorry. It took a hundred years to figure out where you were buried," Koth said sheepishly.

The angel's eyes glowed golden from the depths of its dirty face and it shook dried mud from its hair. When it took a step the rotted tatters of what once was clothing fell from its body and piled on the ground beneath it.

"Are you not yet recovered? Will you speak?" asked Azrael with concern.

Metatron stared into each face before replying, "There is nothing to say."

THE END

The Dispossessed

Book 2

By
Suzanne Madron

CHAPTER I

John Smith had once been known as Virgil Calahan, Jr., but that was in a past life. He had renounced that name and his entire history following his death in a graveyard in Jersey City, New Jersey. Since being known by that name, he had inadvertently helped to kill and then restore The Voice of God, been murdered by his own father roughly two hundred times, become a private detective, opened his own detective agency, been hired by demons, and sent his father to Hell. It had been a very long century, and more recently, an even longer month.

His thoughts swirled in dark and light billows of

cream as he stirred his coffee. He was sitting in an old diner in New York City and the place was mostly empty except for the staff and the few angels and demons who frequented the place. He disliked the perpetually sticky formica tabletops and pleather seats that painfully gripped any patches of bare skin that came in contact with them, but he was always happy to meet there because it meant he might possibly see Cherry.

Smith let out a dreamy sigh. Cherry was a pinup model posing as a waitress to the denizens of Heaven and Hell and she had some serious flirt factor when it came to him. If he was to be honest with himself, he enjoyed the jealous glances from both angels and demons when Cherry made passes at him. They all wanted her, but she refused to give any of them the time of day.

Today was Cherry's day off, unfortunately, and Smith was hungover. It was a bad day all around, and the sudden request to meet with him from out of the blue did not bode well for any chance of an improvement to the day or Smith's mood. The door jangled as it opened, and a dark shape entered the diner.

Koth slid into the booth, taking the seat across from him. Smith glanced at his watch then stared at the demon. He was early. One thing Smith had learned about angels and demons, they were *always* exactly on time. Smith became suspicious and took in the demon's appearance.

It still took some getting used to, gazing into the eyes of demons, even though Koth was one of the more "normal" looking of Hell's minions…for what that was worth. Most of the demons sent topside tended to resemble 1940s hardboiled detectives, thanks to Hell's use of old black and white Noir films as training devices for getting the demons to "fit in."

"Buddy, you look rough," said the demon by way of a greeting.

"Yeah, thanks. It was a long night."

Koth stared at his clawed, pale gray hands and fidgeted.

"You're early. Why?" Smith asked, irritation creeping into his voice.

"I wanted to talk to you before the others got here. How's the transition going, kid? You doing okay? I'm serious."

Smith looked into the demon's silver eyes in surprise. While Koth was the closest a demon could get to being human, the sincere tone of caring was a bit of a jolt. The demon folded his hands and waited politely for Smith to answer.

He let out a long breath and considered the question. It was increasingly difficult to concentrate when he was sober.

"To be honest, it's not quite what I expected. It's damned tough. Like I have two people thinking inside my head, and I can't shut either one of them up, you know?"

Koth sighed and nodded. He really did seem concerned for Smith's wellbeing.

"I wish there had been an easier way. I really do," the demon said ruefully. "You're good people, and there just aren't a lot of you left."

Smith shrugged, uncomfortable with being complimented by a demon. "You're not so bad yourself, I guess. For a demon, I mean. You guys are actually kind of nice."

"We didn't start off as the bad guys, kid," Koth told him with a wink.

Smith rubbed at his head and gave a nod of agreement. It was a good point. He was still suspicious, however.

"Okay, Koth, enough of the bullshit. What's the deal? You're being way too nice to me. And where are Pazuzu and Marduk?"

Koth threw his head back and laughed a deep belly laugh. He raised his hands in surrender.

"You got me," he chuckled, "The demonic duo are on their way. My motives were partly concern for your wellbeing and partly just plain old curiosity. Metatron's never been human before, so it's a bit of an adjustment for us all. Obviously it's important that things run smoothly, you know?"

"Mmm."

Smith returned to staring into his coffee. The whispers in his head dimmed slightly and he rubbed at his eyes. He wished someone would have told him that playing host to the angel, Metatron, also known as "The Voice of God" would mean either getting blind drunk every night or having to suffer perpetual insomnia.

"Coffee any good today?" the demon asked.

Smith shrugged in response. It wasn't as good as it was on the days Cherry made it, but it wasn't as bad as it could be. At least today it wasn't burned.

Koth cleared his throat and motioned to a bored-looking teenage waiter. The kid came over to their table and seemed barely able to keep his eyes open.

"Yeah?"

"Coffee. Black. Preferably hot," Koth ordered.

He watched the kid wander toward the coffee maker behind the breakfast bar and frowned. Smith followed his stare and noticed the track marks all over the kid's arms. *How did I miss that earlier?* he wondered.

The waiter came back to their table, walking slowly. It appeared as if he was struggling his way through a room full of marshmallow fluff. He placed the cup of coffee in front of Koth and meandered back behind the bar. Smith stared as the kid collapsed onto a bar stool, then went face first onto the breakfast bar. His eyes were half-closed and he drooled onto the filthy bar top.

"Is he okay?" Smith asked with real concern.

"Overdose," Koth muttered, disgusted. "We used to get some seriously messed up villains in Hell back in the day. Now we get a lot of junkies who crossed the line from needing their drug to enjoying the pain they inflicted on everyone around them while striving for their next fix." He heaved a sigh. "And here we are."

They looked up as Pazuzu and Marduk wandered in off the street. The sounds of traffic and street noise were abruptly silenced as the door shut behind them, and Smith found himself wishing he could shut off the voice in his head so easily.

Koth motioned for the other two demons to sit down. They slid into the booth, one next to Smith and the other next to their case manager. Pazuzu nodded in greeting to Smith, and Marduk let out a growl that could have been a hello or a curse.

"To what do I owe the pleasure of this reunion?"

the detective-turned-Voice of God asked.

"Well, hang on now, there's back story," Koth said, raising his hand quickly before the other two demons could respond.

"We are looking for someone," Pazuzu told Smith with an annoyed glance at Koth.

"That's it? Are you sure? That sounds awfully simple…. Wait, this isn't another one of my family members who went missing a century ago after killing one of you guys?"

"Now hang on, dammit," Koth seethed, slamming his hands on the table. "Let me tell it. Like I said, there's backstory. And no, it's no one you're related to…at least I don't think you are."

Smith stared at Koth over the rim of his coffee mug, his gaze skeptical. The demon scowled, then turned the look on Pazuzu.

"See? You messed it up, dammit. He probably won't even take the case now."

"Depends," Smith answered, setting his coffee onto the table. "First I need to hear what the case is about, and why you need *me* to help you with it."

CHAPTER II

"Okay. As Pazuzu mentioned, we're looking for someone. Sort of a missing persons thing, but different," Koth began.

"How so?"

"The missing person is one of us," Marduk said quietly.

Smith blinked. "One of *you*? You mean a demon?"

"Yes."

Smith considered this for a moment and the demons watched him in silence. He felt his brow furrow as the question formed on his lips.

"Doesn't Hell keep tabs on all you guys?" he asked.

Koth rolled his eyes. "Come on, man. What do we look like, the NSA? No, we're not tech savvy enough for 'tabs'. We're still playing movies from the 1940s on a film projector, and to be honest, I think even if we had the technology none of us would bother to learn how to use it. Prometheus had to show us how to work the projector. Talk about a sad state of affairs."

Smith stifled a laugh, realized it wasn't a joke, and buried his smirk in his coffee. Koth heaved an embarrassed sigh.

"So here's the story of our guy. It started only

about thirty years ago. Just your run of the mill demon possession. Hell thought it would be good advertising if we started possessions up again, you see? So. Bam. Demon possession of some guy out in Akron, Ohio."

"I'm not going to Ohio," Smith interrupted quickly, dropping his coffee mug to the table with a whack.

Koth growled. "Let. Me. Finish. Guy's name was John Daniels-"

Smith barked out an involuntary laugh. The demons stared at him as if he had gone insane.

"You're joking. Seriously? *John* Daniels?"

"Yes."

"Let me guess–his friends called him Jack?"

Well, yeah, bu—oh." Koth looked as if he had been struck by lightning, then he also began to laugh. Pazuzu looked politely entertained while Marduk scowled.

Smith contained his mirth. "So, John–also known as *Jack* Daniels from Akron, Ohio, gets possessed. Then what?"

"He was possessed for the next thirty years."

"*Thirty years?*" Smith could not hide the surprise in his voice. "I didn't know people could be possessed that long."

"Usually they aren't," Koth explained, "The typical active possession lasts only a very short while, usually until the possessed is either exorcised or is killed in the process of exorcism. The basic point of the whole thing was to keep Hell on the map, to keep humans fearing something. As long as they're afraid, humans will keep doing stupid shit to each other, see? Only this particular possession was a bit unusual."

"What happened?" Smith asked as he took a drink of his now cold coffee.

He motioned for the waiter, saw that the drool puddle had spread across the countertop, and slid out of the booth. He made his way behind the counter and poured his own coffee and cream then held up the carafe toward the table.

"I'll have a cup," Pazuzu said.

Marduk shrugged. "Sure, why not?"

"Koth?"

Koth stared into the dregs of his cup, heaved a dissatisfied sigh and shrugged. "Yeah."

After Smith had finished bringing everyone's coffee to the table he made another pot. He leaned over the waiter and moved to see if the kid was still alive.

He is dead, said the now familiar voice in his head.

He ignored the words and touched the side of the kid's neck anyway. There was no pulse beneath his fingers and the waiter's skin was cold. The others looked at him curiously and he shook his head before joining them back at the booth.

"The service sucks today," Koth said dismally and they all nodded.

"Where's your girlfriend?" Marduk asked with a sly grin.

Smith rolled his eyes. "Cherry's not working today…. And she's *not* my girlfriend. Get back to the story."

"Fair enough," Koth said and sipped at his coffee. "So this guy gets possessed as a kid, right? But his family isn't really that religious, so everyone assumes he just has an imaginary friend and an occasional bout of random epilepsy."

Smith blinked. "*Random* epilepsy?"

"I never said they were the sharpest tacks."

"But a doctor gave them that diagnosis?"

"Oh...no no no. They never brought little Jack to see a doctor about it. They had a friend who saw one of the kid's fits and told them that's what it was."

"Wow. Must have been pretty convincing."

"He was. He was one of our guys," Koth said sheepishly.

"And the point of that convincing speech was what, exactly?"

Koth's expression became more embarrassed. "If they had gone to a doctor, the kid would have been medicated."

"So?"

"Demon possession doesn't work anymore when the possessed get medicated," Koth admitted, "If this kid had been put on anything to stop the seizures, it would have knocked his demon out in the process. We needed everyone to *know* it was a possession and not some medical condition. As it turned out, we'd possessed the wrong family. The demon we sent topside was supposed to possess the *neighbor's* kid. That family was crazy religious."

Smith blew out a breath of air and shook his head. "Okay."

"We realized the error pretty quickly and figured we'd just go ahead with the possession, only with this new family instead. We hoped since they weren't quite as batshit as the neighbors, the possession might even be taken more seriously. Well in the end we didn't realize just *how* non-religious the new family was. When the kid started talking in tongues and telling everyone's deepest, darkest secrets and thoughts, we assumed they would head straight for a priest."

"But they didn't."

"No! Can you believe that shit? They thought he was psychic instead and set him up as a traveling sideshow."

"Oh." Smith stared into his coffee and felt nauseous. He wondered if the sensation was his own or if it belonged to Metatron. Probably a bit of both, he decided.

"It sounds like the kid and his demon have lived happily together for a while now."

"Well, there's the rub," Marduk said, and his tone took on a gossipy quality, "they had a little lover's quarrel."

Koth stared in horror at Marduk. "Shut UP. *I* am telling the story."

"*Lover's* quarrel?"

Koth let out an exasperated sigh and glared at Marduk.

"It was nothing like that. They *did* have a disagreement, yes, but they were most certainly NOT lovers as *this* one suggests. They were close, though. The kid grew up to be a bit of a loner, a misnomer, perhaps, since he had a whole other being living inside him. While he was doing the carnival sideshow circuit, his demon gave him some very lucrative financial advice. His parents did as he told them because they believed he was psychic and would know if they were shafting him–which he would have. When his job as a sideshow act began to fizzle, he cashed in his earnings and lived comfortably like a hermit for quite a while."

"Until...."

"Until an apparent disagreement," Koth mumbled.

"About what?" Smith asked. "What could possibly be so bad after all they'd been through together that would make them split?"

Koth sighed. "Two words: Jehovah's Witnesses."

Smith blinked and struggled to wrap his head around the meaning of the statement. When he realized it was pointless, he asked, "What?"

"Yeah, you heard me correctly, kid. Witnesses. Damn, but they're literally everywhere, even the middle of nowhere, it would seem."

"I'm still not following."

Koth stared into his coffee for a moment. "A few weeks ago, the now-grown John Daniels received a visit from some Jehovah's Witnesses. They knocked, and he actually answered the door. They started talking and he not only heard, but really *listened* to their spiel. When the Witnesses left, he and his demon had a major theological disagreement. Seems Jack had reached the point in life where he had started to consider religion and figured being demon-possessed might hinder his chances of joining a congregation."

"Yeah, probably," Smith said with a wry smile.

"After their fight, the kid started to wonder what else his demon was trying to hide from him, so he starts studying religion on the sly."

Smith arched an eyebrow. "How does one accomplish that? I'd love to know so the next time I've got to go take a dump I can do so with no company."

"I doubt the kid's method would work for your situation," the demon smirked.

"Never know until I try. How did he do it?"

"Porn."

Smith felt his face growing hot and he frowned. "Porn?"

"Oh yes," Koth said lasciviously, "Lots and lots of porn."

Smith wrinkled his nose in distaste. "Yeah, probably wouldn't work for me. My guy seems a little too upright and proper to be distracted by porn."

Upright and proper are considered desirable qualities for one in my position, The Voice said with Smith's mouth.

The demons at the table stared. Koth raised a pointing finger, lowered his hand, and closed his mouth with effort.

"Was that...?"

Smith nodded miserably and let his chin fall into his hands.

"Hey, Metatron! Good to hear you again," Koth said, though his voice sounded strained.

Greetings, Koth. It is good to be alive once more.

"Look, I'd love to continue the little tet-a-tet here," Smith interrupted, "But you guys called me for what I assumed was a paying case, right?"

Koth nodded. His expression was filled with awe.

"Yeah." He passed a hand over his face and let out a breath. "Wow. So anyway, kid starts looking into religion and decides he wants to be some flavor of Christian. He goes to church and starts talking to priests, asking them about demon possession and whatnot until he finds a priest who convinces him an exorcism would be in his best interest.

"They do the deed and something weird happens. After the demon is gone, the kid realizes just how much a part of him his demon was. He's *lonely* without his demon, in fact. After only a week of living with the silence, he goes in search of the priest with one hell of a weird request."

Koth paused to take a sip of his coffee and winced at both the temperature and the taste of it. He pushed the mug off to the side and leaned across the booth toward Smith.

The detective tried to keep his expression both bored and neutral as he stared back into Koth's silver eyes, but he was burning with curiosity. Without realizing he had done so, he leaned in closer to hear what the demon had to say.

"Well?" Smith prompted when the silence stretched into more than seconds.

"See, here's the thing," Koth said, "Possessions are supposed to be cut and dried. Someone gets possessed, they're not supposed to make friends with their demon, and they're really not supposed to live through the exorcism. At least not well. They're definitely not supposed to try to get repossessed."

"Repossessed?" Smith asked. "Like a car?"

"No, stupid," Marduk said. "The kid was trying to find a way to get his old demon to hop back into the skin sack."

Smith tapped his spoon on the formica table top and wondered why someone who was possessed would go to the trouble to be exorcised then try to get possessed again. It didn't make any sense.

"After all of that, he decides he wants to stay possessed. Should be pretty easy, I would think."

"One would think it should be easy, and it would be…. If we could find his demon," Marduk said with a growl.

"A missing demon? What's the big deal?"

Pazuzu nodded and rubbed at the back of his neck. "We have got a missing demon with an awful lot of time on his hands. We are here to assist you in any way we can," he told Smith, but there was no enthusiasm in his tone.

"You'll get half your fee up front, same as before," Koth told him, "And the other half on completion. If you take the case, of course."

Smith leaned back in his chair and considered. Metatron was eerily silent, and it made him uneasy, as if the angel was waiting for something very important.

"What will happen to the demon if I find it?" Smith asked at last.

"It will depend on the circumstances of the case. If the demon's disappearance was a result of a bad exorcism, we really can't punish him for that. If, however, his disappearance was a deliberate attempt to escape Hell, well…then things get a little hairier."

"How hairy?"

"The demon would be cast into the lowest level of Hell and shunned by all the denizens therein until the end of time," said Pazuzu, his voice so low Smith had to lean in to hear him.

The detective sat back into his chair with a heavy sigh. After a long pause, Smith said at last, "All right. I'll take the case. I'll need to know some details. Let's start with where our formerly possessed now resides and what our demon's name is."

CHAPTER III

A half hour later, Smith sat in front of his laptop screen sucking down a tub-sized coffee and using up the free WiFi at a local coffee shop. He was able to find plenty of information on several thousand "Jack Daniels" and "John Daniels", but had finally decided to take a break when none of the men was the one for whom he was looking.

To find the demon, begin with the demon.

"Right," Smith murmured at The Voice, "except that I'm looking for the demon, remember? He's missing."

The other *demon.*

"What's that supposed to mean?" Smith asked, but The Voice had gone silent. He had gotten so used to The Voice thinking inside his head, but it had fallen silent for extended periods since the start of the case, and it was damned unnerving.

Start with the other demon. What other demon? He checked his notes and realized there *had* been another demon, at the very beginning of the possession...the demon who played the "friend of the family." That was interesting...but as he flipped through his notes, he also realized he had no information about that particular demon except that it had been integral in keeping the possessed kid away from seizure and psych medications.

Smith took out his phone and dialed Koth's number. On the second ring, Koth answered.

"Yeah?"

"What was the name of the other demon? The guy with the diagnosis. Can I talk to him or her?" Smith asked, adding the "or her" to be politically correct. There was not reason to assume all demons were male, in fact, now that he thought about it....

There was a long pause on the other end and the line crackled. Finally Koth spoke again.

"The demon's name is Damian–yeah, shut up, I know. He picked his own topside name. Thought it would be funny or something, but the sad thing was none of us had seen the damned movie. Anyway, he'll meet you in five minutes or I'll have his ass. You're at that coffee place around the corner, right?"

"Yeah, how did you–?"

The line clicked and the call ended.

Smith stared at the phone for a moment then set it down next to his laptop. He wondered if Damian would be like the other demons he knew, or if he would be different.

Five minutes later a man in a silk suit so expensive-looking it had to have been custom tailored in Italy walked into the coffee shop. His hair was black, but it was a dye job. His skin was healthy and tanned. Smith turned his gaze back to his laptop as the man approached the counter and ordered a coffee with extra everything and a healthy pour of caramel.

Smith lowered his head behind the laptop's monitor so he could smile at the order and re-immerse himself in his search. The door opened again and a woman entered.

For a moment the entire coffee shop seemed to suck in a breath of awe. She wore a stunning red dress; a smooth, bias-cut drape of heavy silk, the hem ending exactly three inches above her knees. Her legs seemed to go on forever before reaching the stiletto curves of black, patent leather shoes. With every step, her dark hair swayed, framing her exquisite features into a new work of art.

She glanced around the coffee shop, saw the man in the suit and approached him. They embraced briefly. He handed her the coffee he had ordered and Smith hated the man a little.

The pair whispered together, looked in his direction, then both of them came toward Smith. With an immaculate hanky, the well-suited man wiped down the empty chair across from Smith, and when the woman in the red dress slid into that chair, he had to remind himself to close his mouth.

She took off her sunglasses and leveled a silver gaze straight into his soul. Her mouth twisted into a small smile, and the red of her full lips was the exact shade of her dress.

"You wanted me, Mr. Smith?" she said, and her voice was low and sultry.

He struggled to speak, but his heart was throbbing in his throat and blocking the words. Instead he gave a helpless nod. There was a sound in his head, and it took him a moment to realize it was The Voice telling him to be careful. He was unable to process the warning, however, didn't *want* to process the warning.

Demon, that is quite enough.

The woman in red blinked in astonishment and the spell was broken. A slight blush flitted over her cheeks and the man in the suit was instantly at her side. He pulled his sunglasses off to reveal silver eyes matching his companion's, and they stared at Smith in open curiosity.

"The rumors are true," said the woman. "Apologies, Metatron. I did not believe.... Well, it seemed impossible."

She motioned for the man in the suit to sit down then took a sip of her coffee. Smith had difficulty concentrating when she licked the whipped cream from her lips, but her intentions seemed more professional now that she had heard The Voice speaking through Smith's mouth.

"Mr. Smith, it is a pleasure to meet you, and especially to thank you for your part in restoring The Voice. I am Damian, and this is my brother Daimon."

Smith found his own voice at last, blinking with surprise.

"You are not," he searched for a polite way to phrase his concern, "what I was expecting."

"You assumed I would be a male demon?" said Damian helpfully.

"Well, yes."

Damian arched an eyebrow and smiled. "We can be whatever we want to be," she told him, "Same as a human. Our transition is easier, of course, and we can change as many times as we please. Not all humans have figured out shape-shifting yet."

"Koth told me you were a guy, though," Smith said, confused.

"It's been thirty years since I last saw Koth," she

said with a laugh that tinkled like a champagne toast. "I grew bored being a man all the time, so decided to see if the grass might be greener on the other side of the fence, so to speak."

"Is it?" Smith's curiosity was piqued now.

Damian shrugged and waved a hand side to side. "Socially, sometimes. I enjoy free drinks and ladies' nights. The everyday inequality is a bit of a bitch. Sexually?"

Again she laughed and Smith could feel goosebumps tingling all over his body. She went on with a blissful smile.

"I wouldn't trade it for the world. Did you know women have multiple orgasms?"

"I've...I have heard tell," Smith said, gulping uncomfortably.

Damian laughed and crossed one long, perfect leg over the other, sitting sidesaddle in the coffee shop chair. Her very presence made the chair into a throne, and the coffee shop into her personal royal court.

Smith struggled with his own inner turmoil. Part of him was imagining the demon naked and having sex with him right there on the little table while the other part of him was trying to remind himself that she had, at one time, been a man. That part was currently listing all the reasons he wasn't attracted to men, but it was flailing for entries. From the back of his mind, Metatron smirked, then laughed at him.

More important than your base desires is the very real fact that she is neither a man nor a woman, but a demon. Would you follow her to Hell?

Smith recoiled, but then he caught sight of a garter strap peeking out from beneath the hem of Damian's dress. With a sense of impending doom he wondered if Hell was really as bad as the religious folks made it seem.

Demon, Metatron reiterated.

Smith sighed and with a Herculean effort of will he focused on his case.

"I need to ask you some questions," he said after clearing his throat.

Damian raised her eyebrows and waited, motioning for him to proceed.

"You lived next door to John Daniels when he was possessed by a demon named…uh…"

Smith flipped through his notes and frowned. What had the demon's name been? Had Koth even told it to him?

"Dandelion," Damian said with a laugh that cut into his thoughts. "The kid misheard his real name when he first came topside. It's Dantalion, by the way, but he answers to Dandy, Dandelion, and Danti."

The detective struggled to keep his face neutral, but laughter threatened to erupt from him at any moment. A demon named Dandelion? It was almost cute, except for the demon part.

"And you were a friend of the family, correct?"

"Yes, I was a friend of the family. Dantalion was supposed to possess the neighbor's child–a family of religious zealots, but Hell got the address wrong."

Smith nodded and scribbled the demon's various nicknames into his notes. "How long did you know the family?"

"Oh, years. They were quite fun. They were swingers; did you know that?" Damian asked with a wink and a knowing smile. "Really wasn't much of a challenge to sway them one way or the other, if you take my meaning."

"Swingers. Got it."

"It was the seventies," Damian said, and waved a dismissive hand.

Smith took a deep breath and refocused his attention from impure daydreams back to his questions. It was no easy task; somehow Damian kept steering the conversation back to sex.

"Have you interacted with John over the last few years?"

"Indeed. Poor boy had a bout of conscience and wanted to find religion," Damian said in a tone that made it sound as if John Daniels had had the flu rather than a spiritual crisis.

"I take it you tried to bring him back to your side?" Smith asked.

"Of course," Damian laughed. "It comes with the territory, after all."

"And what happened? After you spoke with him, I mean?"

"The silly thing went looking for a priest to perform the exorcism. He thought he would burst into flame if he tried to enter a church or some such nonsense. Really, he was so dramatic. We tried to tell him he could have it both ways. There are plenty of religious humans who are worse than a demon, after all, and they can come and go as they please every Sunday."

Damian paused to take a sip of coffee and Smith watched as her long, pointed tongue flicked over her perfect red lips, capturing the caramel and cream and scooping it into her mouth. He wondered if he kissed her if she would taste like caramel, or something more exotic–like fire and brimstone.

"Jackie was always a bit…wayward," Damian went on. "He went through with the exorcism, and poor Dantalion was out in the cold, ejected from the only home he had known for over thirty years. Such a shame."

Smith considered her statement then asked, "What happened after that? What happens to a demon after an exorcism?"

Damian shrugged. "Typically they go back to Hell, as far as I know. I tend to stay away from the exorcism assignments. I've heard it's a horrid experience."

"Where else could a demon go after an exorcism?"

"Well, that's a good question. A spa weekend getaway?" Damian said and smirked.

Her brother remained silent next to her, but his face split into a wide grin, bubbling with silent mirth. He put a hand over his mouth and turned away from the table as if he might be afraid of offending Smith.

"I apologize," Damian said, reaching across the table and placing a long-fingered hand over Smith's. "That was unnecessary and catty of me to make light of such a serious thing. Dantalion was a long-time friend of mine. I do hope you find him soon."

"So sorry that we could not be of more assistance," Daimon spoke as he rose from the table.

The demon held a hand out for his sister and helped her to her feet. She gave a sigh of disappointment and pouted at her brother.

"I do wish we might have stayed a little longer, but duty calls," she said. "It has been a pleasure, Mr. Smith, and wonderful to hear your voice, Metatron. I hope we can see more of each other...when you find your demon."

Damian leaned across the table, exposing the entirety of her braless chest to him in the scoop of the low neckline of her dress. Smith sat stunned, unable to avert his gaze, and struck dumb as her mouth found his. The kiss was insistent and aggressive without being overly so. It was the kiss of a woman who knew what she wanted and was used to getting it. When she released him from the kiss he fell back against the chair and felt as if all the air had been knocked out of him.

Smith stared after the demonic siblings as they exited the coffee shop. His mouth was still hanging open and probably had red lipstick all over it, but it didn't matter. In the back of his mind, an archangel was laughing at him.

CHAPTER IV

Smith made his way into the restroom. When the door latched behind him and he turned toward the sinks, he snorted at his own reflection in the mirror. Not only was his mouth red, but he looked like the kid who didn't quite know when it was time to put down the red ice pop.

As he wiped off his mouth, Metatron stared over his shoulder in his reflection and laughed. Smith jumped and turned to find no one behind him then spun back to the mirror. Metatron sighed and rolled its eyes.

"What the hell?" Smith cried out at his dual reflection.

You missed some, The Voice told him and pointed at a splotch of red still clinging to the corner of Smith's reflected mouth.

He wiped at it in rough strokes, glaring at Metatron the whole time. The archangel arched an eyebrow and walked around the reflected bathroom, taking in its surroundings.

"How long have you been able to just pop in and out of reflections?" Smith asked after an angry pause.

The angel considered, then said, *This is the first time I have attempted to do it.*

"Well, next time give a guy a little warning, okay?"

Very well.

Smith washed and wiped his hands and leaned against the far wall of the bathroom. He stared into the mirror, considering the angel that stared back at him from the other side of the glass. It was an androgynous being, tall with a fine bone structure. Its face held both infinite serenity and boundless strength. There was a shimmering white aura, almost a glow, surrounding the angel.

"So, now that I can actually see and interact with you a bit, it makes it a little easier to say this: Do you think you can shut up once in a while?" Smith asked, already feeling embarrassed. "I'd have asked earlier, but it felt weird saying something like that without being able to gauge your reaction, you know?"

The archangel blinked at him. *Shut up?*

"Yeah, you talk a *lot*, and the only way I can get any sleep is to drink myself into a coma every night. I was just wondering if you could maybe not talk so much between ten at night and say, eight in the morning?"

Metatron threw its head back and laughed. Smith smiled in confusion and wondered if his mental roommate was crazy or just being a dick.

Apologies, said the angel. *I did not realize you could hear me when I conversed with the Creator.*

"Wait, all those times you were talking, it was with GOD?"

Who else would I speak with?

"I hadn't really thought about it," Smith mumbled. "I just figured you were talking to yourself."

The angel smiled at him from the mirror, and he felt an all-encompassing warmth surround him as the angel hugged his mirror twin. It would be hard to stay mad after a hug like that, Smith decided. The angel released his reflection and the ambient coolness of the restroom settled back over him.

I am sorry. I will try not to talk during the nights. As I am sure you can imagine, the Creator and I have much to discuss.

"Thanks, and yeah, I would guess you guys had a lot of things to catch up on…. Can I ask you something?"

The angel shrugged and motioned for Smith to proceed.

"This case with the rogue demon. What do you think of it?"

Metatron was silent for a moment then said, *Something is not right. There is something amiss.*

Smith nodded. "Yeah, I'm getting that same feeling. I just don't know what it is yet. I guess the next move is to talk to the formerly possessed and get his side of the story."

It would seem a reasonable course of action.

"Is there someplace else, I mean, other than this plane, the demon could be hiding? Can they even *do* that without getting caught?"

Metatron frowned and shook its head. *No. The rules are very clear. After a demon has been successfully exorcised, he or she is to return to Hell at once.*

"Unless they're playing by house rules," Smith mused.

The angel frowned. *'House rules'?*

"Yeah. When you get a board game–or any game, really–there is a set of rules that come with the game, explaining how to play it. Typically, though, rules evolve as people play the game year after year; it has to do with our individual perspectives on the game, you see? These specially modified rules are referred to as 'house rules;' they only apply under this individual's roof, or 'house.' They might be guided by, but they veer from the officially sanctioned rules set forth by the game's creators."

Metatron brightened. *So you believe the demon might have created its own rules?*

"Right. His circumstances may have lead to him changing the game, or something like that," Smith said.

The pair jumped as a knock at the door interrupted them.

"Hey, you alive in there?" came a voice from the other side of the bathroom door. "People out here gotta use the john."

"Sorry!" Smith called.

He opened the door to a disgruntled looking patron. The man shoved past him and closed the door on Smith's apology.

Smith made his way out into the noise of New York and the strangely lackluster light of a city afternoon in autumn. Taking a deep breath, he smelled the carnival air. It was a mix of foods and garbage, asphalt, concrete, river water, sea, and smoke, and it was invigorating somehow, as if the very soul of New York resided in its various scents.

He took out his cell phone and dialed Koth. The demon picked up on the second ring.

"What now? Didn't Damian get there yet?"

"Here and gone," Smith said, feeling a blush at the

mere mention of Damian's name. "Where can I find the guy who was possessed? Might be good to talk to his family, too."

"Turns out you're in luck. They're just outside the city. Okay, I'm lying. They're actually about a two hour train ride from the city in a town called Port Jervis, New York."

Smith paused. "Wouldn't that be a bit of a culture shock for them, moving from the sticks to a place not far from Manhattan?"

Koth laughed on the other end of the line. "You'd think, but no. Wait until you see the place. It's not too far a stretch from Ohio."

"All right, so how do I get to this place?"

"You take the Metro North line out of Hoboken, New Jersey straight to Port Jervis. It will be the last stop," the demon told him.

"Wow, really? That seems way too easy."

"Doesn't it?" Koth replied and hung up on him.

Smith looked around for a street sign and found that he was close to 6th Avenue and 33rd Street. From his previous excursions, he knew the PATH train would take him to New Jersey, but he wasn't sure if the 33rd Street line would do it, or if he would need to switch trains at some point. He decided he would figure it out at the ticket booth.

CHAPTER V

As it turned out, the Hoboken - 33rd Street line would take him directly to the train station in Hoboken. He wandered through the doors into the main waiting area and couldn't help but stare around him. The place was beautiful; it was the kind of place one would imagine a train station should look like.

The architecture was ornate, with elements of the modern encroaching in certain areas. He made his way to the ticket windows and looked around while he waited.

'Tiffany glass," said a voice next to him.

He looked down at the goth girl standing in line in front of him.

"Excuse me?"

She pointed to the skylight and said, "Tiffany glass. I saw you looking around, and I'm a fan of the station, myself. Figured I'd pass the time talking with a stranger while I wait to get my ticket."

"Ahh," he said and smiled in spite of himself. "So you know a bit about this place, I take it?"

"A little. I know it was originally called the Erie-Lackawanna Railroad Terminal and it was built in 1907 to replace the one that burnt to the ground a few years before that. Seems the turn of the century has some of the most incredible architecture, as if they were trying to out-do ancient buildings. For example: this entire building is covered in copper. You wouldn't really know it to look at it since it's oxidized, but the whole thing is *copper*. It must have cost a fortune."

Smith shrugged by way of response. He had no idea how much it would have cost in the early 1900s to side an entire building in copper, but it couldn't have been cheap.

"Do you normally discuss history and architecture with strangers?" he asked her.

"Just the cute ones," she said with a grin.

"Just the...wait, what?" Smith felt a blush climbing into his cheeks.

"I'm *kidding*," she said, "You looked like you needed a friend. Figured I'd fit the bill for at least a few minutes."

"Oh," Smith said, his tone deflated.

The goth girl nudged him in the arm. "You're not *that* bad," she conceded. "I just didn't want you to think I was hitting on you. I have a boyfriend."

"Ah."

"You got time for a drink? I could go for one, and it would be nice to have a drinking buddy," she smiled up at him.

"I guess so?"

Now that he knew she was unattainable, Smith couldn't help but notice that she was quite beautiful under the copious amounts of liberally applied black makeup. She stepped up to the ticket window and he hid a smirk when he saw her stand on tiptoe to better reach the ticket counter.

"Where to?" asked the ticket agent.

"Port Jervis," replied the goth girl.

Smith started in surprise. The ticket agent stated the fare and the girl slid the money to the woman. In return, she got a small strip of paper with pastel logos stamped on it.

When it was his turn at the ticket window, the detective felt strangely guilty stating his destination as Port Jervis. He didn't want his odd new friend to feel like he was following her.

She knows why you are going, said Metatron.

At the unspoken question floating around his head, the angel continued, *She is not quite what she seems.*

Smith had recently begun to wonder if anything was ever as it seemed. He suddenly missed his office and his apartment in Gettysburg very much. Things seemed simpler there, less rushed. He wondered what he would find when he reached Port Jervis.

The goth girl was waiting for him when he moved away from the ticket windows. With a nod of her head she led him through the station to a bar that was so well camouflaged Smith doubted he would have noticed it if he had been there on his own.

"Welcome to the Railhead," the goth girl told him.

She flashed her ID before the bartender had a chance to ask for it and ordered a Jack and Coke. When the drink was pushed across the bar to her she climbed onto one of the seats and settled in with a twenty dollar bill unfurled on the bar in front of her.

The bartender looked to Smith and he ordered a Jack Daniel's on ice. He settled in next to her and she raised her glass in a toast.

"To new beginnings," she said. "And to finding the

answers we seek."

He smirked at her and tapped her glass with his in salute. They sat in silence, sipping their drinks for a moment and then she turned to him. Her expression was vaguely annoyed.

"You really have no idea who I am, do you?" she asked.

Smith shrugged uncertainly. "Should I?"

"C'mon, Metatron, for real?"

"I'm not, well…I sort of am, but at the same time I'm not," Smith faltered in way of explanation. "It's complicated."

She stared hard at him, searching his features for a sign of familiarity. A slow frown flitted across her face.

Of course I knew you the moment I saw you, said the angel through Smith's mouth.

The goth girl jumped. She seemed as stunned as Smith to hear Metatron speaking.

It seems we both have new appearances.

"No kidding," the girl said. Her eyes remained locked on Smith's face as she took a long swig of her drink.

"Look," Smith interrupted, "I get kind of caught in the middle when he starts to chat with people and it gets weird for me. So can we not do this?"

She smothered a laugh behind her hand and nodded. "Sorry about that."

"No problem. My name is John Smith. Nice to meet you," he said by way of introduction, "How did you know about Metatron?"

She arched a perfect eyebrow and smirked. "I know some things. If I told you, I'd have to kill you, blah blah blah," she said with a dismissive wave of her hand. "We've all got secrets, Virgil, but you have made peace with your mistakes and wiped the slate clean. Which is my cryptic way of saying that it is a pleasure to meet you."

She held a pale hand out to him and he shook it automatically.

"And you are…?"

"Just call me Lily."

"OK. Why are you headed to Port Jervis?"

She smiled and took a sip of her drink. "Same reason you're heading there. To figure out where that demon went."

CHAPTER VI

When they finished their drinks she led him out onto the concourse and scanned the area above them. After checking the arrivals and departures board, she rechecked a place just above the trains.

"There we are," she said and pointed.

Smith had no idea what she was pointing to, so followed her blindly. When they reached a particular platform she stopped and turned to face him. She pointed toward the platform.

"Here's our train. And there's your demons."

"My de–?" Smith began.

His voice trailed off when he caught sight of Marduk and Pazuzu waiting on the platform for them. The demons nodded in greeting and motioned to the train. When the hell had demons learned to ride transit he wondered? His first excursion had left him mostly confused, and he was quite sure he would have never found the correct train without help.

As they approached, Pazuzu smiled at Smith's companion and bowed. Marduk snorted and looked away from the gesture as if embarrassed.

"A pleasure to finally meet you, madam," Pazuzu said.

Lily seemed genuinely surprised by the greeting

and smiled at the demon.

"Likewise," she said, "Though I must admit I don't know your name."

"Pazuzu."

"Ahhh. You had quite a high stature in society many years before my time. It is good to meet a fellow castaway."

Marduk glared as Pazuzu hooked his elbow and offered to escort Lily onto the train. Smith stared after them and turned to Marduk in confusion.

"What the hell just happened there? Who is she?"

The demon snorted and climbed the steps onto the train. "We just got put in our place," he said over his shoulder.

"But who *is* she?"

"Don't worry about it," the demon said as Smith joined him in the vestibule of the train car. "She'll make herself known in her own time. Until then, enjoy the quiet while it lasts."

Marduk made his way through the train to a seat across the aisle from Lily and Pazuzu. He glared at them as they sat close together talking quietly. Smith slid into the seat next to Marduk and looked over at the pair.

"Tell me something, Marduk, does *anyone* in Hell make any sense?"

The demon threw his head back and laughed. "Never."

"What brings you guys on the case, anyway?"

Marduk shrugged. "We didn't have anything better to do, and we heard the Nazarene was getting involved. We thought it would be an entertaining time. Little did I suspect that Zu and she would become best friends and leave us out in the cold."

"Wait, *Nazarene*?"

Marduk looked out the window and changed the subject.

"Look, the train is departing the station. Is that not exciting for you?"

Smith growled in frustration and looked back across the aisle to where Pazuzu and Lily were now laughing quietly. To his surprise he felt a small pang of jealousy.

"Don't get attached," Marduk scolded as he settled into the seat for a nap, "She is…out of your league, as they say."

Smith frowned at the demon. He felt like he should say something in his own defense, but found he had no words. He couldn't explain why he felt protective of the girl or why he should feel jealous of Pazuzu. They had just met, she had been friendly and nothing more. Hell, she had even told him she was unavailable. So why did he feel so put out and frustrated?

He shook his head at himself and settled into the seat, following Marduk's lead. A nap was what he needed to clear his head. Once he had gotten some rest he was sure he would feel differently about Lily. What had Marduk called her? To his surprise he had already forgotten the word. Something with an "n", and damn it, it was something important. As Smith drifted into sleep he felt the question nagging at him, but was unable to answer it.

Nazarene.

Smith smiled with relief and the lingering sense of a mild "eureka!" moment. He turned to thank the person who said the word which had been tickling the corners of his mind for what felt like an eternity, but when he looked around himself he saw a misty grayness with a lone figure standing in the center of it all. The angel, Metatron.

I feel it is only fair to inform you that you will not remember to associate that name with Lily when you wake, said the angel apologetically, *She has important things to do and we cannot have you running around telling people who she is before she is prepared to make herself known. I assure you it is nothing personal.*

"Am I talking to...um...God or the angel right now?" Smith asked.

The figure shrugged. *A bit of both, I suppose, as I speak for Him. But you will not hear directly from The Almighty...it is complicated. No questions, please. You need to hear answers.*

"Okay."

The first thing you need to know is that the case you are currently working on is not as simple as they've made it seem. You will need to deduce what is wrong for yourself, as the Creator has taken an oath of non-interference. I tell you this as the angel.

"Like inside information?" Smith asked.

Yes.

"Neat. Except for the non-interference part."

Metatron rolled its eyes and shook its head, avoiding Smith's comment. *Additionally, you must keep the Nazarene safe on this journey. She is your priority above all else. Do you understand?*

"I guess so," Smith said with a frown. "You keep calling her the Nazarene. Does that means she's....you know...."

The angel heaved a sigh. *Mr. Smith, the knowledge you have been given is not to be publicly known for at least another decade. After you wake, you will have no memory of who she really is until the time is right. She is simply 'Lily,' and it is your duty to protect her. Would that it were in my power to punish the demon for revealing her identity..."* The angel sighed. *Remember only that she is our top priority. Now wake up. We've reached the end of the line.*

Smith jerked awake as the train skidded to a slow halt at the Port Jervis station. He rubbed his eyes and looked out the windows, wondering where the station actually was. They passed a building he thought might be the right place, but the train kept rolling, finally stopping in what seemed to be a vacant lot.

As they disembarked onto the concrete slab serving as a platform, Smith noticed a lonely shelter littered with train schedules and a ticket machine. Beyond the end of the platform the tracks continued and multiplied, some with freight engines lurking on the rails like great hulking monsters that growled in the distance. Smith scanned the yard and saw an area with a turntable for trains next to a large parking lot spanning the front of a run-down strip mall. In the middle of the parking lot was a fast food restaurant, but even this greasy island seemed as run-down and forgotten as the rest of the station area.

"Yeah, that look sums it up," said Lily as she caught sight of Smith's expression.

"Was it always like this?" he asked, unable to keep the tone of dismay out of his voice.

She laughed. "No. Back when this place had connecting rails to other cities, it was a much more happening town."

She pointed down the tracks back the way they had come, toward the building Smith had assumed would be their destination. "That was the original station. Not this place."

"Wow," Smith breathed.

"There are a lot of towns just like this all over New York and Pennsylvania," Lily told him. "Back before cars people used to actually like to travel and see where they were going, even meet new friends along the way. Now there are hundreds of towns just like this one that took a hit when the tourists stopped; just a little commute-to-work traffic now."

"Are you from around here or something?" Smith asked her.

She shook her head. "I'm from all over. I like to learn the history and stories of every place I visit. Sometimes I'm lucky enough to have someone to tell them to."

With a smile that caught the rays of the sun she

removed a folded piece of paper from her jacket and looked at it. An instant later Smith was jogging to catch up with her and the demons as they made their way across the mostly empty parking lot toward the main road.

CHAPTER VII

"Where are we going?" Smith asked when he caught up with the trio.

"To see Jack Daniel's."

"The man or the liquor?"

She rolled her eyes. "What do you think?"

"Not to sound like a prude, but you seem to drink a lot," Smith said uncomfortably.

Lily turned to look at him and smirked. "Says the borderline alcoholic. Don't go getting your panties in a wad," she said when Smith bristled, "If you knew half of what I know you might want a drink more often than not. In fact, you *have* been drinking more–I hear you've got to knock yourself out just to sleep since you started hosting The Voice, haven't you?"

Smith grimaced and rubbed at the back of his neck as if trying to remove a barcode tattooed there. She tried to meet his gaze and he avoided it as the angel laughed in the back of his mind; the full baritone was not merry, and it reminded him of the hangover he'd just recovered from.

"Fine. Let's go see Jack Daniels," he mumbled.

As they exited the parking lot, they turned left onto Pike Street and walked for what felt like forever. Smith had to stop himself from asking if they were there yet and how much farther. To him, the streets seemed gray and drab, like a tourist town after a hard winter. At last, Lily stopped in front of a place on the corner that had all the look and charm of an old-world tavern.

Smith stared up at it and could envision songs sung over clinking mugs of mead and ale, a roaring fire and roasting meat just inside the door. The building was Tudor style; it looked like the kind of place where weary travelers would meet up to tell stories while they rested. Like something out of a Canterbury Tale– except for the white and red sign proclaiming that one could watch football in the darkened sanctuary.

Lily held open the door and motioned for them to enter. After getting their drinks at the bar they chose a table toward the back. The spot would afford them an excellent view of the entire place while still allowing them privacy. They sat in silence and sipped their drinks until a waiter walked up to their table.

"Hi, folks. Will you need menus today or are you here strictly for the ambiance?"

The question would have been an insult if not for the waiter's tone and genuine smile. Lily returned the smile.

"Got any burgers?" she asked.

"Sure do."

"Good. I'll have a cheeseburger, medium rare. Hold the salad ingredients, and add some fries if you have them."

"Gotcha," said the waiter and scribbled onto his notepad. He turned to look at the rest of the group.

"And for you, sir?" he asked Pazuzu after a hint of a pause to stare at the demon's eyes and skin.

"Same," replied both of the demons

simultaneously.

The waiter smiled and marked his notepad, then looked at Smith with eyebrows raised in a question.

"Can I get a menu?" the detective asked.

"Yessir, be right back."

"Just gotta be different, huh?" Lily said with a smirk.

"No, I just want to know my options."

"You're going to get the cheeseburger, same as the rest of us," Lily told him.

"Am not."

"Whatever."

She shook her head and smiled into her drink as the waiter returned and handed Smith a menu. Smith glared at Lily then scanned the menu while the waiter smiled patiently.

He thinks you are an idiot, said Metatron from the back of his mind, *And you* are *going to order the burger.*

I am not *ordering a burger!* Smith thought at the angel. *Now shut up and let me look at the menu!*

A few minutes passed in silence. At last Smith closed the laminated pages with a plastic coated slap and handed it back to the ever-patient waiter. He cleared his throat and toyed with his drink glass.

"And for you, sir?" the waiter asked.

The detective rolled his eyes and mumbled, "Cheeseburger."

"Excuse me, sir, I didn't catch that. Could you say again?"

"I'll have what they're having," Smith said and felt his cheeks reddening.

"Good choice."

As the waiter walked away, the others looked at Smith. He could see the laughter in Lily's eyes.

"We could have been eating right now," Marduk growled, "But no, *you* had to be the difficult one."

The demon let out a huff of annoyance and sucked down the rest of his drink. Pazuzu smiled at his companion and shook his head.

Smith glared at the demon for a moment with a fight brewing on his tongue, then turned to Lily. "So how do we know who our guy is?" he asked her.

"Word has it he comes in here almost every day. Figure we can hang out and see who the regulars are, then ask him some questions when we find him."

Pazuzu winced. "Having done the identification by similar means in the instance of finding Virgil Calahan, I would recommend we come up with a better plan of action."

"How about divine intervention?" Lily asked.

The demon considered this and nodded. "Yes, that would be acceptable. Have you received such aid?"

She made a so-so gesture with her hand and shrugged. "My intuition has led us here. I can feel that our guy is close, but that could be because he lives in this town. Sort of a Jackson Pollock approach to people-finding, I know, but it's all I got."

Their food came and Smith could feel his mouth water at the site of a perfectly displayed burger. The cheese peeked out from just under a toasted bun, and the scent steaming off the pile of crinkle-cut french-fries was heavenly. He completely lost the conversation as he tore into his food, only resurfacing when his hunger had at last been satisfied and the only thing left on his plate was a pickle spear.

The others glanced at him as he leaned back, and he saw they had all been equally ravenous. Nearly everyone's plate was empty. Lily took her time, happily munching her french-fries one at a time, each one holding more ketchup than was physically possible.

"I have an idea," Smith said suddenly.

All eyes turned to him and he poked at his pickle with his fork for emphasis. Lily raised her eyebrows, urging him to speak, but said nothing.

"Why don't we ask someone if they know our guy?"

The group looked from one to the other in surprise. At last, Lily let out a laugh.

"Not a bad idea, there, Virg," she said, and the smile was back and twinkling in her eyes. "Seems we thought of everything but the simplest thing: asking for directions. Brilliant. I thought men weren't supposed to ask for directions."

"Yeah, well, I try to be different." He winked at her as he bit into the pickle spear.

When their waiter returned, the group looked at Smith. He had been officially nominated to speak for the collective.

"Can I get you anything else?" asked their waiter.

"Yeah, actually," Smith said, "This may sound weird, but do you know a guy named John Daniels?"

The waiter smiled. "Sure. Everyone knows Jack."

Movement caught Smith's eye and he noticed the napkin holder shift ever so slightly toward him. He glanced around at the others, but no one seemed to have noticed.

"Do you happen to know where we can find him?"

"Yep. Right here."

Smith smirked and said, "Yeah, ha ha. I get it, but we're looking for the person, not the liquor. Do you know John Daniels for real?"

The waiter's grin grew at the looks of expectation. Finally he nodded and thumbed his chest.

"I'm Jack. What can I do for you folks?"

When the napkin holder shifted again, Smith ignored it.

CHAPTER VIII

"Nice to meet you, Jack. We're here because we wanted to ask you some questions."

"Sure, go ahead."

"Recently you were exorcised by Father Victor Kirkpatrick, is that correct?"

Their waiter's expression slipped and his eyes darted around as he leaned down close to them. "Look," he said, "Whoever told you that is lying. I'm fine."

"Did you not call upon a demon named Koth in an attempt to become, for lack of a better word, re-possessed?" Lily asked, her tone solemn.

Jack dropped to his haunches next to their table. When he spoke, his voice was low.

"You guys are friends of Koth?" he asked, and they nodded.

"Look," Jack hissed, "can we talk about this another time? Maybe later? I don't need people hearing about this. It's bad enough I had to see Father Kirkpatrick in the first place."

His eyes scanned the room to make sure no one had heard their conversation as he rose to his feet.

"When can we meet with you?" Smith asked.

Jack's face screwed up in an effort of concentration. "I get off work tonight around eight. We can talk then."

"Okay. What can we do in town for the next six hours?" Smith asked.

"Whatever you want, I guess." Jack said with a shrug as he crumpled up their check and he moved to wait on other customers.

"Let's find Father Kirkpatrick," said Lily, "We can ask him some questions while we wait for Jack to get off work."

They stepped out into the bright afternoon daylight, squinting their eyes against the glare. Lily shielded her eyes and looked around, considering.

"I think I saw a church back near the station," she said at last.

Smith let out a sigh. "So we need to walk back the way we came?"

She nodded and started down the street. She looked back and, with a smile, said, "Look at the bright side, at least it's downhill."

They walked in silence, their pace slower as they made their way back toward the train station. It was as if they were trying to stretch time out so there would be fewer spaces of inactivity.

As they neared the station they passed a Salvation Army thrift store and Lily stopped. She motioned to the Open sign and raised her eyebrows in question.

"You guys want to go do some shopping while we're killing time?"

"Might as well," Smith said as he stared up and down the street for something better to do and came up with nothing.

They entered the fluorescent dimness that seemed to be a mandatory ambiance setting in all thrift stores. The scent, as they stepped into the clothed silence of the store, was one of old attics and basements, of memories and strong perfumes long forgotten. A bored cashier leaned against an open box of clothing ready for the racks while skimming a catalog splayed open on the counter.

Smith was unable to discern if the cashier was a woman or a man. The person had a larger frame, so the breasts hanging over the belly could have been actual breasts or breasts created from obesity. The hair was cropped short in such a way it could have been for a man or a woman.

Androgynous, said Metatron from the back of his mind.

The term fit the cashier perfectly. He or she was unisex.

They are also a hermaphrodite.

Smith blinked. He tried not to be obvious as he wandered through the racks of clothing which seemed to be arranged by decade, then by size. He thought his side-glances had been subtle until Lily came up beside him and gave him a nudge.

"What?" he asked, his tone already defensive.

"You're staring," she said.

"Well, it's not like you see someone who's…" he trailed off, at a loss for the exact phrasing he should use that would be politically correct.

"She's mostly a she," Lily told him, "and you might consider just calling her by her name. It's Taylor."

Even though Smith had found some items he would

have liked to purchase, he felt guilty bringing them to the counter after he had been so rude. Instead he hung back with the demons while Lily bought an armful of clothing and a few dog-eared paperbacks.

When the cashier moved to put the clothing into a plastic shopping bag that was clearly recycled from one of the grocery stores in the area, Lily stopped her. With the air of a magician performing a trick, she unfurled a shopping tote from her pocket and put the clothes into it. She smiled and gently reached out to squeeze the cashier's hand as she slung the tote over her shoulder with her free hand. She leaned in and whispered something to the woman, and the cashier's jaw dropped open in an expression bordering on relief and bliss.

A moment later Lily joined Smith and the demons.

"Ready?" she asked.

"Sure you got everything?" Smith asked.

"I did what I needed to do."

"We weren't really there to shop, were we?"

Lily shrugged as they crossed Pike Street. The demons were almost reverently silent.

"What just happened back there?" Smith asked, pointing.

"I helped someone who had been asking for help," Lily told him. "It's too personal and it's between that woman and her faith, so don't ask me to go into detail. It's private."

They remained silent as they made their way down Ball Street, turned onto Church Street and at last reached their destination on the steps of the Our Lady of Sorrow Church. Smith stared up at the structure then looked to his companions.

"How do we know this is the right place?" he asked.

"Catholic church," Marduk said quietly.

Smith noticed the demons were hanging back, practically standing in the street, well away from the steps of the building. He frowned at the answer.

"Why would that matter?"

"We're looking for Father Kirkpatrick," Lily told him, "typically, 'Father' is a term used by Catholic priests. Also, I think Catholics may have the market cornered on exorcism. Obviously, there are probably some forms of it across the different flavors of Christianity and other religions, but a Catholic church in a small town seems like a good place to start for a Father Kirkpatrick, wouldn't you say?"

Smith shrugged. "I guess."

"And if this isn't the right place, the priest will be able to tell us where we can find Father Kirkpatrick."

Smith had to admit it seemed like solid logic. He followed Lily up the steps, leaving Pazuzu and Marduk standing awkwardly on the sidewalk.

CHAPTER IX

They left the warmth of the sun outside the church as they stepped across the threshold. The sounds of the street were silenced as the heavy doors closed behind them and it took Smith's eyes a moment to adjust to the stained glass dimness of the eerily silent interior.

There was no one in the place, but Smith could feel a presence as if the empty space was filled to the rafters. He watched Lily for any clue as to how he should be acting inside the church and she smirked at him from over her shoulder.

"First time?"

"I think so," Smith told her.

"Don't worry. Takes some getting used to, even for me. I was never one to stuff my entire belief system into a gilded cage, but some folks need that structure and ceremony in order to get into the mindset. I can appreciate that."

She walked down the aisle toward the altar and looked around at the Stations of the Cross and the glittering stained glass. As she made her way to the front, she ran a hand over the pews like a child flying an imaginary airplane.

When she reached the step to the altar she stopped and stared up at the crucifix mounted on the wall. She gave a disgusted snort and shook her head. Smith followed her angry stare to the features of the man who had once claimed to be the son of God. The eyes were staring miserably heavenward, the face an expression of unimaginable agony. The rest of the body was emaciated, ribs and bone showing on the nearly naked frame. While the image was a morbid one, he assumed all Christian churches had a variation on the same theme.

"Is something wrong?" Smith asked as he joined her.

"All the ideas, all the teachings; and all that's left to worship is a mortal body hanging mutilated and in pain on a cross. Really? That's it? Crown of thorns and some idea that suffering is the only way to attain enlightenment? Ugh! Why hasn't anyone figured it out?"

"Huh? I missed something."

"Yeah, so did most of humanity for the last two thousand years."

She stomped away from the altar and folded her arms around herself as if suddenly cold. Smith moved to put a comforting hand on her shoulder and Metatron spoke.

This is a moment best left to her. She needs to process and understand what she sees here.

She doesn't have to do it alone, Smith thought at the angel.

Yes, she does.

Smith heaved a sigh and threw himself into a pew. With a small cry of agony he realized too late why worshippers do not simply flop into the equivalent of a wooden bench with no padding. The sound of his body hitting the wood echoed through the church and Smith cringed, even though they were the only ones to hear it. The crash, coupled with his evident discomfort, seemed to shake Lily out of her mood and she laughed at him.

"It's not that funny," he mumbled at her.

"Yes it is."

"You try it and see if you're laughing then."

"I'll just stand, thanks," she replied. "I hate sitting on anything that makes me feel like I'm hanging out in an old transit waiting area."

Smith gave a nod of agreement at the description of the pews and got to his feet. They turned at the sound of footsteps and saw a tall, thin man dressed in black hurrying toward them. His disheveled, graying hair flew about his head and his eyes looked around as if searching for damage done to the church. His hands shook as he tucked the traditional white tab into the collar of his shirt.

"I heard a noise," he said in way of greeting.

Lily motioned to Smith with a grin. "My friend here." She extended a hand toward the priest in way of greeting. "Father Kirkpatrick?"

The priest shook her hand and Smith could swear his eyes lit up.

"Yes, but I suspect you already knew that, didn't you?"

"Very astute," Lily said with a smile. "You're one of the good ones, I'm happy to see."

The priest shrugged, smiling. "To what do I owe the honor?" he asked.

"We wanted to ask you some questions about the exorcism you performed on John Daniels."

Father Kirkpatrick gave a heavy sigh and sank into a pew without even genuflecting toward the altar. He ran a hand over his brow and was silent for a moment, weighing his words.

"Father?"

"I knew that would come back to bite me," he said at last.

Lily sat down next to him and asked, "How so?"

"Just a feeling. Like something wasn't quite right. I should have known better and left it alone, but the allure of being one of the few priests to perform an exorcism, well…" he smiled at her ruefully. "My pride and my vanity blocked my vision to see what was right."

She placed a comforting hand over his and gave a squeeze.

"You meant well, and ultimately that's what counts. Can you tell us what happened during the exorcism?"

The old priest shrugged. "He died."

Smith jerked to attention. "He *died*?"

Lily gave him an impatient look and motioned for him to be quiet. Father Kirkpatrick stared down at his gnarled hands.

"We brought him back," he said defensively, but his voice lacked conviction.

"Brought him back?"

He nodded. "Yes, CPR. I had a doctor with me the entire time."

"Hmmm. What was the doctor's name?"

"Kain. His practice is just up the road."

"What's his first name?" Smith asked.

The priest blinked. "You know, I have no idea.

Isn't that strange?"

"Very," Smith said, his tone flat.

"Are there any more details you can give us?" Lily asked, adding quickly, "I'm not asking for his confession–assuming he made one beforehand."

The priest's cautious expression brightened with relief. "Thank you for not asking. I would have been in a bad spot if you had," he admitted. "Could I really say no to you?"

Lily shrugged and rolled her eyes. "You *could* I guess, but I'd have to send you to Purgatory."

She smiled to let Father Kirkpatrick know she was kidding, but the old man was still visibly shaken. His mouth worked for a moment but no sound came out.

"There is one thing," he said at last. "During the exorcism. He didn't scream or curse or any of the things one would expect a demon to do when being exorcised. He just…went."

"No fight at all?" Lily raised an eyebrow and looked skeptically around, considering the new information.

"None," replied the priest. "It was as if he wanted to be expelled."

Lily shook the priest's hand and thanked him for his help, though her expression said all he had done was given them more questions than answers. When they exited the church, they found Pazuzu and Marduk sitting on the curb outside, looking very uncomfortable.

"Well?" Marduk asked before the doors had even finished closing behind them.

"Not much help, I'm afraid," said Lily with a sigh. "Come on, we have one more person to see."

"Who would that be?"

"The attending Dr. Kain."

"Why do we have to question him?" Pazuzu asked with genuine curiosity, adding quickly with a sidelong glance at Lily, "Or her?"

"Because *he* is the one who brought Mr. Daniels back from the dead during the exorcism."

The group stood on the sidewalk outside of an office building with Kain's name on it. The good doctor's office was closed, and it looked like no one had been seen there for weeks.

"So where do we find this guy?" Smith asked.

"We ask John where he is," Lily told him and started walking.

They made their way back up to the bar in relative silence. When John Daniels saw them, his brow furrowed first in confusion, then in worry.

"He's going to make a run for it," Smith whispered to Lily.

"No he's not," she whispered back through a radiant smile aimed at the waiter.

She waved him over and he came, but his steps were unsteady. Smith watched him with suspicion, sensing the man was hiding something. Then again, he thought, wasn't everyone hiding something?

Lily spoke to the waiter briefly, her smile and manner reassuring the man so that he relaxed. At last he gave a relieved nod, wrote something on a slip of paper, signed it, and handed it to Lily.

"This should do the trick," he said in a louder tone so they could all hear him. "If Dr. Kain has any questions, he can reach me here."

Smith glanced at the clock and inwardly groaned.

It was only three o'clock. Five more hours to kill.

CHAPTER X

They left the bar once more and started walking. After a block Smith could stand it no longer and stopped short.

"Aren't there any damned taxis in this town?" he burst out. "We've done nothing but walk since we got here!"

Lily and the demons turned to look at him in surprise. Smith blushed and stared at the pavement as if he could hide beneath the layers of leftover pebbles and cinders from last winter's snow removal efforts.

"Finished?" asked Lily.

He nodded.

"Good."

Without another word she turned and continued walking in the direction she had started. The two demons trailed after her with cast looks of amusement backward in Smith's direction. When he met their eyes he scowled.

If the trek from the train stop had seemed long to the detective, the walk to the doctor's home office was even worse. They wandered streets deserted of even hope and by the time they reached the address John had given them, Smith could practically see the raincloud that surely hovered over his head.

"Here we are," Lily said at last.

She double-checked the address and the number on the door, gave a nod, and knocked. Smith looked at the building skeptically. It looked more like a rundown house instead of a doctor's home practice. Before he had time to voice his doubt, the door opened a crack and he could see the glint of a chain lock in the opening.

"Yeah?" said a gruff voice from behind the door.

"Doctor Kain, may we come in?"

"I'm not a doctor anymore," came the reply.

"We don't need anything in that regard. We wanted to ask you some questions about," Lily paused, searching for a delicate way to phrase it. She decided to be direct. "We're here to ask you what happened at the exorcism."

"Shit."

The door closed and the sound of a chain rattling could be heard from the other side of the wood before it opened again, wider this time. The man standing on the other side was not what Smith had expected, and judging from the looks on the others' faces, this new piece to the puzzle had not been what they were expecting, either.

"*Qayin?*" Marduk stared at the man as if he had just slapped the demon.

The man started, glancing around the empty street before he ushered them inside. Once they were across the threshold, he slammed the door and locked it behind them.

"Did anyone follow you?" he asked, motioning for them to find a seat.

Smith looked around for a spot after Lily and the

demons took what appeared to be serving as both a couch and a bed. There was a folding chair, and Kain opened it with a flourish and handed it to the detective.

"No one followed us," Pazuzu answered when they were settled.

"Good." He looked hard at Smith. "Buddy, seriously, sit down. You're making me nervous."

Smith sank into the wooden folding chair and observed their host. The man was tall with the unkempt and un-showered appearance of someone who spends his nights watching out the window. Dark circles surrounded his wild eyes and stubble littered his sunken cheeks and chin, shading his neck down into the open collar of his wrinkled shirt. Just beneath, Smith could see burn scars in the shape of human hands, as if someone with fingers made of flame had tried to strangle the man.

Kain ran a hand through his greasy hair and slid down to sit on his heels, his back against the door. He opened a pack of cigarettes and Smith held back the urge to take one when the man offered.

"Suit yourself," Kain muttered around the cigarette in his mouth.

He lit it before thinking to ask if anyone minded. Clearly he was a longtime bachelor used to living alone, Smith mused.

"You are rumored to be dead," Pazuzu whispered. He stared at Kain as if he was a walking miracle.

"The exorcism," Kain said after several long drags and exhales, ignoring the demon's words completely. "What a mess that was."

"You were nothing more than ashes," Marduk interrupted, "I saw your body."

"Look, people change, okay? Circle of life and all that bullshit. Now do you want to hear about what happened to *your* guy or not?"

"But you were *dead*," Marduk argued. "Not much change in that."

"Not entirely true," Lily said, her voice quiet and thoughtful, "But we're not here to find out what happened to Qayin, we're here to find out what happened to Dantalion, so let's stay focused."

"Koth and Belial will not be pleased."

There was a click and Smith flinched when his eyes focused on the barrel of the gun suddenly aimed at them. Slowly he held his hands up, more out of instinct than any logical thought.

"Hey, Doc, come on, we can talk about this w–"

"The fuck we're going to talk about this!" Kain exploded. "This is exactly why I didn't want to get involved, but I thought maybe if I helped out I'd get some points upstairs, you know?"

Smith watched helplessly as the barrel of the gun waved around the room with Kain's expressive hand. Kain pointed it at Smith and the detective could see madness in the man's eyes.

"Qayin, take a breath and think about this," Lily spoke.

Kain's eyes seemed to clear at the sound of her voice and the barrel of the gun wavered. He did as she said, drawing in a deep breath and letting it out slowly.

"We won't tell anyone we saw you," Lily said with a threatening glance at Smith and the demons. "Will we, guys?"

Smith shook his head. "I don't even know who you are."

Marduk and Pazuzu were more reluctant to make the promise asked of them. Marduk eyed the gun with deep unease before slowly nodding his agreement to the terms, his fingers picking at the frayed edges of the burn hole in his favorite shirt where a bullet had once entered his chest.

After an eternity of considering their promise of silence, the gun barrel lowered, shaking with Kain's grip. He settled the gun into his lap and his head hit the door as he stared up at the ceiling.

"We good now?" Lily asked.

Kain gave a short nod and they could see tears glittering down his cheeks in the dusty light coming through the window. He lit another cigarette and curls of smoke swirled around the small room.

"Dantalion," Kain said at last, then gave a bark that could have been a sob or laughter. "*Dandelion*. He was a piss-poor demon. He and the kid were friends. Did you know that?"

He took another drag on his cigarette and watched the smoke motes billowing from his nose. Without waiting for an answer he went on.

"*Friends*. Probably more even. Who the hell knows anything anymore? At any rate, the exorcism. That's why you guys are here. You want to know what went wrong, right?"

Lily gave a nod and Kain contemplated his cigarette cherry for a moment.

"Yeah. The kid was my patient for the last couple of years. Bet he didn't tell you that."

"Why would he?" Smith asked.

"Because he was sick," Kain told them.

"Sick? How sick?"

Kain focused on Lily and his smile was bitter. "Dying sick. He had cancer."

"You're saying 'had' as if he doesn't still have it," Smith said.

Kain nodded. "Once he was exorcised, it vanished. He goes in to the oncologist; all his tests are negative. After that, he stopped going to doctors."

"Faith healing?" Lily proposed.

Kain laughed and shook his head. "He stopped going to churches, too. I guess he got the God bug out of his system. The only time I see him is at the bar, and he avoids me like the plague."

Lily tapped her lip thoughtfully, but said nothing. The demons stared at Kain, always keeping a close eye on the gun still resting in his lap.

"How did you do it?" Marduk finally asked, his curiosity winning over his fear of bullets.

"Do what?"

"How did you come back?"

Kain closed his eyes, resting his head against the wall as he inhaled. He blew a cloud of smoke toward the ceiling, contemplating. Finally he said, "I wish to God I knew. I'd give anything to have stayed dead."

CHAPTER XI

Lily checked the position of the sun as it sank on the horizon. The second they reached the sidewalk, the door slammed behind them and they could hear the chain sliding back into place and a deadbolt being thrown home. She sighed and rolled her eyes.

"He always did overreact. Let's start heading back. Our guy should be getting off work soon."

Smith kicked at small bits of gravel as they made their way to the bar. For such a small town, it felt endless to him now. Pieces of the case were falling into place, but there were canyon-sized holes in the stories that worried him. He reviewed the details in his head, trying to find the piece which would solve the mystery.

The devil is in the details, Metatron spoke from the back of his mind.

No kidding, really? Smith thought with as much sarcasm as he could muster.

Really.

You're no help, you know that?

The angel seemed to shrug at him and Smith could almost feel its smugness. It was times like this he hated the angel in his head. He would have sworn at it, but somehow it felt like that would be a sin.

The quartet reached their destination and found Jack sitting alone in an empty bar, head down. His position and the eerie quiet was unnatural and the hair on the back of Smith's neck stood on end as he paused in the door. Lily turned to look at him, a question in her eyes.

"Something's not right," he whispered.

The grim set of her mouth told him he had just confirmed her own suspicions. She gave a small nod and motioned for him to come in.

The two demons had clearly had the same feeling and stood a cautious several paces from the table where Jack was sitting with hands folded and head resting on them as if he had taken a nap.

"Oh crap. He's dead, isn't he?" Smith muttered.

The napkin holder on the table where Jack sat launched itself across the room, missing Smith's head by mere inches. The detective dove to the floor with a cry.

"What the hell?!"

The waiter's head snapped up. The man was clearly terrified.

"It's not what you think!" he cried as they rushed toward him.

More napkin holders flew off the tables at them along with silverware and paper placemats. They ducked and dodged until they reached the waiter and grabbed him. Heaving him to his feet, they pulled him out of the bar and onto the street.

As soon as he was outside he shook them off, his face twisted in anger. Tears rolled down his cheeks and he wiped at them.

"What the hell are you doing?"

"What are we doing? We're saving you from a poltergeist!" Smith snapped.

"You weren't saving me, dammit! It took me forever to get him to come back!"

"What?" asked Lily.

Jack's head fell forward so his chin rested on his chest and he continued to wipe at his eyes. He shook his head in response and started walking back into the bar.

"Hey! Get back here, it's not safe in there!"

"He needs me," said the waiter.

"Who are you talking about?" Smith asked after him, but it was already too late.

The waiter entered the bar and closed the door behind him. They heard the door lock and Lily growled in frustration.

"What the hell just happened?" she muttered and slumped onto the curb, chin in hands and elbows propped on her knees.

Smith stared at the bar for a moment, then looked around them. He replayed Jack's words in his head and thought about the details of the case.

You are getting closer, Metatron told him.

So why don't you just tell me the answer, since you obviously know it.

It would not be a learning experience and a chance to grow spiritually if you were given the answers to all of the questions, the angel said and fell silent.

"No damned help at all," Smith mumbled angrily out loud.

The demons glanced at him from their position on the curb next to Lily. Smith joined them and they sat in silence.

"What now?" Smith asked.

Lily stood and helped him to his feet. "Hotel. Sleep. We'll deal with him tomorrow."

"What if he escapes?" asked Pazuzu.

Marduk rubbed at the bridge of his nose in annoyance. "Enough of this."

He walked up to the door and waved a hand in one aggressive semi-circle. The door shattered and the demon stepped across the threshold.

The rest of the group ran to catch up and found Marduk standing over the unconscious form of the waiter. Pazuzu placed a hand on Marduk's shoulder as if to hold him back and the other demon shrugged it off.

"This is not my doing, he was like this when I entered."

CHAPTER XII

Smith walked over and checked for a pulse. As he felt along the man's neck, his fingers touched something hard hiding just below the surface of the skin. The last piece of the puzzle fell into place with an almost audible click. When he met the eyes of the others he gave a nod. "He's alive. Just unconscious."

"Help me lift him," Lily told them.

Smith took the waiter under the arms and Pazuzu lifted his legs. They carried him over to an area away from the spent maelstrom of napkins and placemats and set him carefully into a chair.

The demons began to tap out a pair of cigarettes and Smith cleared his throat at them. They looked up, annoyed until they realized he was holding his hand out for one rather than telling them not to smoke.

"I didn't know you smoked," Lily said with surprise.

Smith shrugged and let out a short laugh while Pazuzu lit the cigarette dangling from his lips. He inhaled, held it, and exhaled a plume of smoke with gusto at the ceiling.

"I've been trying to quit. Old habits die hard, though."

"What *is* your deal, anyway?" she asked.

Smith looked at her through a set of smoke rings

and raised an eyebrow in question.

"I mean, you're hosting The Voice, right? But who were you before that? What happened to Virgil Calahan?"

"Long story. Nutshell version is I don't really remember the man I used to be before all this," he motioned to himself, "and I'm okay with that. I've made amends for the wrongs I committed in that prior life, and I'm working on keeping the slate clean in this one."

She nodded thoughtfully and watched the smoke rings float toward the ceiling and dissipate into the murky air.

"How about you?" he asked her, "What's your story?"

She smirked and shook her head. "Can't tell you yet. It's a secret."

"Women," Smith muttered with mock contempt, "Always backing out of their half of the Show Me Yours, I'll Show You Mine game, huh?"

Lily rolled her eyes and nudged Pazuzu. She motioned for a cigarette and the demon looked affronted.

"I can't go around judging someone if I have no clue what it's all about now, can I?" she asked as she inhaled the proffered cancer stick.

When she finished coughing she handed the lit cigarette to the nearest demon, motioning she didn't want anymore. After they had finished laughing, Lily included, they snuffed their respective cherries and turned their attention to the unconscious man once more. Smith tapped him lightly on the cheek.

"Come on, Jack, wake up."

At last the waiter's eyes rolled beneath fluttering lids and he suddenly jerked to his feet. He stared around him in open panic and looked ready to make a break for it.

"Hey, hey, hey, easy! We're all friends here. Why don't you sit down and tell us where you've been all this time, Mr. Daniels? I mean the *real* Mr. Daniels."

Everyone blinked at Smith and he smiled.

"How did you know?" the waiter asked.

Smith shrugged, trying not to appear smug. On the inside he was smug incarnate.

"I missed something," Lily said, her tone flat, voice still hoarse from the cigarette.

"We all did. The whole time we've been running around looking for a demon, but we should have been looking for a missing human."

Pazuzu and Marduk tilted their heads in confusion at him like a pair of demonic dogs and the detective bit back a laugh. The waiter settled back into his chair, his eyes darting to each of them.

"You going to fill them in, or should I?" Smith asked.

Jack motioned for him to continue.

"Okay, I think I got all the details, but if not, feel free to chime in." He took a breath and continued. "It all started when young Jack Daniels got possessed by a demon named Dantalion. From what we've gathered, most demonic possessions are a short–term thing, but this one ran long enough for something interesting to happen."

"And what was that?" asked Marduk, leaning forward as if he was hearing a wonderful story.

"The same thing that happens to mice left in a

python's cage too long. The relationship went from predator and prey to friends of a sort. In the case of Jack and Dantalion, I suspect it may have gone a little deeper than that. Am I right?" Smith asked, looking toward the man in the chair.

Jack nodded, his face pale. "We…"

"And we'll leave it at that," Smith interrupted when it seemed as if Jack would tell them all the sordid details of his relationship with the demon. "Fast forward now. Something happens to make Jack the Human start thinking about religion. My guess is that lump on your neck by your jugular is cancerous, isn't it, Jack?"

The waiter's mouth fell open and he nodded. Everyone stared in shock, including Pazuzu and Marduk, who now resembled devout soap opera watchers following their favorite show.

"With the threat of death staring you in the face, and your soul in danger of heading to Hell with your buddy, you sought out the help of a priest to get exorcised so you could go to church with a clean soul. Am I right?"

"Not quite," Jack said. "You're right about everything up to the exorcism for the most part, but we didn't get exorcised for the reason you're thinking."

"Then why get exorcised?" asked Lily.

"I'm dying, yes. Yeah I know, we all are, right? I got my pink slip on life about three months ago when they found the tumor in my neck. It couldn't be operated on because of the location, and chemo didn't work. Dandelion couldn't help either. Poor Dandy beat himself up over it, too. Religious people have this idea of how demons are, but they're not all bad. It was driving him nuts that he couldn't heal me and that we'd most likely be separated after…well…*after*. I hated seeing him hurting, grieving, I guess. Dandy's my best friend. I love him. I sure as hell didn't want to lose him, either."

The waiter wiped at a tear and tried to laugh. Instead it sounded more like a sob. Lily handed him a napkin and he smiled gratefully.

"Go on," Pazuzu told him when he had regained his composure.

"Well, we thought it over and talked about it, and that's when we realized something."

"What?"

"Demons don't get cancer."

Pazuzu and Marduk turned and blinked at each other as if seeing one another for the first time.

"How many cigarettes have you guys smoked since you got topside?" Jack asked and the demons shrugged. "See? You guys can smoke like chimneys and you don't get sick. You can drink without getting alcohol poisoning–"

"We get hangovers, I assure you," interrupted Marduk.

Smith and Pazuzu tried unsuccessfully to hide their smiles. Marduk glared. Not quite understanding the joke, Jack continued.

"'Kay. So anyway, Dandy and I wondered what would happen if *I* were a demon for a while; what if the shoe was on the other foot? Not in the strictest sense, of course, but what if a demon occupied my body without me? Would the cancer go away?"

Smith looked to Lily; she gave him a look that said the idea might actually have some merit, especially as a last resort.

"We planned it out and contacted a bunch of priests. We nagged the hell out of poor Father Kirkpatrick until he finally said yes."

"But how did *you* end up getting cast out instead of your demon? It's only supposed to work one way," Lily said.

"It was easier than it seems. In fact, that was the plan all along. Cast *me* out instead of the demon, and Dandy stays. Our idea being that if he took over my body, the cancer would go away. The tricky part came with getting *me* back *into* my body. Dandy was used to living in the ether, but we hadn't considered the obvious. After the exorcism, I was a ghost, not a demon. I had to hide from a very terrifying dark angel so he wouldn't take me."

He escaped Azrael, Metatron suddenly spoke in Smith's head. *Azrael will not be pleased.*

Smith gave a mental nod in response. Azrael was definitely the scariest angel he had ever encountered, next to Metatron. He briefly wondered if all angels were scary before pulling his attention back to the story.

The waiter paused and rubbed at his eyes. "I gotta tell you, it feels weird to be back in my skin," he said after a pause. "But I wouldn't trade it for anything after what I saw while I was out of my body. There's some crazy things out there that we don't even know about or see. *Scary* things. I don't know how Dandy dealt with it all those years."

"He is a demon. We *are* the scary things out there."

Everyone but Pazuzu turned to look at Marduk, who was smiling darkly at them.

"It's true," he shrugged.

"So you hung around and played poltergeist?" Smith finally asked after a pause.

"Sort of. It took me one hell of a long time to get back and focus. Dandy was holding mini séances every night to try and draw me back in. We hadn't really thought about how souls generally don't head back into their bodies after they die."

"How *did* you end up getting back in?"

"This is going to sound weird, but I heard you guys saying my name and it pulled me here. I started trying to get everyone's attention so we could figure out how to get me back in my body. When Dandy came back inside, I accidentally hit him in the head with a napkin holder and knocked him unconscious."

The waiter looked apologetic. He held his hands out to them, palms up.

"And here I am. As soon as Dandy got knocked out, I got sucked back in."

"That doesn't make any sense," Smith said, "Surely he must have fallen asleep at some point. Couldn't you have just jumped back in then?"

Jack looked confused. "I don't know what you mean. Dandy never slept."

CHAPTER XIII

Smith looked at Pazuzu and Marduk. "You guys don't sleep?"

The demons shrugged.

"Generally, no," Marduk said. "Unless we've been made to drink, of course, then we can sleep if we wish."

"What my companion is saying is we do not require sleep to function," Pazuzu explained.

Lily chuckled. "Evil never sleeps?"

Smith laughed in spite of himself at the old cliché. Two clichés, to be exact, with a third if he counted Dandelion.

"So," the waiter said to the room in general, "Now what? Is Dandy in trouble?"

"Huh. I have no idea," the detective said, "I was just paid to find him, and I found him. Case closed."

The demons whispered amongst themselves for a moment and Lily frowned at them. She ran a hand through her hair and looked toward the ceiling as if the air vents might give her guidance. Without warning, Smith's mouth opened of its own accord and Metatron spoke through his parted lips.

"This has been a case of mistaken identity, it seems. Since Dantalion's actions were made with pure intent

to save the life of his human, he has been pardoned. When John Daniels' time on this plane is complete, both he and Dantalion may continue onward together rather than be separated."

The waiter covered his mouth with a trembling hand as tears streamed from his eyes. When he spoke, it was with two distinct voices.

"The archangel Metatron! Thank you! Thank you so much!"

Lily stepped forward and hugged the waiter to her. She leaned in close to his ear, whispered, and he smiled through his tears at her.

"I'm not afraid anymore," he told her.

She gave a nod and Smith could see tears brimming in her eyes. She hugged the waiter to her tightly.

"Then go in peace, brother," she said at last. "You will have no pain. It's the least I can do for you and your partner."

He held her hands in his, then brought them to his lips and kissed them. "Thank you, and may you find peace at the end of your journey."

Lily wiped at her eyes. "I wish," was all she said before turning and walking behind the bar.

She rummaged through the shelves and brought out a bottle of sour mash whiskey. It made a loud clacking noise as the glass hit the bar top along with five shot glasses. She poured out the shots and slid them down the bar toward them.

"To happy endings," Lily said and raised her glass.

"I'll drink to that one," Smith said and grabbed up a shot glass.

The others picked up a shot and toasted, clinking glasses before downing the liquor. Each made a face resembling ecstatic pain before slamming his respective shot glass onto the bar.

An hour later, Smith stood on the platform with Lily and the demons. In the distance they heard the approach of a train from the yard. As it pulled into the makeshift stop, they boarded.

Already the case felt like a dream, and Smith wondered if the others felt the same way; as if the entire thing had been imaginary. He glanced over at Lily as she stared out the window and watched the scenery flow past.

"What did you whisper to Jack?" he asked.

Lily sighed. When she turned to face him, Smith saw she had been crying.

"I gave him a choice," she said. "I told him I would heal him, and he could live out his life to a ripe old age if he wanted to."

"I thought Dandelion had cured his cancer?"

Lily shook her head. "You felt the lump. It wasn't going anywhere. In fact, he's got about a year left, maybe less. He chose to die and be with Dantalion."

"And you made it so his death would be painless," Smith said reverently.

She nodded. "It was the least I could do. I'm a sucker for a good love story."

Lily fell silent, and when Smith looked she was sound asleep. Even the demons were taking a nap, and the detective rolled his eyes. He settled back against the seat and tried to sleep, but it was impossible with all that had happened. When everyone disembarked in Hoboken the silence was awkward.

"We should go, Mr. Smith. You will be paid for your services," Pazuzu said by way of farewell.

Smith nodded and turned to Lily. Without a word, she placed a finger on his lips, removed it briefly to kiss him, and put it back.

"This goodbye is best left unsaid," she told him.

He watched her walk away, her black-clad form disappearing into the entrance to the subway. He felt an odd pang. He touched his lips reverently, unable to comprehend just how quickly she had gotten under his skin. Without a thought he moved to follow after her, and Pazuzu and Marduk caught hold of him.

"It would be best to forget her," Pazuzu told him. "She has no time for you."

The demons gave him a sympathetic clap on the back and he blinked at them as if he were waking from a dream. They led him into a tear in the fabric of existence, Pazuzu giving one, last backward glance of longing.

THE END

The Resurrectionist
Book 3

By
Suzanne Madron

PROLOGUE

The day had been unbearably hot when the men of the 44th New York Infantry discovered him facedown in a stream known as Plum Run. A comrade had warned him to avoid being discovered drinking from the tainted water, but he was hungry and thirsty, and to his thinking, it was better to drink from the dead than to feed on the living.

Bodies floated past him, carried on the current, but he drank greedily, only pulling away when he heard the crunch of approaching footfalls. He looked up at his comrades and knew he must leave that night if he were to survive–if they allowed him to live until nightfall.

The soldiers stared at him, disgust written across each of their faces. It was not the abundance of floating dead which repulsed them; it was the stream from which he drank. Water reddened by the blood of the dying dripped from his lapels as he leapt to his feet, and the body of the dead man he had been draining bobbed to the surface and joined the current once more, continuing downstream.

"My brothers, I can explain," he began.

The surrounding eyes hardened at his foreign accent and he started to back away, hands held out in supplication.

"What in God's name were you doing?" asked one of the soldiers.

"I was so thirsty. You must all be thirsty?"

Another of the soldiers scratched at the stubble on his face and said, "We're all thirsty, but we aren't drinking the way you drank from that stream. Too much blood and not enough water. From the looks of you, I'd say you enjoy drinking blood."

He opened his mouth, closed it again. He knew there was no reasoning with them at this point. They had seen too much, and the battle had set everyone on edge. There was nothing that would save him, not now. The silence was broken by his brief cry as one of the men drove a bayonet through his heart.

Pain sliced through him and he fell backward to the ground. The blade of the bayonet slid out of his chest, the metal lubricated with his blood. He lay on his back, staring up into the sky as he gasped his last breath. Blood drained from his chest and mingled with the water of Plum Run, painting the stream red in grasping tendrils. The small group of soldiers gathered around him, one nudging his lifeless form with a boot. Another soldier leaned close and listened at his mouth then at his chest for any signs of life.

"Is he dead?" asked one man.

The soldier laid a hand over his eyes and closed them, then gave a silent nod while another soldier sneered.

"Pray he is. Men like him are not men at all. They are monsters."

CHAPTER I

John Smith had not always been a heavy sleeper, but recently he slept the sleep of the dead. His nights were dreamless, from what he remembered upon waking, and he was fine with that. He chalked his constant exhaustion up to the last few months and the events that had left him dead, reborn, and severely jaded.

Before receiving payment for his last case involving a dislocated soul, he had asked for a few minutes to pay a visit to the gravesite of his father, younger brother, and the body of an angel called Metatron. They were all buried in the same place. For some reason he could not fathom, wandering spirits made him feel morbidly nostalgic. He had told the demons Pazuzu and Marduk he would meet them at the diner and after bringing him to the cemetery, they had left him

The grave was an old plot, and it took him a moment to recognize the patch next to the acid-eroded marker where the grass was not quite as complete as the surrounding grounds. He had stared at the earth for a long time and contemplated life, then had ventured into the city via a New Jersey PATH train. When he reached the sleazy diner where Koth and his crew had been waiting, he found he was no longer interested in collecting his payment. He stayed instead for the company.

Cherry had been working that day.

It seems like a lifetime ago, he mused as he returned to the present, and Smith rolled over to face the warmth pressed against him. He smiled and stroked the smooth, pale skin, letting his fingers follow the ridge of high cheekbone before plunging into the depths of thick red hair.

Cherry's eyes fluttered and opened, her mouth curling into a slow and knowing grin. She reached up to touch his hand and pressed his palm against her lips. The sensation sent a deep thrill through him and her grin widened when he moved to kiss her. She pushed against him and covered his mouth with her free hand.

"Sorry, Cal, you're going to have to wait until the next date. I need to get to work on time or the damned demons will raise holy hell that their coffee's not ready."

Smith laughed and it took her a moment to realize what she had said. She shook her head and joined in his mirth before sliding from the bed, gathering clothing as she made her way toward the bathroom, her hips wiggling from side to side in a seductive dance he couldn't help but watch.

She left a hint of her perfume in her wake and Smith breathed it in. Heliotrope. She always wore Crown Heliotrope in the winter months as a kind of summons for spring to arrive. Then in the summer, she wore Crown Esterhazy, which had a much lighter, almost citrus scent to it.

He blinked at this sudden thought and wondered if

it was a buried memory of his own, or Metatron's injection into his consciousness. He found he didn't care as the heady cherry-vanilla scent lingered in his bed sheets to haunt him with every shift of his position.

He watched as Cherry moved across his bedroom, the sunlight playing over her curves. It cast her skin in a pale gold light and turned the strands of her bob cut hair into filaments of sunset. She looked like a fire goddess. His fire goddess. From the back of his mind he felt Metatron smirk at him and he rolled his eyes.

Fine, she wasn't solely *his*, but he liked to pretend there were no others in her life. When they had made love for the first time–at least that he remembered–she had told him exactly what to expect as far as her affections. He had gone along with it, sure that his prowess and their attraction to one another would somehow win her over so she would choose to be with only him. He had been naïve.

Since that first night, he had learned to sit back and enjoy himself because it was one hell of a ride. He no longer asked if she had other dates or other men–or even other women. Cherry was a complicated woman with many tastes, as he re-discovered every time they slept together. He knew he could ask the angel renting space in his head, but it was unlikely he'd be granted a straight answer. Anyway, it was best not to think of where she had learned some of the tricks she knew or how long she had been practicing them, he decided.

He heard the shower turn on and fumbled for the pack of cigarettes he now kept in his nightstand. An empty whiskey glass clinked as he pulled at the drawer handle, finally prying it open. The powdery floral scent of heliotrope seemed to intensify and he paused with the lighter halfway to the cigarette pressed between his lips. Instead of lighting it, Smith put it down and slid from the bed. Naked, he crossed the room to the bathroom and watched for a moment at the door while Cherry showered. She was in silhouette behind the shower curtain, her movements graceful as she wet her hair. He grinned when he realized she had been singing softly to herself and he listened more closely.

The tune was lilting and held the gaiety of an early 1900s Irish aire, its familiarity tickling over the back of his mind. When Cherry's voice rose slightly at the chorus, Smith was shocked to find himself singing along with her, though he had no idea how he knew the words to the song.

"Call again, call again—"

"Mr. Calligan," he interrupted with out-of-tune bravado.

Cherry gasped and Smith let out a low chuckle. She poked her head out from behind the shower curtain and raised an eyebrow at him through dripping, dark red strands of hair.

"I thought you had no idea who you used to be, Cal," she teased, and though her expression was playful, there was a crackle of unease in her voice.

He shrugged. "I don't. Something about that tune, though. It's familiar. I knew the words."

She smiled. "I used to sing it to you when you walked me home, but instead of 'Calligan' I always sang 'Calahan'." Her smile became shy. "You used to say how much you liked it when I said your name."

Smith leaned across the small bathroom and kissed her, his words spoken into her open mouth. "I still do," he told her, his voice low.

Their kiss deepened and she pulled him into the shower with her. He struggled to keep his footing on the slick floor of the tub as they washed each other, kisses shifting between mouths and necks, hands wandering lower and touches becoming more insistent.

"Enough," Smith said and his voice was a growl of longing. "There's no way we can safely keep this going in the shower."

"Where's your sense of adventure?"

"To hell with adventure; we're going to run out of hot water."

She laughed as he scooped her up and carried her out of the tub. When he passed the neatly stacked towels he motioned for her to grab two. She did so, holding one on her chest and using the other to start drying their hair. The towel covered their heads, and Smith leaned in closer so Cherry would be able to reach the back of his head. As he did so she kissed him and they continued into the bedroom under the cover of terrycloth.

Smith set her onto her feet next to the bed, his focus taking in everything but the second pair of feet behind Cherry's dripping bare ones. They continued to kiss, and he wrapped the second towel around them in a cocoon, drying both of their bodies as she continued to dry their hair. When he deemed them both to be dry enough, he tugged the towels away and dropped them to the floor, their kiss deepening as he lowered Cherry onto the bed.

Her body stiffened against his and he opened his eyes. On the bed directly beneath them, Koth lay sprawled. Smith had practically straddled him in his efforts to continue with Cherry and the demon smiled up at Smith with a wink.

"Well, this is awkward, huh?" asked the demonic caseworker.

"Awkward? Yeah, that's one word for it."

Cherry growled as Koth attempted to shift her more comfortably over his lap and she sprang to her feet, but not before she had taken a chunk out of the demon's face with her fingernails. Smith had never seen her look so feral, and he had to admit that, as much as it turned him on, it also scared the hell out of him. Koth wiped at the silver blood pooling from the wounds next to his eye, arched an eyebrow at her, then licked his gray lips with a long, pointed red tongue, undaunted by the attack.

Smith let out a groan as the first twinges of blue balls settled over his groin. *Nothing like a surprise demon visit to kill the mood,* he thought bitterly, *and I was worried about a cold shower.* From the back of his mind, Metatron nodded sympathetically, making the entire situation that much more uncomfortable.

"What in God's name are you doing here, Koth?" he asked with some effort.

"Hey, keep it clean, I'm not alone."

Smith and Cherry spun around to find Marduk and Pazuzu carefully averting their eyes. They *were* laughing, however.

Smith spun back to face Koth. "I do have an office, you know. You could have gone there and waited like a normal person."

He grabbed a towel from the floor and wrapped it around his waist as he sat down in a chair, shifting himself uncomfortably and with a small groan of pain. Cherry continued to glower at their demonic guests, unapologetically naked and ready for a fight.

Koth's grin widened. "You forget, we are not exactly normal, and we are most definitely not *people*. Besides, what fun would going to the office be? No way we'd have gotten this kind of show in a boring old office."

"Good point. Next time we'll have sex in the office so we can get some damned privacy."

The demon laughed and shook his head. "We're here, Mr. Smith, because it's *important*. Looks like some weird shit is about to go down, and we wanted to give you a heads up."

"Really?" Smith asked as he climbed to his feet and fumbled for the cigarette he had set on the nightstand. He leaned in as Koth flicked his nails and produced a flame with his fingertips. "A warning? That's why you're here? Come off it."

He fell onto the head of the bed with a bounce, took a deep drag on his cigarette, then pulled another one from the pack for Cherry. She settled on the bed next to him, away from Koth, and took the cigarette from Smith.

"Need a light, honey?" the demon asked and waggled his eyebrows.

"Not from *you*," Cherry said and spat at the demon.

Koth seemed to shudder with pleasure. "I do love a feisty woman. They're the reason behind The Fall you know. The hosts of heaven are suckers for a hot temper and a strong will. And you, sweet meat, you have both in abundance."

She glowered at the demon and moved as if to burn him with the lit end of her cigarette. Smith caught her by the wrist and gave a small shake of the head, the message clear. Koth was not worth it.

He released Cherry's wrist when he was sure she was no threat to the demon, then released a plume of smoke in a sigh. "Get to the point, Koth."

The demon laughed and said, "Would you believe we're here because internet porn just isn't as entertaining as the real thing? No? Well, it was worth a shot."

Koth lounged on the bed and Smith caught a whiff of coffee and brimstone overpowering the underlying scent of heliotrope. He waited for the demon to speak, staring at the chiseled, pale features through a plume of swirling smoke tendrils. A thought, unbidden, crept into his mind and he wondered suddenly if Cherry had ever slept with Koth. He shook his head to clear it and searched in the recesses of his brain for Metatron's voice. For once the angel was strangely silent. Waiting–but for what?

"You will soon get a client," Koth said after a pause, "He's a bit…odd. Not human, but certainly not one of us, either."

"What is he then?"

"Damned bloodsucker," Marduk spoke from the corner.

Smith turned to face Marduk, startled for a moment. Both Marduk and Pazuzu had been so quiet he had almost forgotten they were there. The expression on the demon's face was one of disgust and hatred.

"Bloodsucker?"

"What Marduk means is your next client is a vampire."

"So what do you want me to do, feed him?"

Koth shook his head. "Not necessarily, although it may come up in conversation."

Smith said nothing but took a deep inhale on his diminishing cigarette. He reached for the bottle of whiskey on the side table and filled the glass, then contemplated the liquid for a long moment. He removed the cigarette from his mouth, and downed the drink. It helped ease the traveling discomfort in his groin and calmed his nerves enough to take the tremble from his voice when next he spoke.

"Get out."

The demons blinked at him in collective surprise. Koth sat up and stared. Smith motioned to the door.

"Door, window, crack in the fabric of space-time, in a damned clown car, I don't care how you got here and I don't care how you leave. Get out. Come to the office during business hours. And this?" Smith motioned with the hand that held the cigarette to the bedroom in general, "This appearing in my bedroom shit will not happen again. Am I clear?"

"Well, hell, you don't have to be a dick about it," Koth said, pouting. "Come on, guys, we'll let these two get to work."

The demons walked to the door and left. Smith waited, listening until he heard his front door open and close before moving. Cherry stared at him in awe.

"Geez, Cal. You really put those guys in their place," she said with a grin.

Smith's voice shook from anger and suppressed fear. "Yeah, well, boundaries, you know? If I let them in this time, then it's a damned free-for-all."

"Got that right," Cherry said, nodding. She took a drag off her cigarette and tugged the glass out of

Smith's hand. She filled it, downed the whiskey, and refilled it. "I hate that guy."

"Who? Koth?"

She nodded.

"Why? He seems likable enough when he's not being a pain in the ass."

She shuddered. "He makes my skin crawl. I can't explain it, but I don't like him."

Smith remained silent and avoided eye contact. He didn't have the heart to tell her when she was done being a waitress on this plane she would be at Koth's mercy for all eternity.

CHAPTER II

When Smith and Cherry said their goodbyes after one more round of lovemaking–let the demons wonder where they were–Smith waited while Cherry made a tear in the fabric of existence and stepped through. He had not yet mastered the trick, and stood for a few minutes examining the air where Cherry had stood moments before. He tried concentrating, poking at the empty space, then pulled at it, but nothing happened. Mentally he poked at Metatron, but no answer came from the angelic realm, either. He didn't like the angel's growing silence of late, but he had a client who may or may not drain his blood to worry about.

Finally, with a shake of his head, he made his way to his office in a way that very much resembled walking. He unlocked the door of his suite to find the demons sitting at his desk.

Koth rose from his lounging position on top of the wide desk and began kicking the air with his legs like a bored kid. Smith rolled his eyes at the demon's smile of greeting and hung up his jacket. He nodded to Marduk and Pazuzu in way of hellos then moved behind his desk. He dropped into his chair and stared up at the case manager with raised eyebrows as he threw open the window. He reached into his desk drawer and pulled out his "work" cigarettes, noting he was about to smoke the last one in the pack. He wondered if it would be a good time to quit smoking.

"Well?" he asked, breathing a plume of smoke out the open window.

"You kept us waiting," Koth said with a mock pout. The anger flickering in the demon's eyes was very real, however.

"Yeah, well, if you can't guess why then you have no business flirting with my girlfriend." Smith felt his own anger at the morning's interruption bubbling to the surface again.

The demon snorted and shrugged. "I'll be honest, Mr. Smith. I'm in it purely for the pain I can inflict, and your lady has earned some pain."

The detective clutched the armrests of his chair to keep himself from punching the demon in his smiling face. He clenched his jaw and cleared his throat, counted to ten. With slow movements he gently stubbed the cigarette on the outside portion of the windowsill and set the cylinder onto the desk blotter. From the back of his mind, Metatron seemed to be watching closely.

Take care. Koth is baiting you.

Finally awake, huh? Good for you. Smith thought at the angel irritably.

"Why would you say something like that to me?" he asked out loud when he had regained control of himself.

At this the demon laughed. "Are you serious, man? After all that little tart put you through? I would think you would thank me."

Smith stared coldly, silent.

"You don't remember," Koth said and knocked himself on the forehead. "Right. I keep forgetting.

Never mind. You two seem like you're getting on really well now, so, congratulations." The demon leaned in close to Smith and flicked at a stray ash on the detective's collar before returning his chrome gaze to his face. He was close enough for the detective to feel his breath on his lips like heat from an open oven, and when next he spoke his voice was low and more demonic than Smith had ever heard it. "Just remember this: she's mine, Cal. After all is said and done, after you are merely dust and forgotten memories, I will have her for the rest of always, so don't get too attached to your little whore."

Before he realized what he was doing, Smith was out of his chair and Koth was sprawled on the floor. Silver blood oozed from between the fingers wrapped over his face and for a moment the demon's appearance shifted to reveal something not human.

Marduk and Pazuzu rushed to hold their superior and the detective apart from one another as Koth's face shifted between his true visage and the one he wore when he was topside. Smith struggled against Pazuzu's grip and spittle flew from his lips as he hurled expletives at the demonic case manager.

Marduk struggled to hold onto his charge, his grip slipping as Koth at last dropped his human skin to the floor. Smith stared in horror at the puddled features pooling around the demon's feet as Koth grew to his true height and spread enormous wings across the span of the office.

"Go ahead, hit me again, you little prick," the thing said from a face so horribly beautiful it made Smith drop his eyes and bite back a scream.

Koth lifted Smith's gaze by hooking the claws of

one gnarled gray finger under his chin and cutting into the flesh, lifting upward until their eyes met. The detective flinched at the sensation of nail on bone, but to scream would be death. He stared up and the demon smiled, row upon row of razor teeth glinting down at him.

"I will eat your soul after I have made you watch what I intend to do to your woman, you mortal wretch. You forget your place. Do you think you are more powerful than I? You are *nothing*!"

"Enough, demon. You would do well to recall this man is the Vessel."

Koth blinked at Metatron's words and shrank back into his human form. The discarded skin slid back up onto his body with a horrid sucking noise, ending with the human face swallowing the demon and seeming to zip closed around a tight smile.

"Yeah, no problem, Metatron. Sorry about that. Sometimes I forget," said Koth as he straightened his suit and tie then adjusted the skin around his hairline.

Smith cleared his throat and glared at the demon. Without a word he opened his desk and grabbed a paper towel from the drawer, then pressed it over the puncture wound beneath his chin. The demons watched him in silence until he again settled into his chair. From the back of his mind he could sense Metatron staring out of his eyes, cautious and ready for another fight. He could feel the angel's wrath coursing through his blood along with his own anger, and a large part of him wanted to tap into that strength and find out what happened. With a deep, steadying breath he reminded himself Koth was not one of the bad guys; he was doing the job he had been created to do, and in a strange way he considered him a friend. Koth was not a friend he would trust, but one he might depend on for a ride to the airport or to help him move. The humor of the idea chased away the rest of his anger and he stared at his demonic audience. He picked up the cigarette from the blotter and relit it. He took a long drag and stared at the demons through the exhaled smoke, no longer caring if the building manager cited him for smoking inside.

"Should I be worried about tetanus or any other bullshit infections from this little puncture wound you gave me?" Smith asked the demons.

They looked to one another, then back to the detective. They shrugged.

"No one has ever lived after being injured by a demon," Marduk told him. "But they are also not usually in one piece."

"Ah." Smith reached into his desk drawer and took out the bottle of Dewar's hiding in the back of it. He splashed some liquor onto the clean part of the paper towel and pressed it to the underside of his chin with a wince.

"So why are we here, guys?" he finally asked, his voice as tired as he suddenly felt. "I mean for real. Why did you get me out of bed?"

"Perhaps I should speak for us," Pazuzu interjected as Koth opened his mouth. "You both need a 'timeout', I believe."

Marduk clapped a hand over his mouth to hold back a bark of laughter. The demons had had a crash course in topside vocabulary, but instead of watching programming for adults, they had instead spent most of their spare time watching children's shows because they liked the colorful characters and the songs. They had especially liked the songs.

Smith gave a nod, mostly to hide his own mirth at being told he needed a timeout by one of Hell's minions. "Go ahead."

"Your next client will be investigating the murder victim found on the battlefield."

Smith sat up in alarm. "What victim on the battlefield? I didn't hear anything about it."

"You will. Today."

"Look, if you guys had anything to do with this—"

"I assure you, we are not to blame. The body was found shortly after sunrise by park rangers."

"So why am I getting involved if the rangers already found it?" Smith asked, confused.

"You will see that for yourself. As to why we are interested in the case...." Pazuzu paused then looked to Koth, motioning him to wrap up the story.

The case manager scowled, but said, "We suspect the murderer to be one of the men who made a deal with Hell a long time ago. It was during the Civil War, and he made a deal that he and his friend would survive the battle. They lived, as per the deal, but when their demon came to collect payment for services rendered, they were nowhere to be found."

"So? Good for them."

Koth ground his teeth and twisted his head with a horrible snapping sound. He twisted it the other way with similar result then focused on Smith once more.

"*So*," he said, "They upset the balance, just like you and your idiot father and brother did when you summoned Metatron and then killed it."

"Get to the point."

Koth growled. "Humans who counteract fate throw everything out of whack, that's the point. These two guys were supposed to die in the Civil War and they didn't. Then they were supposed to die when Hell came to collect, and they didn't."

"Where does the body on the battlefield come in?" Smith asked, flicking ashes out the window.

"Getting to that," the demon answered. "We've tracked one of the two to Gettysburg, and we think the body is proof positive he's here. Once we find him, he can tell us where his friend is."

"Let me get this straight," Smith said with a slow, derisive grin, "It took you guys one hundred and fifty years to track down someone who owed you something? Can you give lessons to collections agencies? I think the human race would convert to your side en masse out of gratitude."

Pazuzu stepped between the pair and glared at them. "Enough. We have said what we came to say, and now it is time to leave. Mr. Smith, as always, it has been," the demon paused, searching for the right word, "interesting."

"Yeah, no kidding," the detective said with a snort.

He nodded to Marduk and Koth as they exited behind Pazuzu. Marduk smirked and shook his head at him before stepping through the doorway in the air, leaving Smith to finish his last cigarette and wait for his mysterious, undead client.

CHAPTER III

The man who eventually came to Smith's office was not his demonically predicted client, but he was undead. Somewhat. Mostly dead, at the very least.

Smith was rummaging in his desk looking for any cached cigarettes when he heard the click of the door latch. Without looking up, he motioned to the two chairs in front of his desk and said, "Come on in, have a seat."

He heard the scrape of the chair legs moving over the industrial berber carpet, followed by the creak of someone sitting down. Instead of cigarettes he found the last pen in his drawer and the notebook he had kept for actual, non-otherworldy cases and shoved the stashed bottle of Dewar's into the back, well out of client view.

With a flourish, Smith sat up and managed to say, "What can I do for you?" before further words died in his throat.

He felt his jaw fall open and hang there, but the sensation was distant. He dropped the pen and notebook onto his desk, his hands suddenly weak as he stared at his new client.

"I need help," the man said quietly.

"You need a hospital, my friend." Sometimes

sarcasm was a kneejerk reaction, Smith decided.

The man nodded. "I think I might have already been in one." He reached down and tugged at something Smith was unable to see beyond the bulk of his desk. There was a small snapping noise and a moment later the man rose with a slip of paper in his hand. He pushed it across the desktop toward the detective and Smith pulled it the rest of the way.

It was card stock and had a loop of broken string attached to it. Smith looked closer and noted the name and date of death printed neatly on the toe tag. He was amazed there was a place still using the things. According to the tag, his new client's name was Roger Norton, fifty years old, died in town with "unknown" written in the cause of death area. Without a word he pushed it back toward the man in the client's chair and the man took it. Smith eyed him up, noting that the man was remarkable in that he was unremarkable in every way: bland features, medium build, and a middle-aged face. He was the living embodiment of a deceased Everyman.

"Okay, you're dead. Really, Mr. Norton, isn't everything else spilled milk at this point?" Smith asked lamely.

"Please, call me Roger," said the dead man.

"Roger, then."

"And no, it's not 'spilled milk', Mr. Smith. I have unfinished business."

"Such as?"

"I want you to find the person or people who killed me."

Smith let out a long breath and leaned back in his chair. He stared at his new client and wondered if this was his personal form of Limbo for the wrongs committed in his own past life.

"Maybe you'd better start from the beginning."

The man gave a small nod. "It's as good a place as any, I suppose. It started with the nightmares. Past couple of months, I've been having some horrible nightmares, like I was fighting in the war all over again. I'd wake up and feel worse than when I went to bed."

Smith nodded, brow furrowed. He contemplated the bottle of Dewar's in his desk drawer and wondered if it would be unprofessional to offer his client a drink.

Norton went on in his lightly southern-inflected voice, eyes staring intently at Smith while he spoke, though Smith had stopped paying attention. "And so I woke up face down in Plum Run by the Devil's Den, except I wasn't awake enough for them to think I was alive."

Smith jerked himself out of the beginnings of a mental doze at the last words. "What?"

"I said I woke up face down in Plum Run."

"When?"

"Today. Haven't you been listening?"

Smith shrugged apologetically. "Been a rough morning."

"*You* had a rough morning?"

Norton crossed his arms over his chest and Smith suddenly realized the man was naked but for a white doctor's coat. How the hell had he missed that detail? He rubbed at his eyes. Not enough sleep; he was starting to lose it, he decided.

"You're the body they found this morning?" he asked.

Norton nodded impatiently. "Only what I been saying while you were off in your head somewhere."

"How did you die?"

"If I knew that, I wouldn't be here now, would I?"

Smith grimaced. "Fair enough. So how did you come back to life?"

Norton seemed to consider this question for a moment before idly scratching at his neck. Smith noted with some alarm two holes located directly over the man's jugular.

"Dunno exactly. I remember hearing and feeling water around my face and ears, then men talking but muffled like when you're in the pool, you know? They pulled me up and checked me over, but I had no pulse. My eyes were open, but I couldn't move," the man gave a little shudder. "I guess I must have passed out because I'll be honest, I was screaming my damned head off inside my own head. After that, I think I woke up in the morgue, but things are kind of fuzzy, you know?"

Smith nodded.

"So, you'll help me, then?"

"I actually have a case pending, but I'll see what I can do, okay?"

It was the man's turn to nod, resigned. He stared down at himself for a moment and looked back up at the detective.

"Don't happen to have any clothes, do you?"

Smith looked the man up and down, then opened a drawer in his desk and threw him the spare set of clothes he kept there for "just in case" and late nights. Norton caught the clothes gratefully and pulled them on after shedding his doctor's coat. Smith turned his head and let his new client have a semblance of privacy, though he suspected the man was long past caring.

"I don't mean to rush you out of here, Roger, but I'm expecting another appointment."

"Ahhh. I'll be out of your hair in a minute. Can I come by later? In case maybe your other case doesn't pan out?"

Smith considered the request but shook his head. "Your family is probably worried sick about you. You'll want to let them know you're okay."

"Got none," Roger said, "Wife died, never had kids, rest of the family's all gone and there's just me left."

Smith rubbed at the bridge of his nose. "I have a date tonight," he lied.

Norton thankfully got the hint and let the subject drop, but his expression was so forlorn Smith felt like he had kicked a puppy. Smith groaned, already regretting his next words before they were out of his mouth.

"Where can I reach you?" the detective asked with exasperated guilt.

"If you have a couple of bucks I can go to the pub on the square and you can find me there. They took all my belongings when they brought me to the morgue."

Smith gave the man the grand total of forty dollars from his wallet. Roger took the cash and gave Smith a hard, earnest look.

"I will get this back to you, Mr. Smith. You have my word."

The detective shook his head and clapped the man on the back as he walked him to the door. "Don't worry about it. I'll see you around six, okay?"

Roger nodded and walked down the hall without another word. Smith closed the door and leaned his head against the cool, frosted glass. What the hell was going on? He wished he had more cigarettes and wondered if he had enough time to run to the convenience store before his actual client arrived.

He turned to face into the room and nearly jumped through the glass of his door in surprise. Instead of an empty office, a man sat in the chair next to his desk, watching him expectantly.

"Who? How?" Smith stammered.

The man's smile was thin beneath his full beard and mustache, his face showing quiet strength in spite of his touristy sunglasses and baseball cap ensemble. He removed his hat and gave a nod toward Smith in way of greeting, then motioned for him to sit down as if it were not Smith's office.

"I believe the demons alerted you to my arrival?"

Smith could only stare at the man as he made his way behind his desk and fumbled for his chair. The man waited patiently, folding his hands and resting them in his lap.

"Yeah," the detective said at last. "What can I do for you?"

The man took in a slow breath and let it out as he surveyed the office. "I would like you to find out who killed Roger Norton."

Smith was momentarily at a loss for words. At last he said, "Okay, why?"

The man removed his sunglasses and Smith fell back into his chair. The detective glanced behind himself at the wall of windows and pointed, the words stuck in his throat. The man smiled then, revealing gleaming white teeth that ended in points on the canines.

His eyes glittered in the afternoon sunlight coming through the windows, an uncanny amber gold. He fixed Smith with an unblinking stare and his smile faded.

"First, I would like you to find his murderer so that I may continue to exist well below the radar, as it were." The man ran a hand through his tousled hat hair and sighed. "Secondly, the trouble in this instance is that there are men who would enjoy seeing me brought up on murder charges and whom I suspect would not be averse to setting a murder scene to look as if I had committed the crime. The only way to stop that from occurring is to catch them."

"But why would they do it?"

"To expose me."

"'K," Smith tried again, "Now, *Why*? Everyone has a reason for doing something, so what did you do to piss these guys off?"

"I killed their brothers and fathers in the war."

Smith was confused. "The war? As in Gulf, Afghanistan, Iraq, Vietnam? You look a little young for the world wars or Korea. Help me out here."

"The Civil War."

"I see. So," Smith paused and contemplated the drawer containing the Dewar's bottle, "How many of you guys are there in town?"

"Only a handful of us. Worldwide, perhaps only a few hundred, if even that many."

"How do you— That is to say, *do* you drink blood?"

205

The vampire threw his head back and laughed. "God, man, no! Not all of us are bloodsuckers. Some feed on energy or emotions, some on a rare steak or animal blood, and some don't need to feed at all. They just *are*."

Feeling silly, Smith toyed with a pencil lying on his desk. "Okay, look. I'll level with you." He leaned over his desk toward the man. "It's been a hell of a day and it's not even near over. Since you're a friend of the demonic dream team, I'll let you in on a secret: I need a drink and a cigarette. Not want, *need*. I only have alcohol, though, so I am going to reach into this drawer and pull out a bottle of Dewar's. Would you like some, Mister….?"

The vampire smiled so wide Smith could see his back teeth. "McGuffin, but call me Mac. And yes, please."

CHAPTER IV

Within an hour Smith and his second undead client were drunk, only stopping because they ran out of anything to drink. Smith struggled to focus on McGuffin, using his glass to point at the man across his desk.

"You," he declared, "are not what I expected. D'y'know that?"

The vampire laughed and rested his head against the back of the chair. "What did you expect, Mr. Smith? Bela Lugosi?"

Smith considered this and shook his head. "David Bowie, I think."

McGuffin laughed again, settling further into his chair. "I apologize for instilling a sense of disappointment, then, sir. Truly, I do."

Smith waved a dismissive hand. "Nah. It all makes sense. You're here, you're trying to live a normal life, keep secrets and stuff, and everyone's gonna notice a damned rock star running around town and..." his voice trailed off and he stared into the distance as he lost his train of thought.

"Are you the guy who made the deal with Hell to stay alive?" Smith asked suddenly.

McGuffin's smile was rueful as he shook his head.

"No. My condition is hereditary."

"Mmmm." Smith nodded lower and lower until his head was propped up in his hands.

The vampire smirked at him, clearly able to hold his liquor much better than either a mortal or a demon. "Ready to hit the pub, detective?"

Smith's eyes widened. "Crap, I forgot I was supposed to meet whatisname there! Norton! What time is it?"

"Just enough time to restore you to a semblance of being coherent enough to get you in the door, but I cannot promise they will serve you."

Smith held up a hand. "Oh God, no. I'm good on drinks for now."

McGuffin helped him to his feet and they stumbled out onto the street. From Smith's office it was a couple of blocks' walk, but the vampire took back alleys and side streets instead of the more direct main roads.

"Cigarettes. Need to get cigarettes. And juss so you are aware," Smith warned, waggling a finger, "I've got The Voice of God in me. So, you know, no funny business."

The vampire laughed and shook his head. "Mr. Smith, I am attempting to give you a chance to sober up without being seen by any stray police who happen to be patrolling the area. There is no need to add a public drunkenness arrest to your otherwise relatively spotless record now, is there?"

Smith narrowed his eyes then gave a nod. "Good point."

They wandered to the convenience store where Smith waited outside while McGuffin entered and bought his cigarettes. As the detective stood on the sidewalk waiting for the vampire to return, he felt distinctly underage. He glanced up at the feeling of eyes on him and noticed a shadow ducking into a doorway across the street. He squinted, watching the spot, unblinking, until his eyes watered and the world spun around him. No one emerged and he shook his head at the tricks his imagination was playing on him.

McGuffin exited the shop and handed Smith three packs of cigarettes. "Use them wisely, sir."

Smith smiled and tapped the pack against the palm of his hand, then opened it. The scent of fresh tobacco wafted up to his nose and he inhaled, his smile turning to bliss as he placed one of the cigarettes between his lips.

"You know," he told the vampire, "I din't always smoke. Din't know I did 'til my father gave me a cigarette."

"How's that?"

"Pass life regr…ession," the detective said with a bitter laugh, concentrating to say the words without slurring.

When at last they made their way to the pub on the square, Smith extinguished his third cigarette in the ashcan outside the door and scanned the patrons until he saw one waving at them. They approached the man and joined him at his table.

"Roger, this is Mr. McGuffin—I mean Mac. Mac, this is Roger," said the detective, with much effort to remain coherent.

Their server approached and Smith ordered coffee from the very familiar waitress. He blinked and tried to remember where he knew her from, but came up blank.

"Hey, Mr. Smith," she said brightly. "Good to see you again. How's your friend been?"

"My friend?"

"The older gentleman you were in here with a while back?" she tried.

The memory clicked at last and Smith bit back a gasp of shock. Sobriety coursed through his veins on adrenaline and he gave a short cough.

"Oh, ummm. He's fine," Smith lied, feeling awkward.

"That's great to hear. Send him my best. Now what can I get you all?" she said and readied her notepad and pencil, her eyes never leaving Smith.

The vampire ordered a cheeseburger and coke while Smith's freshly undead client looked a little green around the gills at the mention of food.

"Can I just get a water?" he asked, pushing aside the now watery drink he had been nursing all afternoon.

"Sure thing. Mr. Smith, did you want any food to go with your coffee?"

"Just some fries."

She gave a smile and nod, then practically skipped off to put the order in and get the drinks. McGuffin watched her go, his face scrunched in confusion.

"I've never seen Janice look so happy to wait a table," he murmured.

Smith folded his hands in front of him and stared down at his whitening knuckles. "I hope she isn't expecting the same tip she got last time I was in here."

The vampire stared at him for a moment, then asked, "Who was she talking about?"

"My father," the detective replied.

"Not a great guy, I'm guessing?" asked Roger, the newly undead.

Smith gave a harsh laugh. "He apparently murdered me over two-hundred times before it finally caught up with him. He was the head of a very powerful group of men, and when shit hit the fan, he more or less sacrificed all of us for his own agenda. 'Not a great guy' is an understatement."

"What happened to him?" asked the vampire.

"He's in Hell."

"Hell?"

"Yeah. Hell. Fire, brimstone, demons. *Hell*."

They sat in uncomfortable silence as Janice brought their drinks, carefully setting the places in front of them with silverware folded in napkins. "Your food will be out in a few," she said, her attention once more focused solely on Smith, and left them.

"Gentlemen, I'm no good with awkward situations, so forgive me if I'm too abrupt," Norton began, "but can we talk about my case and what this man has to do with it?"

"Yes, of course," said Smith while rubbing at the bridge of his nose. "Mac has hired me to figure out who 'killed' you, for lack of a better term, and why they did it."

"Ahhh. Mighty generous of you," said Norton, turning to look at the vampire. "Now mind telling me why, mister?"

McGuffin's smile was thin. "There are those who would have the authorities believe I am the one who ended your life. I promise you I am not. In order to draw attention away from me, the best thing we can do is to find the person or persons who *did* kill you. This will most likely involve you having to to convince people you are neither dead nor undead."

Roger considered this as Janice brought the food to their table. At last she took notice of the others as she set their plates down. McGuffin smiled at her and she returned it with a small blush.

"Sorry, didn't see you there before. How are you tonight, Mac?" she asked the vampire.

"Doing well, thank you, and yourself?"

"Busy." She motioned to the crowded bar. "Been like this all day. Must be something going on up on campus."

The vampire gave a shrug for response.

"I'll be free this weekend if you want to get together."

"I would like that very much. Shall we meet in our usual place at the usual time?"

Janice laughed and brushed a stray strand of hair out of her eyes. "You make it sound so wrong, but yeah. Same time, same place. See you then."

As she wandered back into the crowd she gave a quick glance behind and smiled. McGuffin returned it and gave a little wave, then turned to face the blatantly curious expressions of Smith and Norton.

"We are meeting at the library to discuss literature," he said defensively.

"That girl wants to do more than discuss books with you, friend," Roger said with a wolfish grin.

Smith nodded his agreement. "You get her phone number?"

The vampire scowled. "No, of course not!"

"Whoah, whoah. Easy now. I didn't ask if you slept with her."

McGuffin glared at them. "A lady must be wooed only *after* a friendship has been established. It would be forward of me to assume she wanted more than my friendship, especially considering my…condition."

Smith rolled his eyes. "Come off it, Count Doom and Gloom. You've been a regular guy up to this point, and now you're going to go mess it up with the tortured monster bit? No way."

"But I—"

"But nothing! You can eat food, you can go out in daylight, and you don't drink blood. Apparently the only weird thing about you is your inability to age. So ask her out."

The vampire huffed, then shrugged. "I had not thought of it from that perspective."

"Yeah, well, never thought I'd be giving relationship tips to a vampire." Smith said as he bit into a french-fry.

Roger watched both of them for a moment. "Is that what I am? I'm a vampire?"

McGuffin cringed. "Apologies. I failed to mention it earlier."

"You were distracted," Roger said helpfully.

The vampire's smile was rueful. "Yes, I suppose I was."

He glanced over the crowd toward where Janice was working behind the bar. As if sensing his gaze, she looked up. When she smiled at him he dropped his eyes, a blush creeping into his cheeks.

"Vampire?" Roger reminded him.

"Ahh. Yes. My guess is during the night you were attacked in your home or a secluded place then moved to someplace more public in order to be discovered.

The reason you survived was as a result of your becoming a vampire," McGuffin paused, his gaze far away, "I don't know if your attackers intended for that to happen, however. We will need to keep watch over you to ensure your safety. While it is a good thing you are not *technically* dead, questions will be asked. We need to speak with the coroner and convince him or her that they were mistaken and you were merely in a very deep coma."

"How are we going to do that?" Smith asked from around a mouthful of french-fries.

McGuffin smiled. "I can be very persuasive when necessary; more importantly, I will teach Roger how to make his heart beat again."

CHAPTER V

When dinner was complete and they had outstayed their welcome at the pub, they agreed to meet the next day and visit the police station. It gave Smith a chance to sleep in for a change. Cherry had plans that night and wouldn't be coming over, and McGuffin planned to bring Roger back to his home until they could retrieve the dead man's belongings from the police.

"Can you show me where they found you?" Smith asked.

"When, now? Are you kidding?"

The detective shrugged. "Good a time as any."

"It's night, and the park is closed," Roger told him.

"And I'm walking after midnight with two real, live, undead men. What's your point?"

The vampire stared at him for a moment, contemplating. "You're Dutch," he muttered. "Can I borrow your phone?"

"Sure, and then you can tell me what the hell the Dutch have to do with any of this." Smith handed over his phone and lit a cigarette, watching his companions through the curls of smoke.

Roger dialed a number, his face already cringing as a woman's voice answered. "Hi, Chris," he said quietly, "It's Roger. Sorry to call so late, but could you do me a favor?"

He paused, listening, and said, "It's a really long story, but a couple of friends and I need to get up by Little Roundtop tonight. Think you could give us a tour?"

His face flushed as laughter erupted from the phone. "I'm being serious, damn it!"

More laughter, followed by a click. Roger handed the phone back to Smith with a sigh. "Sometimes her sense of humor is a little too good."

"So what do we do now?" asked the detective.

"Go up there and hope we don't get caught."

As they walked along, Smith opened a fresh pack of cigarettes and held it out in offering. Both vampires accepted and smoked as they walked.

The night was eerily quiet, and it seemed they were on Taneytown Road for a small eternity before reaching Wheatfield Road, and finally Sykes Avenue. They turned right onto the path that would bring them near to the stone monuments at Little Roundtop. The stone structures reminded Smith of giant chess pieces in the moonlight.

As they wandered down the hill toward Devil's Den, a gleam in the shadows of the boulders caught Smith's eye. He stared in horror as the largest, blackest snake he had ever seen slid along the boulders, disappearing inside one of the many crevices.

"Did...did you guys just see that?" he asked, his voice weak.

"The eyes play tricks out here after dark," McGuffin warned. "And if you're talking about the snake, best to forget you ever saw it. Bad luck, that thing."

Smith shuddered as they approached the small trickling noise of water. He cast nervous glances over his shoulder at every sound on the night air, afraid he would see the serpent approaching them from the shadows if he was not vigilant.

"Here it is," said Roger. He had stopped at a small bend in the stream and pointed at the ground.

McGuffin stared at the spot. "Are you sure?"

"Yes, sir. Man can't forget a thing like that."

"Why?" Smith asked. "What's wrong with that spot, Mac?"

"It is the exact place I was killed when I was a soldier in the war. Plum Run was much bigger back then, big enough to carry bodies."

They were distracted by the echoing sound of a bugle being played across the fields. Moments later the sound of distant gunfire came to them and McGuffin looked ashen.

"Gentlemen, I have no desire to reunite with my former brothers in arms. Might I suggest we leave now?"

The three men returned the way they had come, walking briskly and ignoring the shadows darting between the trees. They remained silent until they reached McGuffin's house, none of them willing to admit to having heard or seen anything strange as they retreated.

Smith was surprised to discover the vampire lived in a lovely old Victorian rather than a mausoleum, but who was he to judge? One might incorrectly assume the human playing host to The Voice of God would live in a church instead of a small apartment off the square of a small town, after all. He blew out a puff of smoke in appreciation of fresh tobacco and raised a hand at the vampires.

"See you tomorrow."

"Mr. Smith? Be careful," McGuffin told him with a worried glance up and down the street.

The detective laughed. "Always, Mac."

He gave a last nod and went on his way, the old vampire's words sending a chill up his spine. As he walked back to his little should-be palace, the detective found himself dozing on his feet in spite of his unease. Several times his cigarette fell from his lips, and several times the garbled voice of Metatron spoke from the back of his mind with the same message.

Be alert.

"Why should I?" Smith mumbled. "And where the hell have you been?"

Something is not right.

"Shut up."

Smith attempted to sound surly as he lit a new cigarette from the glowing cherry of the previous one, but the angel was correct in its statement–something was off. It was as if the air was made of liquid glitter, fog rolling and sparkling beneath sodium-colored pools of light from the streetlamps before disappearing into the blackest shadows Smith had ever seen.

He heard the crunch of boots on crumbling sidewalk behind him and turned to see a tall, human-shaped shadow slip into a doorway. Beneath his jacket, his skin began to prickle with gooseflesh and he continued on his way with a quickening pace.

The footfalls started again, the steps matching his in tempo until he was running. To hell with looking behind him, he decided. He had seen enough to know he didn't want to find out what the shadow-person wanted.

As he reached the doorway to his apartment building, the footfalls stopped. He glanced out of the corner of his eye while fumbling with his keys and saw the shadow gliding toward him, its feet hovering a full six inches above the ground.

"STOP."

The shadow paused for only a moment, then continued forward again. *Oh hell, it's not afraid of The Voice of God*, Smith thought wildly while continuing to search his keys–when the hell had he acquired so many damned keys?? He stared down at the seemingly endless ring of nondescript metal, wondering which one would open his front door, then looked back up as the thing bore down on him. Frantic, he reached up to use the cigarette as a weapon only to find it was gone, dropped during his attempt at escape.

Smith pressed against the wall of the building, biting back a scream of terror as the shadow thing came into the light of a streetlamp. It had the face of an anglerfish, with jagged teeth curving to points outside its horribly misshapen mouth and white eyes staring dead from its gray and sunken face.

He brought the hefty weight of his keyring around in an arc that connected with the side of the thing's face. He wasn't sure what he expected, but it certainly wasn't no reaction at all. His keys glinted as they shivered with the creature's movements, the clink of metal muted by gray flesh as the thing cocked its head at him as if asking what he had intended by such an action.

"Oh shit," Smith whispered.

He watched, dismayed, as his keys were shaken loose, hitting the sidewalk with a metallic clink. He grabbed at them, ducking and weaving to avoid the creature's outstretched claws.

"WAKE UP."

The angel's voice was loud, and Smith clutched at the sides of his head as the shadow creature growled and closed the distance between them. The stench of rotting flesh was strong around it as it came in close enough to sniff him, its breath like wind through PVC piping. Smith pressed flatter against the side of the building, eyes squeezed shut and every muscle tensed in anticipation of the fatal blow.

"WAKE UP!"

Smith screamed at the pain as he sat up and smacked his head off the bricks of his apartment building. He found himself half-sprawled on the sidewalk and half-leaning against the wall, ordinary keyring in hand and no sign of a monster–or anyone else nearby. He flinched as the last of the glowing tip of his cigarette burned through his pants and singed his flesh. He batted at his leg and jumped to his feet, snuffing the cigarette into the sidewalk with the tip of his shoe.

"What the hell was that?" he mumbled to himself as he slipped his key in the lock and pushed the door inward.

A bad dream.

"Yeah, no shit."

It had felt so real. Smith rubbed at his face, his shaking hands brushing over the stubble of five-o-clock shadow as he made his way up the stairs. On the landing outside his door he fumbled the cigarette pack out of his jacket pocket and pushed a fresh cigarette between his lips. He would have loved to have lit the thing right then and there, but he knew his non-smoking neighbors wouldn't appreciate it, regardless that he had been scared half to death. He decided after his current cases were solved he would try to quit again, but not tonight.

Pausing on the landing, he looked down at his keys in confusion. Mere moments ago he could have sworn he owned an endless ring of the things, and now he held a small fob with only four keys on it. He slid the one to his apartment into the deadbolt lock and gave a small sigh of relief when it clicked. He needed sleep and was looking forward to falling into bed.

"Bad dream," he said, the statement more like a mantra as he fished in his pockets for a lighter.

He walked through the door of his apartment to find Cherry already there and waiting for him. Naked. So much for sleeping in, he thought, hand holding the lighter paused halfway to his lips.

Her skin shimmered in the glow of the streetlamp outside the window, her body gloriously bare but for a pair of large, white wings protruding from her back and a Carnivale plague mask firmly tied to her head, obscuring most of her face. This was a new look for her.

Smith paused in the doorway, unsure. He could hear the muffled sound of Cherry's cheeks rubbing against the inside of the mask as she smiled. Her grin was in direct opposition to the expression of the half-mask, the papier-mâché pushed and molded into an obscenely long nose and angry, glaring holes for eyes. It was painted all over with the most incredibly intricate designs Smith had ever seen, each one seeming to shift in the dim lighting as if alive.

"You're a sight for sore eyes."

"Bad day at the office?" she asked, her voice distorted and made hollow by her costume.

"You have no idea."

Cherry laughed and held up a whiskey bottle. "Come on in and relax, then. Drink?"

"God, yes."

He watched her pour the liquor into a rocks glass with the anticipation of a shore-stranded fish catching sight of water, shoving the now-forgotten lighter back into his pocket and resting the cigarette in one of the many ashtrays littering his apartment. After taking a large gulp of the offered liquid he grimaced.

"What the hell is this?" he asked as he tried to turn the glass toward the light.

"The blood of virgins."

The detective smacked his lips and frowned. Her description was exactly what it tasted like, if the virgins were emergency room drunk. He put the glass onto an end table, retrieved his cigarette and lit it, then threw his jacket onto a chair.

"What's with the outfit, or rather the lack thereof?" She turned toward him and he inwardly recoiled at the sight of her demonic appearance. "And what's with that mask?" he asked, motioning to his own face for emphasis, the cigarette smoke encircling his head like a halo.

"Do you like it?" Cherry asked "The design is Enochian."

"It's beautiful," was all he could think to say, in the same tone a husband would tell his wife her hair looked great when in fact it didn't and she needed to find a new hairdresser sooner instead of later.

Behind them the door swung slow on its hinges until the click of the latch broke the silence stretching between them. Cherry took a step forward and the wings swished the air as she moved, sending a cloud of musky perfume wafting toward him. In the back of his mind it felt as if Metatron was trying to say something, but its voice was muffled, the words blocked. Mentally he closed an inner door on the agitated angel and focused instead on where his night with Cherry might go.

"You've got wings."

"I do," she said, her smile widening enough to show a glint of teeth beneath the mask, "What do you think?"

He stared at them and took a long drag on his cigarette, contemplating, and her smile began to fade. At last he nodded his appreciation and he heard more than saw her smile return beneath the mask. He had to admit, the wings in contrast to the mask were damned near sexy. As beautiful as the craftsmanship of the visage was, the mask itself was hideous to the point of terrifying and he found himself lost in his own horror of the thing, unable to look away from it.

The metallic sheen of the painted symbols seemed to glow in the shifting light and appeared to crawl over the surface of the plaster like insects. He could only stare in fascination as Cherry moved closer. She lifted the mask to reveal her real nose and the curve of her full, red lips.

"You know what you want to do," she whispered, "So do it. Promise I won't bite…unless you ask me to."

Instantly his misgivings were forgotten and he groaned with longing as he snuffed his cigarette and pulled her to him. It didn't matter that she had possibly given him blood to drink, or that she had wings, or that she was wearing the most horrifying mask he had ever seen, or that everything about the scenario was wrong. He would worry about it all in the morning after he woke up and dealt with his inevitable hangover.

They kissed their way toward his bed, her hands deft as they unfastened his pants, tearing his belt through the loops in one swift motion and leaving it spread across the floor like a dead serpent in their wake. He growled and bit her lip as she massaged him through his underwear, the desire in him so strong he felt as if he might tear her apart while they made love.

His eyes snapped open when he felt intense heat on his back. The symbols covering the mask flickered in what could only be firelight and Smith frowned at the suffocating stench of burning. He turned to look at his bed, noted the flames engulfing the mattress, and recoiled in shock.

"We have to get out of here!"

Cherry placed a long finger on his lips, silencing his fear. "It's okay. Trust me. Tonight we are embracing the inferno and drinking the blood of the unrighteous."

He pulled back from her and stared. "What the hell are you talking about? My bed is on *fire*!"

With a laugh she fell into him, pushing him backward with the combination of her weight and momentum. As he went screaming into the pyre she held onto him, her legs locked around his waist. He howled in agony as the first of the flames licked his flesh and she pulled him into her with an ecstatic sigh. He struggled against her as he burned, his throat raw from a combination of screaming and smoke inhalation. This only made her more excited and she rode him to climax, her cries of orgasm mingling with his anguish.

Fire seemed to burst forth from her as she peaked, flames caressing her body with a lover's touch as she smiled down at him, immune to the burning of her own flesh. Her wings were the first to go, incinerated to bloody stumps within seconds, leaving what remained wriggling at her shoulders before they blackened to cinders. Next to burn was Cherry's skin, strips of it peeling away like autumn leaves and floating upward on the backdraft from the fire below and around them. He stared in horror, his own discomfort suddenly distant, as finally the mask burned away to reveal the true, charred face beneath.

Smith awoke drenched in sweat, the cry of terror choked in his throat. He scrambled over his bed for a moment, searching for something to hold onto, to escape the flames in his mind before he blinked and realized he was no longer inside an inferno. Sunlight bathed his bedroom and he stared down at himself in disbelief. There was no evidence of his ever having gone through a fire, but there was evidence of a wet dream. He wasn't sure what disturbed him more, the nightmare or the fact he'd had an orgasm during such a horrible ordeal.

"Sweet Christ," he whispered and shook his head.

With a motion that had become automatic he reached out to grab the bottle of Jack Daniel's that sat as an insomnia companion on his nightstand. Without another thought, he twisted off the cap and drank straight from the bottle until his hands steadied enough to handle a smoke.

Propping the bottle between his legs at the knees, he next reached for his cigarettes. He fumbled and dropped one before finally getting it lit, his hands shaking around the lighter. He alternated between smoking and drinking for what felt like a long time before finally letting his head drop back against the headboard of his thrift store bed. As the low-key buzz from the alcohol began, he glanced at his watch to see it read seven in the morning. It felt much earlier than that, he decided, and took comfort in the fact that somewhere in the world it was happy hour.

"What a night," he told no one in particular.

Indeed, said Metatron, its voice haggard.

"You didn't sleep good either, huh?"

He felt the angel shake its head in response and he took another swig from the bottle of whiskey. "What the hell was that all about? Something from the other side?"

Again, he felt the angel shake its head. *It is unclear as to the source of the dreams. The objective was clearly to frighten you.*

"Yeah, well, kudos to them because they succeeded."

The phone rang next to him and Smith nearly jumped out of his skin. He swore when the whiskey spilled onto his crotch as he reached for the receiver. Who the hell would call so early? Better not be the damned demons again.

"Hello?"

"Hello, Mr. Smith. You don't know me, but I

believe we have a mutual friend," said a tinny voice into his ear.

The detective glanced at the receiver in confusion while he waited for the other person to continue. It had sounded as if there were flies buzzing around in the earpiece and into his head. In the back of his mind, Metatron came to instant attention.

When the man remained silent, Smith asked, "Right, well, I've got a lot of friends, it's early, and I had a rough night. Forgive me for being abrupt, but who's our mutual friend?"

"Lily," The Voice replied.

Smith sat up a little straighter. "Really? And who might you be?"

"Her husband."

CHAPTER VI

Smith felt his mouth go dry and his stomach clenched at the words. Lily had never mentioned she was married–had she? Had he been that smitten with her he had ignored a wedding band and all mention of a spouse?

"I didn't catch your name," he said, his voice barely above a croak.

"Luke."

In the back of Smith's mind he felt Metatron begin to pace.

"What can I do for you, Luke?"

"It's better if we speak in person. When can I come by? You're in Gettysburg, correct?"

"How exactly did you hear about me?" Smith asked as warning bells sounded. "And how did you get this number?"

Ignoring his questions, the man continued, "I'll be at your office in about an hour."

He glared at the phone as he heard a click and the hum of dialtone instead of flies. What the hell just happened? In the back of his head he could feel Metatron moving from one side of his skull to the other, back and forth, back and forth.

"Spill it, angel, who was that?"

Metatron was silent for a moment before speaking. *He cannot be here, it is not time.*

"Who?"

First let us meet him. A positive identification is necessary before any actions can be taken.

"Always with the mystery."

The detective climbed out of bed and wandered into the bathroom mumbling under his breath about the nonsense he had to put up with as a result of Heaven's need-to-know mentality. He peeled his soiled pants and underwear off, wincing as body hair tugged with the material, and threw them into the hamper with a disgusted grunt. Worst wet dream ever, he decided, flicking ashes off the end of his cigarette into the basin of the sink.

When he glanced into the bathroom mirror he felt like punching the reflection of the angel as it stared back at him from the glass. Being able to see it didn't improve his mood. "For The Voice of God, you're kind of a jerk, you know that?"

Metatron shrugged and tried to appear unaffected, but Smith could see something was weighing on the angel's mind as it now paced around the bathroom behind him instead of inside his head. He growled and the image of the reflected voice of the Almighty slanted as he opened the door to the medicine cabinet and grabbed his bottle of aspirin. As the angel slid back into view he glared at it.

"Is this going to get me killed again?" he asked as he snuffed out the last of his cigarette and pitched the distorted filter into the toilet where it joined several other spent smokes.

Metatron sighed. *I sincerely hope not. I must admit*

I have come to enjoy being partially human.

"Yeah? Why's that?" he asked as he dropped two pills into his mouth.

Sex.

Smith choked on his aspirin. As he scrabbled for the faucet to take a drink he tried to forget what he had just heard, as if to forget knowing angels enjoyed sex would somehow keep his innocence intact. It had to be another nightmare, he decided as he struggled to swallow the rest of the pill lodged in his throat.

When he looked back at his reflection, Metatron was sitting on the edge of the tub and staring thoughtfully at the wall. Smith didn't like the expression on the angel's face. It said it had not been joking about the sex.

"I didn't think angels cared about physical attraction."

Nor did I. Metatron smiled ruefully at him. *When the Watchers were cast out, the entire host of Heaven believed it to be a just decision. The Watchers had defiled themselves, after all, and none of us had ever known the pleasures of the flesh. Having recently had a sampling, I now feel as though my judgment may have been made in haste.*

"Watchers? The what?"

There are Watcher angels who—

"Yeah, I get that part. What do you mean by 'cast out' and 'defiled', and what the hell does it have to do with sex?" Smith asked as he got out a can of shaving cream and lathered his face.

The angel looked uncomfortable. *There were several Watchers who discovered sex and they...experimented.*

Smith winced as the razor he had been dragging down his cheek nicked him. "They got cast out for having sex?"

It was more complicated than that, said Metatron, *Had it been merely sex, and with one another, they might have been forgiven. They had intercourse with every creature on earth–every one they could physically penetrate–and even some they could not. Human women were the only ones who provided them viable offspring, however.*

The detective let out a yelp as the razor cut him again and blood mingled with the remaining shaving cream on his face.

"Offspring? Like babies?"

Metatron nodded.

"They don't really go into those details in the Bible, do they?" The detective was proud of his Bible study since becoming possessed by The Voice of God, however, he could not recall any mention of a human-angel crossbreed anywhere.

There are many things left out of the current version of the book, the angel said with contempt, *and still more is omitted by choice and ignorance. Let us not forget all of the elements added to the texts in order to control the population through interpretation and fear.*

Metatron rubbed at the bridge of its nose in a familiar exasperated gesture Smith recognized as his own. He was rubbing off on the angel. It sighed and stared back out of the mirror at him; Smith felt almost sorry for The Voice of God. He wondered how many years it had watched, unable to act, as humans corrupted what started off as a good idea.

Nevertheless, there is mention of the children. They are referred to as Nephilim.

"Oh, yeah. I do remember something about them. So what was their story? I mean the real one."

The angel shrugged. *'Nutshell version' as you might say, angels had offspring with women, and the flood was sent as a means to destroy said offspring when they began devouring all of the resources of the earth–including humans. The flood drowned most of them, thus saving mankind from extinction.*

Smith felt a chill run down his spine. "'Most of them'?"

He tried not to think of the implications of vengeful Nephilim wandering the earth as he rinsed his razor, tapping the blade against the side of the sink in order to dislodge any stray shavings. He had always believed the flood was sent to kill the sinners of the earth, but it made more sense it had been sent to destroy a genetic hybrid that never should have occurred.

Metatron sat on the reflected edge of the tub. It seemed tired suddenly, as if all the weight of time had suddenly crushed its will to go on with life. *Some Nephilim escaped*, it said.

"Okay, and then what?"

And they went on to be as gods…and even monsters among men.

Smith blinked at the angel. "What exactly do you mean by that?"

The gods and monsters of myth, of Olympus, and the various other stories of impossible feats accomplished by mere mortal men; all of these stories stem from Nephilim involvement. The angel smirked, the expression foreign on its divine features. *Not all of the Nephilim were giants and hideous to gaze upon. Some were able to disguise themselves as men and women. Those same Nephilim are alive today, living in society, but they are not completely human.*

"So heaven knows it didn't get them all, and yet the survivors are still around?"

Metatron nodded. *After the flood, a line was drawn. The survivors live within those boundaries and fear to cross that line. The children born of the union between a Nephilim and a human have been taught to stay in the shadows, to blend in, or they will bring down Heaven's wrath. They hide their gifts and their longevity, and they live as humans, for the most part.*

"Someone broke the rules," the detective said with a smirk and Metatron nodded.

Some Nephilim have always failed to blend in, and still others are distorted by their own genetic structure. They know they are not like humans; they know of their own power, and it drives them to madness. One such Nephilim nearly took over the planet before he was stopped.

"Wait. You're telling me this for a reason, aren't you? This isn't about having sex anymore," Smith said, eyes locked with Metatron's reflection as he dried his face and wiped off the remnants of shaving cream clinging around his ears and jawline.

It nodded. *One of your new clients is descended from the original bloodline.*

He dropped the towel, fingers suddenly numb. He stared at the angel's grave expression and the chill returned.

"McGuffin?" he asked, his voice barely a whisper.

Again the angel nodded. *McGuffin is not pure*

Nephilim, and he poses no threat to you, but others of his kind might, always remember that. You understand, I must not interfere directly with the natural proceedings of mortal men. However, I felt obligated to warn you of the potential dangers you may face, as I have a vested interest.

"Oh hell," said Smith miserably, "How am I supposed to defend myself if one of them decides to attack me? *Can* I defend myself?"

Metatron smiled wryly. *You did an excellent job of defending yourself against me, therefore I have no doubt you will do well.*

He winced. "Oh, yeah. Sorry about that. I still don't really remember it, if that's any consolation?"

No. It is not.

The angel walked up behind him and wrapped its arms around him as if to embrace him. The gesture sent an odd chill of déjà vu through him as instead of hugging him it whispered into his ear, *If the time comes when you must kill a Nephilim, aim for the solar plexus.*

"I thought you had to stake a vampire in the heart?"

Metatron shook its head and tapped just below the bottom of the reflected Smith's sternum. The detective felt a slight pressure between his navel and sternum where the angel's reflection touched him.

The modern term for the Nephilim is 'vampire', but they are not so simple to define. If you must kill one, hit it here. It is their only true weakness, aside from decapitation, burning, and drowning - though drowning only kills the body for as long as it is submerged.

"What's so special about that spot?" Smith asked,

touching the area.

It is where their soul resides.

He looked up and locked eyes with the angel. As if reading the question in his mind, the angel spoke again.

Yes, it is the same for humans as well.

Smith ran a hand over his face and turned away from the mirror. "I didn't want to know that." He wasn't sure why the knowledge of a soul's location made him uncomfortable, but it did.

He glanced at the clock as he exited the bathroom and swore. He had roughly ten minutes before he was supposed to meet Lily's husband. For reasons he could not explain, he obsessed over his outfit and dressed up more than he would have for a regular client.

The detective arrived at his office with enough time to unlock the door and jump behind his desk as the elevator dinged. He was craving a cigarette and a drink while repositioning himself to look nonchalant when footsteps paused outside his office door.

"Come on in, it's open," Smith called out.

Tentatively, the door latch clicked and a man who could have been a model for a quirky fashion magazine walked into his office. All poise and confidence the detective had mustered before the man arrived promptly left him and he felt visibly deflated. The angel in his head had no such reaction, however. Smith felt as if he had touched an electric socket with a metal fork when Metatron caught sight of the man as he strode across the office, hand out, and a dazzlingly white smile flashing at the detective.

"Hi, Mr. Smith, I'm Luke. We spoke earlier? I hope you can fit me into your schedule this morning.

It's important."

Smith shook the offered hand and felt another jolt, this one more physical than spiritual. His hand trembled as he motioned for his guest to have a seat. Luke settled into a chair with the grace and poise of a dancer, his entire body completely at ease in its new environment as if he visited on a regular basis. He ran a hand through perfectly wavy fire engine red hair, streaks of yellow highlights glinting just before his smile faded like the sun going behind a cloud.

It took Smith a moment to regain his composure as Metatron all but bounced off the insides of his head. *"Cut it out!"* he mentally shouted at the angel, relieved when Metatron seemed to vanish from his mind. He turned his attention back onto the man seated across from him, a man good-looking enough to have been an angel himself.

"What can I do for you, Mr....sorry, I can't remember your last name."

"I never mentioned it. It's Morgenstern. Please, Mr. Smith, Luke is fine."

"Luke Morgenstern?" the detective asked with a smirk.

"Junior, yes."

"What are you, the antichrist?"

The man stared at him with a mixture of surprise and annoyance. "What?"

Smith chuckled. "Your name, it just-" he looked at the man in front of him and his humor drained. "Nevermind. What can I do for you, Luke?"

Luke Morgenstern, Jr. took a deep, shaking breath. "It's Lily. She's missing."

CHAPTER VII

"Missing?"

Lily's husband nodded.

"How long? Have you gone to the police?"

Luke arched a perfect, dark brown eyebrow. "Mr. Smith, we can't exactly go running to the police where Lily's concerned, now can we? I think you know that. Besides, I'd like to keep this quiet."

"Your wife is missing," Smith said, hating the taste of the words in his mouth, "One would think you would want to shout it from the rooftops in order to find her."

The man leaned back in his chair, everything about him catlike as he blinked at the detective. He folded his fingers behind his head and somehow managed to lounge in the uncomfortable plastic chair.

"Make no mistake, Mr. Smith, I *do* want to find her, but I happen to know there are others who are *also* trying to find her and their intentions are not nearly so noble as mine. Do you understand me now?"

The detective rolled his eyes. "Yes. Now tell me about the last time you saw her."

"It was back at our place. She was heading out to get coffee and she didn't come back."

Smith felt his stomach flutter with excitement and

he carefully folded his hands in front of him on his desk. After a pause, he asked, "Is it possible she left you, Mr. Morgenstern?" He kept his gaze focused on his intertwined fingers, struggling to contain his elation at the possibility Lily might have just gotten tired of married life and walked out.

"Of course not! She'd never leave me. Why would you say that?"

The detective lifted his gaze to meet Luke's and shrugged. He leaned back in his chair, positioning himself out of arm's reach, before continuing.

"Women leave their husbands for all kinds of reasons." He blinked slowly and pursed his lips. "Abuse...."

The detective left the word hanging in the air between them, the implied accusation more than apparent. Luke bristled, open-mouthed with rage, and Smith held up a placating hand at him.

"I'm not saying you hit her or abused her in any way. She could have left because she was bored, or just needed to get away for a bit."

Lily's husband grimaced, the expression so out of place on his handsome features as to be comical. After a moment of thought he nodded.

"I admit, she may have needed a break. She's seemed burnt out over the last few weeks."

"See? There you go," Smith said with more confidence than he felt, "She's probably vacationing in Port Jervis as we speak."

Luke stared at him blankly, clearly not understanding the reference. Suddenly, Smith realized he didn't trust the man sitting across from him, and now he disliked the man's claim that he was Lily's husband. There was something not quite *wrong* but not quite *right* about him. If Metatron's initial reaction to Luke Morgenstern, Jr. and subsequent silence was any indication, he should not believe a word the man said.

"She would not have gone anywhere without telling me where she was going. Lily just isn't like that."

"But you've never heard her mention Port Jervis? We were just there not too long ago, she and I. Seems odd she would never mention it to someone claiming to be her husband."

The detective regretted his words when he saw the obvious pain mixed with jealousy and concern in the man's eyes. The emotions were real enough, but there was something Luke was hiding from him. Of course there was. Secrets and truth evasion were par for the course in his line of work.

"How long has she been missing?" he asked and hated himself.

The man relaxed at the change of topic, a look of relief flooding his face. "Three days."

"Where was she last seen by anyone?"

"At the coffee shop around the corner from our place in the city." He paused, his expression filled with nostalgia. "She liked to go there and get coffee for the homeless."

"Seriously?"

Luke stared at him as if he had grown a second head. "Yeah. So what?"

Smith shook off his surprise. "I didn't think people actually did things for other people anymore. Getting coffee for the homeless sounds, well, really nice. Refreshing, even."

"Lily's a wonderful woman underneath the makeup. Possibly the only truly good person left on the planet."

Luke dropped his gaze to his folded hands and for a moment looked like a repentant sinner. Again, Smith got a chill up his spine, a tingling in his gut that said again something was not right about this guy.

"I know what you mean," was all he could say in response.

The conversation was interrupted when the phone rang, causing them both to jump. Smith grabbed the receiver, fumbled it, and finally caught it again between his hands, shoulder, and ear.

"Smith," he said and held up a finger toward Lily's husband in a universal "one second" sign as he listened. "Damn, I forgot. Where are you guys? I'll come meet you as soon as I can."

He grabbed a pen and paper and jotted down an address, smiling apologetically at Luke. "OK, got it. I'll see you soon." He hung up and did his best to look embarrassed. "I need to get going. Clients."

Luke nodded, then brought out a cellphone from his back pocket. He dialed a number, waited for an answer, and said, "Hold."

The detective stared at him, curious as to what the hell he was doing. He glanced down to the locked drawer of his desk and wondered if he would have time to get his gun out if he needed it. Probably not.

"Mr. Smith, I am willing to pay three times what your current clients are paying. All you have to do is say yes."

The detective let out a low whistle. "That's a hefty pricetag, Luke; my clients value my services rather highly. You sure your bank account can handle it?"

"Yes."

Smith scratched the back of his head, his face screwed up in thought. "The thing is, I can do both cases at the same time. However, the other guys get priority because they came to me first, you see?"

Luke's smile didn't reach his violet blue eyes. "Fair enough. You'll take my case, then?"

"Yes. For Lily."

The man raised his phone back to his mouth and said, "Bring it in."

The door opened and a demon in a black suit and tie walked in. His bald head gleamed in the daylight, and his silver eyes flashed toward Smith in what appeared to be recognition. The demon's gaze was so intent it forced Smith to engage in conversation with the creature despite the terrible feeling deep in the pit of his insides. He couldn't explain it, but he hated the demon with every cell in his body. If given half a chance, he would have liked to kill the thing, in fact.

"Do I know you?"

The demon smiled, the zigzag lines of his teeth more fitting for a shark than a human. "Of course you do, Cal," he said with a wink as he placed a briefcase on the detective's desk.

"You got the wrong guy, Crowley," interrupted Luke, his voice full of sudden authority. "This is *John Smith*, no one you knew. Now get out. Oh, and Crowley?"

"Yes?"

"Don't go lurking out there. Just get back where you came from. Got it?"

The demon flinched and hurried from the office

without another word. Smith saw a flash of light in the hallway as the demon called Crowley created a tear in the fabric of existence and disappeared in a puff of brimstone-scented smoke.

"That was a demon," Smith observed.

"Yes, it was."

"And you gave it orders. *You*, a mere mortal."

"Yes, well. We have an understanding," Luke said and pushed the briefcase toward Smith. "Go ahead, open it up." The man's words cut through Smith's thoughts, scattering them before he could form a coherent idea of what had just transpired.

The detective was savvy enough to know one does not open a mysterious briefcase brought by a minion of Hell on first invitation, however. Warning bells went off in Smith's head and he frowned. "You open it."

His newest client laughed and turned the latches of the briefcase toward himself instead of the detective. "You're a trip, you know that?"

Smith flinched as the latches snapped open, expecting something with more bang. When Luke turned the briefcase around to face him, the detective took an involuntary breath at the sight of neatly stacked and wrapped hundred dollar bills. He glanced up at his new client, able to smirk after he had had a moment to regain his composure.

"What's with the cloak and dagger money briefcase?"

"I prefer to run a cash business."

Smith glanced toward the door to make sure Crowley had indeed gone and pushed the briefcase full of money aside. "OK, seriously now. Who was that guy?" he asked. "Seemed like he knew me pretty well."

"I just gave you a briefcase full of money, Mr. Smith."

"Yeah, that's great. Who was he?"

Luke frowned. "Stacks of hundreds not enough?"

Smith waved it away impatiently. "Look, I have plenty of money to live off of right now, so I really don't need all this," he motioned to the cash, "But I do need to know if that demon really knew me."

"I suspect he may have, in another lifetime. I am a firm believer in reincarnation." Luke rose from his chair, leaving the briefcase open on the desk. "New life, new start, right?" He extended a hand. "It was nice to meet you. I wish it had been under more pleasant circumstances."

Smith shook the offered hand, the jolt still present but less jarring, and nodded. "Likewise."

Luke gripped Smith's hand tighter. "Promise me you will be the one to find her, Mr. Smith."

"I promise I'll do my best."

The man's smile lost some of its brilliance. "That will have to do, I suppose." He released the handshake and handed the detective a piece of folded paper. "Here is the address of the coffee shop along with a recent picture of Lily."

Smith took the paper with the address and the photo, but didn't look at them. "Thanks. I'll get started as soon as I can."

He waited for Lily's husband to leave before glancing at the photo and collapsing into his desk chair. The picture was borderline professional, with Lily smiling out at him. He felt a tug at his heart, at the core of his very being when he looked at her, replaced quickly with a sense of guilt when he remembered he'd just taken a stack of hundreds from her husband and that he had a date with Cherry that night.

He stared at the open briefcase full of money for a moment, then unlocked the desk. He snapped the case closed and slid it into the drawer, pushing aside mini bottles of liquor and his gun. It was a lot of money to find a single missing person, he thought. The guy must really miss her. A darker voice in his mind whispered that Junior wanted to make it look good when the cops came sniffing around for a body.

With a heavy sigh, the detective made an effort to wipe women from his thoughts, then made a mental note to ask Pazuzu and Marduk who Crowley was and how he may have known the demon. He'd have asked Koth, but somehow he felt as if he and the demonic case manager were not exactly on speaking terms.

CHAPTER VIII

Smith's mood had deteriorated from sadly optimistic to borderline hostile by the time he reached the pub where the vampires waited for him. He scanned the afternoon crowd tucked toward the back of the shadowy interior and soon found his clients in the darkest corner. From the looks of it, McGuffin was in the middle of a story and people had gathered around the table to listen. As Smith drew nearer he was able to hear the vampire's words, as well as the slur in them.

"During the war there was a man in our company who firmly believed everyone had rabies." The vampire paused and held up a calming hand as the crowd burst into laughter. "Now, now, this is no laughing matter when one is attempting to win a war, ladies and gentlemen. Paranoia can kill just as effectively as a bullet or bayonet, you see."

A pretty brunette woman who looked to be not quite legal drinking age leaned toward Smith and whispered, "Isn't he great? I love history and everything, but I've never seen a re-enactor take it to this level out in public."

Smith nodded politely, sure that the girl was both mistaken and inebriated, while McGuffin went on with his story. The whiskey in the vampire's glass lowered with each pause, and the man was visibly drunk.

"We would march all day in one hundred degrees, dressed in uniforms that had practically grown into our very flesh from sweat and blood, and if one of us dared to say we were thirsty this fellow would swear we had rabies. We were unable to bathe lest he misinterpret the soap suds as our having broken out in body rabies."

The crowd broke into laughter once more, the humor of the sort that only the very drunk would find entertaining. Two college students with Greek letters silkscreened across the front of their t-shirts ordered the vampires another round of drinks with much protesting from McGuffin.

"No, gentlemen, we mustn't. We have business to attend to this day."

One of the students laughed, saying, "Oh come on, man. You've been entertaining as hell. No one tells funny stories about the battle."

The amused twinkle in the old vampire's eyes extinguished instantly. "I suspect it is because there were no amusing stories to be had during that time," replied McGuffin. "It is only with the span of over a century and a half that I may finally look back on those days with our comrade and see humor lurking there."

"Who were you with during the battle?" asked another patron.

"The 44th New York Infantry."

"What was your rank? Who are you supposed to be?" shouted another voice.

"What happened to the rabies guy?" called out a third.

Norton and McGuffin suddenly resembled deer in oncoming headlights at the barrage of questions.

Smith, sensing an imminent riot of drunken vampire proportions, stepped forward and held his hands up at the crowd.

"Folks, please head back to your tables. My friends like to get a little drunk and pretend they were soldiers at Gettysburg, that's all. They're *not* re-enactors; I doubt they even sat in on a history class." Smith focused on the half empty glass in front of McGuffin with a long pause. "Judging by the rabies story, I can see my friend has had exactly one more drink than he should have. Keep going past that, and you get to hear about the deer he hit with his truck, and how he gutted it and took home for dinner." He paused to let the visual of a roadkill meal settle into the college crowd listeners, waiting for the looks of disgust and abhorrence to surface through the haze of alcohol before saying in his most apologetic voice, "Yeah, I know. Thanks for playing along and being such a good audience, but I need to get these two sobered up and home to their wives."

Reluctantly, the crowd dispersed back to their respective tables and a low hum of conversation ensued, the focus shifting from an old soldier's personal tales, to the old guy who ate roadkill and made up Civil War stories, then on to things more relevant to them. Smith slid into an empty seat and smirked at his clients. "Looks like you two have been having fun."

"There was nothing 'fun' about the war," McGuffin said, his demeanor grave.

"Hey, focus, Mac. Two minutes ago you were laughing about a guy who thought everyone had rabies and now you're going mopey? No." Smith slammed his hand on the table in front of McGuffin. "Remember where we are? War's been ended for over a hundred and fifty years. No need to pretend you were in the 44th anymore, right?"

The vampire stared into Smith's eyes. "But I *was* in the 44th."

"I believe you believe that, but you've had a bit to drink. If anyone asks, that's what I'll tell them and it's what you should tell them, too. Unless your secret really isn't that important, of course."

Realization dawned in the old vampire's eyes and he blinked away the anger and gravity that had begun to take hold of him. He shook his head as if to clear it then laughed at himself. "You're absolutely right, Mr. Smith."

"That's why I make the big bucks," Smith said, waving away the attempted compliment, "And now, in all seriousness, what *did* happen to the rabies guy?"

Mac winced. "He met with an unfortunate accident after he tried to put one of us down."

"Ouch."

"One cannot repeatedly attempt to murder his fellows in arms and expect no retaliation."

The detective scratched the back of his neck and nodded. "Yeah, I can see your point. Kill or be killed."

"Exactly!" said the vampire with a smack of emphasis on the table.

Smith contemplated the man for a moment then said, "So what was your story back then? Your accent is not quite New York, if you know what I mean, yet it's still there even after a century and a half, which leads me to believe you aren't a born and raised citizen. The short version," he held a palm up politely, "please."

McGuffin sighed. "I came to the United States around 1830 as a result of a misunderstanding."

Smith glanced at Roger and the two leaned closer. "Do tell," the detective encouraged.

"At the time of my leaving my, err…country of origin, there were men known as resurrectionists. I was mistaken for one."

"Say for a moment I have no idea what a 'resurrectionist' is," Smith said with a drawn out pause.

The vampire laughed and shook his head. "Apologies. They were body snatchers, to put it bluntly. They would steal the freshly dead from their graves and sell them to doctors who would cut them up and explore the human anatomy."

"Oh," said Roger and Smith simultaneously.

The old vampire rolled his eyes. "I *said* it was a mistake. I was trying to aid a fellow vampire before he suffocated in his coffin, not steal a dead body to sell to science."

The detective leaned back in his chair and blew out a breath. "That is morbid. So you came over here and ended up fighting in the Civil War a couple of decades later."

"More or less. I left the war after the Battle of Gettysburg."

"Because of the rabies guy?"

McGuffin stared into his whiskey, his jaw set. "No, it was a bit more basic than that." He took a sip of his whiskey and looked at them. "I was killed."

Roger stared at him, his mouth open to ask the obvious. As if sensing the inevitable request for information, the old vampire went on.

"I drank from the water of Plum Run, or 'Bloody Run' as it was known during the height of the battle of Little Roundtop. More significantly, I had been caught drinking from the dying."

His listeners cringed, but he was too lost in his memories to notice their reactions. He tilted his glass and the amber liquid sloshed languidly before he took a long swallow. When he looked at them again, his expression was hard, that of a soldier, eyes haunted.

"It was done out of mercy. There were so many bodies! So much blood. I couldn't bare the screams in the night, the cries for help that would never come, or worse, of those who would die of infections or on makeshift operating tables. I gave them a quick and painless alternative."

"Sorry I asked now." Smith rubbed his temples and took a deep, steadying breath. "Total change of topic: do you guys have an update for me?"

"Yes," Roger said, perking up from his own musings and happy to change the subject. "We've gotten my stuff back and managed at length to convince everyone involved that they made a mistake when they pronounced me dead."

"That's great news."

"Yes and no," said Roger with a meaningful glance toward McGuffin.

"Good that we were easily able to rectify the situation, yes," said the vampire, "However, it is still bad we will need to remain vigilant. Those who attempted to kill our friend here will be alerted that they failed to kill him and may try again. I fear they may be more thorough with their next victim."

"But we *do* have a lead," offered Norton.

"OK, let's have it, then." Smith paused to give his drink order to the waiter then turned back to his clients.

"There was an anonymous tip–that is the person gave a fake name to the police the day I died."

"How could you possibly know it's a fake name? What name did they give?"

"Thorium G."

Smith tapped the table and considered the name. "Maybe it's a codename? Mac, do you know anyone who goes by that name?"

The vampire shook his head and stared into his nearly empty rocks glass. He glanced up briefly when their waiter came back with Smith's drink and a fresh drink for him as well. He smiled his thanks, the smile fading as soon as the waiter had turned away from them. In a low voice he said, "The tip came from someplace local, but not next to the battlefield."

"So where did it come from?" Smith asked as he took a sip from his drink.

McGuffin's smile was predatory, his eyes shifting peripherally as he tapped the tabletop with his index finger. "Here."

"Here? This bar?"

The vampires nodded.

"Have you asked the staff if they know the person?"

"We decided to camp out here and wait for Mac's girlfriend to show up for her shift before we started asking questions," said Roger, the most recently undead. "Figured it would be the easiest way to go about it."

Smith nodded. "When does she come on?"

McGuffin shrugged. "I think she starts work at six o'clock."

"You *think*?"

"I try not to stalk ladies whom I would like to court at some point."

"We'll be here all day. Wonderful."

"I am unsure what passes for 'all day' in this century, but an hour is not overlong to wait."

Smith glanced at the clock over the bar with a frown. "That can't be right."

The vampires followed his glare then looked back at him in confusion.

"What?"

"That clock says it's five thirty."

McGuffin smirked. "Because it *is*. Close to, anyway. They set the clocks a half hour ahead so they can get people out of here by two at closing time."

Smith and Roger blinked at the old vampire and he smiled.

"One learns the tricks set in place in establishments serving alcohol. Specifically, how long one has to finish one's last drink of the night before he's invited to leave."

Smith shook his head and let out a snort. "That's all fine and well, but I woke up at nine this morning. I was in the office before ten. There's no way in hell I spent an entire lunchless afternoon talking to a new client."

CHAPTER IX

"New client? Hold on, what about us and our case?" Roger asked indignantly.

"You guys get first dibs on my time," Smith answered.

The newly undead man relaxed. "All right then. Who is it? Anyone we know?"

"I don't think so," Smith said, distracted. "And anyway, I can't tell you. Privacy and all that."

"Fair enough," replied the vampire as he sipped his drink. "Can you tell us if the other case is related to ours in any way?"

The detective smirked. "Technically, no, I can't, but it's not related as far as I know. Missing person case, and that's all you get out of me."

The waiter approached their table and Smith motioned to him. "Can I get a cheeseburger and fries, please?"

"Sure. How would you like that done?" he asked, pulling an order pad out of his pocket and scribbling.

"Medium."

"You got it. Do you need a refill on your drink?"

"I'll just have a Coke, thanks."

He nodded and jotted, then turned to the others at the table. "Can I get anyone anything else?" he asked, looking around hopefully.

McGuffin held up his glass and gave a nod and a smile. Roger shook his head and went back to nursing his mostly full glass.

"Your burger will be out in a few minutes. If you don't mind, my shift is ending so I'll go ahead and close you out." He looked at Smith and said, "Janice is coming on in a few, so she'll get your bill squared away."

"No problem."

With a move that was almost sleight of hand, he slid the vampires' check in its discreet black folder onto the table. McGuffin held a hand up as he was about to move away and placed several bills into the folder.

"There you are, please keep the change. And one more thing, would you be so kind as to tell Janice we're here when she starts her shift?"

The waiter took the folder, glanced inside to ascertain there would be enough cash to cover the bill, and nodded with a wide smile. "Of course, sir. Who should I say is waiting?"

"Tell her Mac. She'll know."

As their waiter walked away, Roger leaned in toward the vampire and asked, "How much did you put in there?"

"Enough to get his attention."

Smith snorted and rubbed at his eyes. When he yawned and leaned in on his hands, McGuffin looked at him for a long moment, scrutinizing him until the detective glared back at him.

"What?"

"Have you been sleeping?"

"Now that you mention it, no, not really."

"Any particular reason?"

"Nightmares. Horrible, really realistic nightmares." He rubbed at his eyes again and stared down at the table.

The old vampire glanced over at Roger then back to Smith. "When did they start?"

"Funny you mention that," Smith said and stared into his drink. "They started that night we got drunk, while I was walking home."

The old vampire came to attention. "*While* you were walking home?"

The detective nodded. "I guess I passed out cold on the sidewalk. Had one hell of a nightmare."

"What did you dream?" asked Roger with a nervous edge to the question.

Smith slammed his drink glass on the tabletop and stared at the two vampires. "What the hell does it matter? Suffice it to say it was horrible, and every time I thought I was awake it was just another nightmare."

"Got all that, but *what* specifically did you dream?" asked Roger with more urgency. "Was it a scary bastard who seemed to be made of shadows? Did he follow you?"

Smith stared. "How did you know?"

"I dreamt of him, too, just before I woke up dead in Plum Run."

"Hell, that can't be good," said Smith and mentally poked himself between the eyes. "*Hey, Metatron, wake up. You've been too quiet. What's your take on all this?*"

He waited for a response, but the angel was maddeningly still. What the hell was going on with it?

Smith wondered. It wasn't like Metatron not to chime in with opinions and monologues or at least a murmur of distaste for such an extended period of time. He tried to think of the last time he'd even heard so much as a sigh from the angel and narrowed it down to Luke Morgenstern Jr.'s arrival. Did Lily's husband have something to do with Metatron's silent treatment?

He was brought out of his thoughts by a plate of food being set in front of him. He looked up to see Janice smiling at McGuffin and felt his unease fade slightly.

"Hi, Mac," the waitress said with a broad smile.

"Hello, Janice. It is good to see you again."

A slight blush crept across the young woman's face and she dropped her eyes. The old vampire stared at her, longing hiding behind his gaze. Roger rolled his eyes and knocked a fork against his drink glass loud enough to be heard over the din in the pub. Remembering himself, McGuffin cleared his throat and cast a quick look toward his comrades.

"I have a question for you, if you have a minute?" he said.

Janice's smile broadened and Smith felt sorry for her. He supposed she thought it would be a different sort of question than the one the vampire was about to ask.

"Do you know anyone who goes by the name 'Thorium G?'"

Her brow furrowed and the smile collapsed in on itself. "Is that a joke?"

"No. Have you heard of it?"

She shook her head with a confused laugh. "I thought everyone had seen *Dr. Strangelove*, but I guess not." Observing their blank expressions, she went on, "Thorium G was referred to as 'cobalt thorium g' in this cult film by Kubrick. It was part of the Doomsday Device. Really? Doesn't ring a bell?"

McGuffin shrugged apologetically, his cheeks reddening.

"Does anyone working here have a particular love of that film?" Smith asked.

"Just me, unfortunately."

"Didn't happen to call in a corpse on the battlefield the other day, did you?" he asked with a skeptical chuckle.

Janice cringed and dropped her eyes. "They said it was supposed to be anonymous. How the hell did you find out about it?" The three men stared in amazement and her eyes blazed defiance as she held her order pad like a shield. "I did the right thing. I couldn't just leave the guy there for some tourist to find, it would have wrecked the entire season." Then in a softer voice, her face paling with what could only be sickness, she went on, "Besides, it was supposed to get hot that day and I didn't think it was right to leave a dead person out in the sun like that."

Smith held his hands up defensively. "No one's saying you did a bad thing. We thought maybe someone else had called it in."

Norton smiled apologetically at their waitress and said, "If it's any consolation, I got better."

Janice looked confused and angry, mouth opening to tell the man off as Smith jumped in to diffuse the situation before it got to the point he was banned from his favorite hangout. "He was passed out drunk," he said in a conspiratorial tone.

"Drunk?" She looked skeptically from the detective to the vampires.

Roger nodded and looked embarrassed. "It's true. I was at a friend's bachelor party the night before, and we all had a dare going on to see who could spend the night on the battlefield."

"No one's supposed to go on the battlefields after sundown."

"I know…I know. We all knew. We did it anyway. Needless to say none of the others made it through the night, and I think the only reason I did was because I was passed out cold before midnight." He smiled up at her. "No hard feelings?"

Janice let out a sigh of relief. "You scared the shit out of me, you know. And you were face-down in that stream up there."

Roger cringed and nodded. "Yep. Damned lucky you called it in when you did, or I'd have drowned. When they got me out of there, all that bumping must have knocked the water out of my lungs and gave my heart a thump. You saved my life. Thank you."

She shrugged and brushed a stray strand of hair off her face. "No big deal. Glad to help. You must have really freaked out the coroner."

"When I went back to pick up my stuff, you mean? Yes, I definitely freaked out some staff at the morgue."

Janice laughed and shook her head, then looked over her shoulder back at the bar where the manager was watching them. "Do you guys need anything? I'll have tables getting pissed if I took this long chatting and come back empty handed."

"I'll have another Jack Daniel's," McGuffin said, handing her his empty glass.

"And I'll have another order of fries," Smith chimed in, discovering he fully intended to eat every last one of them, so ravenous was he.

When she had walked away, the three men visibly deflated.

"Back to square one," Roger said miserably.

"Back to square one," Smith agreed. He downed the rest of his drink and took the pack of cigarettes out of his jacket pocket. He tapped out a cigarette and let it dangle between his fingers, contemplating.

"What are you thinking?" asked the old vampire, squinting at him.

"I'm thinking I need to visit some friends and maybe kill two birds in the process."

"But you just ordered fries," Roger reminded him.

"I didn't mean right now. I'll get an early start tomorrow. My friends may have information they forgot to mention earlier. In fact, I'm sure of it."

CHAPTER X

On the walk back to his apartment, Smith gritted his teeth and called Koth's phone number, hoping there were no hard feelings between them. The phone was answered on the second ring.

"Koth," said a voice that sounded very much a demon and not at all human.

"Hey, it's Smith. Before you hang up on me, can I say something?"

The voice shifted to something more human, smoother, that of a purring tiger. "Wasn't going to hang up. What have you got?"

"First, I wanted to apologize. I know we haven't exactly been getting along lately, and—"

"We haven't?" the demon asked with genuine surprise.

"Well, no. At least I don't think we have been." Smith paused. "Have we?"

"Why are you talking nonsense? Are you mad at me, Cal? Is that it? Because I said shit about your girlfriend?"

"Yeah, that too. Koth, what the hell is going on?"

"You're the detective. You tell me. Come on over."

"Where are you?" Smith asked, suddenly paranoid and scanning the buildings for a face in a window.

As if sensing his actions Koth said, "I'm not there, stupid. Hang on a minute."

A tear in the air appeared before Smith's eyes and a gray hand extended out of it. There was a glint of gold on the pinky finger and Smith wondered when the case manager had started wearing jewelry. The hand motioned for him to come through, and Koth's voice spoke, tinny and distorted through the phone speaker.

"What the hell are you waiting for? Come on. This is hard to keep open."

Smith stepped through into a large and lavishly appointed bedroom. Koth lounged on the bed, naked but for the gold pinky ring and a smile as he placed the handset back into the cradle. The coiled phone wire wrapped around the base like a serpent and Smith marveled at the sight of the heavy antique phone.

"Welcome to my place," said the demon with a slow grin. "Have a seat."

Koth patted the bed next to him and Smith had a hard time averting his eyes from where the demon was trying to make him look. The detective took out a cigarette and lit it without asking if it the demon objected, turning away and scanning the room for a chair in which to sit instead of next to the demon's lap and what lurked there.

"What is it with you guys?" he muttered. "If you're not trying to kill me you're trying to sleep with me. Make up your minds."

Koth let out a laugh behind him. "You can't blame a guy for trying. It's nice to have voluntary sex on occasion, so I need to 'catch as catch can,' as the saying goes. Pull that chair in the corner over while I put on some pants."

Smith did as he was told, puffing on his cigarette while he listened to the sounds of the demon getting dressed behind him. When the chair was in place, he sat down and kept his eyes on the floor. At last Koth settled onto the bed in a sitting position. He wore deep crimson silk pajamas that looked like they cost more than Smith's monthly rent.

"All clear. Now. What can I do for you, Cal? You never call me, much less come to visit."

"Two things. First, I reached a dead end on the undead case."

The demon laughed and pointed at him. "Good one."

The detective blinked. "What? Oh," he said with sudden understanding, "Yeah, ha ha. Second, I got another case, I think from one of your guys."

"My guys? Pazuzu and Marduk?"

"No, no, no," Smith said quickly as the case manager's eyes narrowed with suspicion. "Some guy. Looked like a model straight out of a magazine. He had at least one demon with him."

"What was the name?"

"Of the demon?"

Koth nodded.

"Crowley."

"And your client's name?" the demon asked nervously.

"Luke Morgenstern, Jr."

Koth's face paled. "He's here? *Now?*" he said more to himself than to the detective.

Smith's grin was tight. "See, that's the same thing Metatron said just before it went on radio silence, and I have to admit it scares the shit out of me. Who is this guy, aside from Lily's husband?"

The demon almost fell off the bed in shock. "Husband? Lily? Wait–*What*?"

"I didn't know she was married either, and the whole thing stinks. So can someone, from either Heaven or Hell, just give me a straight answer?"

"You're sure he said his name was Luke Morgenstern?"

Smith nodded, a ripple of fear running through him as he noticed the demon's hands were shaking. "Junior…. He's not human, is he?"

Koth shook his head.

"What is he?"

"He's early, that's what he is, and he's unannounced, dammit. We're supposed to get advanced warnings about this shit. What the hell did we invent memos for if we never use them?" The demon mumbled to himself as he picked up the phone and dialed. "Pazuzu? Koth. Grab Marduk and get your asses over here. We have a situation." He paused, listening. "Yes, it's important! That's what 'have a situation' means! Boss already sent up the damned anti—" Koth stopped himself, remembering Smith was in the room. "Just get over here," he finished and slammed down the phone.

"Old rotary phone," the detective observed. "Don't see those anymore."

"Hmm? Oh, yeah. Well, Hell doesn't get the greatest connection with a push button phone. Too many electronics in the way."

"But you have a cellphone."

The demon glared at him. "Hell works in mysterious ways, okay? And when I slam a phone down, I need a damned phone that won't break. Now shut up. I need to think."

Smith leaned back in the chair, taking a last drag on the finished cigarette and pulling the pack out of his jacket to light a new one while they waited for Pazuzu and Marduk to show. Koth held a hand out and Smith placed a cigarette into the upturned palm.

"Thanks."

"No problem. Calmed down a little?"

"Yeah."

"Going to tell me what's going on now?"

The demon stared at him, contemplating. "Why did Luke Morgenstern hire you?"

"Lily's missing."

Koth tried hard to conceal it, but the look of surprise was there, lurking below the surface of his forced neutral expression. He leaned in toward Smith, voice low. "Drop the case, Cal. Whatever he paid you, I will personally match it. Just drop the case."

"Why?"

"If you care about her, drop it." The demon stared into his eyes so intently it made Smith uncomfortable. With a flick of his fingers Koth lit the end of the cigarette jutting from his mouth and Smith took a deep drag, watching the flames flickering in the chrome of the demon's eyes. "And while you're at it, I would recommend not seeing Cherry for a while."

"Drop the only two women on earth I care about? Right."

"Look, I'm not going to try to force you to do anything. Hell is pretty clear about free will. We love it, in fact. Gets people into all kinds of trouble." The demon smiled thinly for a moment and took a drag on the cigarette. "I'm telling you this as your friend–believe it or not, I think of you as a friend–and it would bug the shit out of me if something bad happened to you."

"Touching. You should write greeting cards."

"I'm being serious, Cal. Both of those dames are bad news, and you know it. They're going to get you killed if you don't watch your ass."

"Killed? What's that supposed to mean?"

"Can't tell you anything else. Already said too much. Just trust me, okay?"

A tearing sound in the other room distracted them and they turned toward the door. Koth looked over at Smith in near panic and moved his fingers across his lips as if closing a zipper. The detective nodded, though he was unsure why they needed to stay quiet about their conversation.

Pazuzu and Marduk knocked and walked into the bedroom, their expressions becoming awkward when they caught sight of Koth and Smith sitting next to each other. For a reason he could not explain, Smith also felt self-conscious, as if something forbidden and intimate had occurred between the case manager and himself, though he had no recollection of it.

"Sit, you two."

The demons carried in chairs with them and brought them next to the bed. Marduk looked from the case manager to the detective and motioned to the cigarettes.

"Do you have any more?"

Smith nodded and took out the pack, motioning to Pazuzu, who nodded. He handed out the cigarettes and they stared at one another after the ends had been lit.

Within moments the air was hazy with tendrils of smoke.

"Why did you summon us, Koth?" Pazuzu finally asked, breaking the silence.

The case manager's face was grim. He looked from Smith to the two demons and ran an unsteady hand through slicked black hair.

"You-Know-Who is topside already. Yeah, we heard rumors about it, and Cal here just confirmed it, officially," he said at last. "What we didn't know was that, according to him, at least, he's married to Lily."

Both Pazuzu and Marduk blinked at him, then glanced to each other. When the information had processed, they glanced nervously at Smith.

"Should we be discussing this *ithway imhay erehay*?" asked Marduk, motioning in a not-so-subtle fashion toward the detective.

"Seriously? *Pig* Latin?" Koth asked in disbelief. "You speak *real* Latin, idiot! If you didn't want *imhay* to *understanday*, you'd think speaking in fluent, actual Latin would be more effective." The case manager rubbed the bridge of his nose and shook his head. "I've said it before, and I'll say it again, you guys suck at this. Might as well let the cat out of the bag now. Jeez."

He looked around them as if fearful the walls could listen to him and motioned for them to come closer. "Everything discussed here is totally off the record and it goes *nowhere*, am I clear?"

Everyone nodded and Koth took a deep, shaking breath. Suddenly he looked up at Smith.

"That goes for you, too, Metatron. I know you can hear me and you're listening."

Smith's mouth opened and The Voice of God

spoke. *"You understand I am a conduit, correct? Communications with the Creator cannot be 'off the record'. Choose your words wisely if the information is sensitive."*

The demon considered this, then nodded. "Fine. This has gone on for too long as it is. Honestly, I'm sick of all the He-said-She said crap. I like it here and I don't feel like seeing it destroyed in some final battle, much less fighting in said battle." He looked hard at and into Smith's eyes, addressing Metatron. "Can you put in a good word for me with both parties? Let them know I'm not trying to pick sides here?"

Smith's head nodded and he cringed at the sensation of having someone else controlling his body. The case manager relaxed.

"OK, I'll come clean. You have to promise not to get pissed at me, Cal."

The detective shrugged. "Sure, fine. What's the big conspiracy?"

Koth flinched and said, "The vampire case was a bunch of bullshit."

CHAPTER XI

Smith stared for a moment, unable to grasp the demon's meaning. "Excuse me?"

"The whole thing. It was a total ruse, meant to distract you while I hid Lily from a couple of unidentified wayward demons who were a little too hellbent–pardon the pun–on world domination."

"But…but, Roger Norton, and McGuffin," Smith began and Koth shook his head.

"They're real enough. The case is real enough. We do have a debtor on the run and they did turn Mr. Norton into a member of the undead to mess with McGuffin, but that hasn't been the *real* case."

"Enlighten me, then."

"It started just after you got back from Port Jervis. You and Cherry hooked up," the demon paused and winked at him, "Kudos, by the way. But I'm betting you noticed she's started going out more and working longer hours the last few weeks?"

Smith thought about it, then nodded. He hadn't seen Cherry outside of nightmares for most of the time he had been working the vampire case.

The demon noted his expression and scratched at the back of his neck. "Yeah. I was afraid of that. I'm sorry, kid."

"What happened to Cherry?" the detective asked, his mouth dry.

"Not entirely sure," Koth admitted. "She still works at the diner, but she's different. Can't quite put my finger on it."

"She doesn't smack you when you flirt with her anymore," Marduk said with a smirk. "There is clearly something amiss."

Koth glared at his subordinate and shook his head.

"And what about Lily? Is she okay?" Smith asked, steering the conversation back to relevance.

Koth nodded. "She's fine."

"Where is she?"

"I'd rather not tell you that right now, not until we figure out exactly what's going on here and who's pulling all the strings." As he said the words, Koth took out a folded paper and passed it to Smith with an intent stare. "Let's get some rest then meet up tomorrow at the diner and you can see what I mean."

"Yeah, it's late. I should get back to my place and get some rest," Smith said, taking the demon's hint. He wondered what was written on the folded paper as he tucked it into his jacket pocket for safekeeping.

Koth split the air in front of him and gave a wave, motioning for Pazuzu and Marduk to wait. As the air closed behind him, Smith found himself back in his own apartment.

He took out his cellphone and dialed McGuffin's number. The phone on the other end rang three times before the old vampire's voice growled out a tired greeting.

"'Lo?"

"Mac, it's Smith. Listen, I found out the details of

Roger Norton's death."

"Mmm."

"Good news is, it was just to mess with you. Kind of letting you know they're still alive and well."

On the other end of the phone McGuffin sighed. "In that case, it would have to be Arden Langer. That bastard never knew when a joke wasn't funny anymore."

Smith gave a tired laugh. "Looks like we've been running in circles for nothing."

"Well, Mr. Smith, I thank you for your time, and I apologize for wasting it."

"Not a waste at all," Smith said. "I had a great time."

"Then perhaps we can continue to meet for drinks at the pub?"

"Call me and I'm there. Have a good night, Mac."

"You too. And be careful."

Smith stared at the phone long after the click and silence signaled the call had been ended. "Be careful;" it seemed to be the running theme in the advice area these days.

He put his phone in his pocket, glad to be home. As he stepped forward, the scent of brimstone filled his nose and he crashed to the floor, unconscious.

When he came around, the scent of burning was stronger and he looked around in panic. A dark form stood over him, gently tapping his face. As he blinked away the haze, the form backed away and he could make out a familiar musk scent beneath the burning smell.

"You're awake," Cherry said. "Finding you on the floor was a bit of a surprise, I admit. You must have been tired, you poor thing." She helped him to a sitting position, pushing him up from behind. "I hope you don't mind, but I burned some incense while you were out. I think it gives the place a little romantic ambience, don't you?" As if to emphasize her point, she walked through the smoke to where it seemed twenty sticks of incense smoldered in a bowl she had filled with salt.

"Sure," he answered, muffling a cough as he got to his feet, relieved the smell wasn't a fire. He moved toward her silhouette in the incense haze, and she glanced over her naked shoulder at him. He stopped short, realization hitting him like a train. The smell. Cherry wore either Crown Heliotrope in the early spring, fall, and winter, or Crown Esterhazy in the summer. She never strayed from those two scents. Whoever this woman was, she smelled like musk.

As if sensing the change in his demeanor she said, "Well, that's disappointing. I had hoped for more time, but I can see you know I'm not myself anymore, Cal."

She was wearing the mask again and Smith fell back a step. For some reason he was suddenly terrified of her.

"I know I've done things in the past," she went on, her sultry voice distorted by papier-mâché. "I had hoped you might love me anyway, but you don't."

"No," Smith whispered, his voice weak, "Of course I love you."

"You don't even know me," she said, laughing. For an instant the mask shifted with her words, the mouth stretching open into a frowning maw in direct contrast to the madness of her mirth. The darkness inside the gaping mouth was punctuated by row upon row of jagged, yellow-gray teeth.

She caught herself, and with an extreme effort that caused her to grunt, she forced her features to separate themselves from the mask. When she took a step toward him, he took another step backward.

"You should have listened to Koth. I hate to say it, but he was right. He was right about everything."

"Like what?" he asked, unable to push his voice above a whisper.

"Like staying away from me. Like dropping the other case."

"What other case?"

"Coy Cal." She tutted. "I know about the other case. Now why don't you sit down and talk to me?"

Smith inched closer to the door, keeping his eyes fixed on the eyes of the mask in an effort to draw her attention away from his movements. She curled her index finger in a motion he assumed was meant for him until he felt the seat of a chair hit the backs of his knees. His legs folded and he fell hard into the chair and stayed put as it slid across the floor toward Cherry, the arms encircling him in a wooden embrace that crushed the air from his lungs.

"Talk to me," she commanded.

"It's private." When the arms of the chair tightened he screamed, "I can't tell you anything!"

She emerged out of the smoke to stand before him and her features melted into those of the mask. Her red hair grew out gray and gnarled, flowing around her head in a corona of age, and her body sagged into that of a squat, twisted creature. She climbed into his lap and began to tear at his pants with talons, spittle flying from the frowning mouth with her efforts.

"Help!" Smith screamed, struggling against the

wooden embrace of the chair. He was too terrified to care how he sounded at that moment, or to question who might show up to help him.

"Wake the hell up, you idiot!"

He blinked, relief washing over him as he caught sight of Koth standing in the murky shadows. The case manager approached, and the thing in Smith's lap shrank away with a howl of rage.

Koth grabbed it by the neck before it could escape and turned to look at Smith with a smirk. "Please tell me you didn't sleep with this thing and not me."

"What?" Smith asked, struggling away from the bedside chair to stand next to Koth. "I haven't slept with anyone but Cherry."

"Yeah, about that," the demon said with a shake of his head. He held his free hand up at Smith when the detective opened his mouth to respond. "You can yell all you want, but first let's get to the waking world, shall we?"

Smith nodded, confused.

"Good. This may hurt a little."

Before he could ask what he was talking about, the demon punched Smith in the face. The detective went sprawling, knocking his head against a very solid bedframe.

"What the hell did you do that for?"

"Mostly for fun, but also to make sure you're good and awake."

Koth stepped through a glimmering veil, his form solidifying with each step. He held out his free hand, helping Smith to his feet and Pazuzu and Marduk led him to sit on his bed.

The detective stared at the struggling, snarling

thing still clutched in Koth's other hand. It twisted and scratched at the demon, attempting to sink tiny razor sharp teeth into the pale gray flesh of the case manager's arm, but he held it too far out of reach to do any damage.

"What the hell is that?!" Smith cried.

"My guess would be a troll of some sort," Koth said, narrowing his eyes as he looked over the creature squirming in his iron grasp, "but on closer inspection…she's one of ours. Damn, Cal, you lucky whore. I take it back. I'd sleep with her, too, if she ever asked."

"Lucky?" Smith's voice came out in a choked gag. "Whore?"

"Come on, show him the real you, Damian," Koth commanded. "Or so help me, you'll get to clean the pit when we get back to Hell."

The thing in Koth's grasp squirmed and morphed into a pale and naked woman. Her long black hair cascaded around the case manager's hand, covering her nakedness as she glared at her captor, red lips sneering.

"Don't be rude, say hello."

"Hi, asshole." She glanced over her shoulder at Smith and her lips curled into something more playful. "Hi, Cal."

"Damian? Okay, what is going on here?"

The demon wriggled out of Koth's grasp and crossed her arms over her ample breasts. "Koth is spoiling all my fun is what's going on here."

The demons stared at the detective with open envy when Damian sauntered over to him and tried to sit in his lap. He shoved her away, scurrying sideways over the bed to escape her advances. He remembered a time when he had fallen in love with her just from watching her drink a cup of coffee and marveled at how he loathed the sight of her now.

She pouted for a moment before lounging at the opposite end of the bed, regarding them all with cold, chrome eyes. Pazuzu and Marduk made an effort to look anywhere but directly at her, but Koth had no such reservations.

"So," he began, "Are you going to tell us who hired you and why?"

Damian blinked at him in a way Smith assumed was meant to be sultry, but which ended up appearing more like the expression of a predator, feral and catlike. She leaned back on the bed, staring up at the ceiling, and ignored the question.

"Ahhh, the hard way," Koth said, and his teeth glinted a little sharper with the words. He motioned to Pazuzu and Marduk and the demons moved toward Damian.

"Cal, you have the option of watching how Hell interrogates, or staying out of it. If you choose to remain ignorant, we'll take Damian to my place."

"I'll pass on the interrogation," said Smith, feeling queasy at the idea.

Koth nodded and motioned for Pazuzu and Marduk to leave with Damian. The demons obeyed, dragging their screaming prisoner through the rent in the air. The case manager turned to Smith once the others were out of earshot.

"Been a productive night. I'll see you tomorrow."

"All of that, just to catch Damian?" Smith asked.

Koth nodded. "Yeah, sorry about using you for

bait, but it couldn't be helped. I'd better get going before the demonic duo get their asses handed to them."

Smith caught him by the arm as he turned to leave. "Hey, what about Lily? Where is she?"

Koth patted him over his heart. "She's right here."

He didn't have time to ask what the case manager meant. Without another word Koth was through the tear in reality and gone, leaving behind a faint hint of brimstone on the air.

Smith rolled his eyes. "'Right here', what the hell is that supposed to mean? Follow my heart?"

In the back of his head Metatron seemed to be laughing at him. He inwardly glared at the angel and moved into the bathroom to the only mirror in his apartment. From the reflection, the angel looked out at him. Its smile was evident now that he could see its face.

"What's so funny? And where the hell do you keep disappearing to?"

Metatron arched an eyebrow, amused. *Check your pocket, not your heart*, it said, avoiding the second question.

Smith patted the outside of his jacket and heard the crinkle of paper. His eyes widened with sudden realization. "The note. I forgot all about it!"

The angel nodded and Smith pulled out the folded paper from inside his jacket. He unfolded it and cocked his head in confusion.

What is it? Metatron asked.

"It's an address."

CHAPTER XII

Smith stared at the ceiling for the rest of the night, too excited to sleep. Koth had ensured he would be unable to visit the place on the note without first speaking to him by omitting the city in which the address was located, and an internet search provided too many possibilities to even start.

The morning seemed to take forever to arrive, and the detective tossed and turned until at last Metatron spoke up.

Perhaps it would be more productive to wait for Koth at the Diner.

Smith punched his pillow and sighed. "Wish we could, but they're probably closed."

The Diner never closes.

"Okay, but trains don't start running until five in the morning out of Harrisburg, and I don't feel like driving into Baltimore, so we're going to just have to wait it out."

The angel seemed to roll its eyes at him.

"What?"

There is another way to travel to the Diner.

"Yeah? How?"

The air crackled and opened next to the bed and Smith jumped to his feet. Without pause he pulled on a shirt, pants, and shoes, grabbing his jacket as he leaped through the crack in reality. He landed hard on the scuffed floor of the diner, knocking into a table of angels as he tried to regain his balance.

"Sorry," Smith mumbled, and the angels stared at him with open curiosity.

He made his way through the diner toward the booth at the back. There he sat and scowled at the dingy formica tabletop.

"How long have you been able to do that?" he whispered to Metatron.

Always, replied the angel.

"Why the hell didn't you say you could do that?"

It was never a topic of conversation.

Smith's reply was cut short by a waitress standing over the table. He looked up and into Cherry's pale face. Her lips curled into a hint of a smile and she slid into the seat across from him.

"Hi, Cal."

"It's good to see you." He reached across the table toward her, but felt suddenly both awkward and leery. Was this woman actually Cherry?

A hint of Crown Heliotrope wafted toward him and he relaxed. She was definitely Cherry.

"I've missed you," she said with a slight blush.

"Things have been pretty crazy," he said with a nod.

"I heard you were seeing someone else," she blurted out, "I stayed away because I didn't want to interfere. You know, in case you found someone to love you."

Her eyes blurred behind the tears as they fell, silent rivulets over her porcelain skin. Smith stared at her in surprise, unable to answer for a moment.

"Who told you that?" he finally asked.

Cherry wiped at her eyes and sniffed. "Koth."

He was going to punch the demon, he decided, and not in a metaphorical way. He was literally going to punch Koth the moment he came close enough.

Smith reached across the table and took Cherry's hands in his. "He lied. Well, in a way. I didn't realize it wasn't you."

She looked at him and her expression was filled with both anger and confusion. "You didn't know it wasn't me? Cal, that is the worst excuse anyone has ever given me."

"No, it's true!" he stood up and pulled her to him as she made to leave. "It was Damian posing as you, but I didn't realize it. I should have, but I assumed you were trying out a new perfume."

She stared at him, doubtful. "What the hell does that mean?"

"It means nothing and I'm sorry. That's what it means."

She shrugged. "Guess I can forgive you for it, since you forgave me all those years ago."

He pretended to plug his ears. "Don't want to know, Cher. Let's just call it even. Deal?"

She smiled and wiped away more tears as they fell. "Deal," she said, then added, "I'm going to scratch out Damian's eyes next time I see that bitch."

"Hit her once for me, too."

Cherry arched an eyebrow at him. "Really now, Cal, I didn't take you for that kind of man."

"You haven't been through what she put me through."

Closing the subject and pushing his own darkness away, Smith looked at his watch. It felt like time should have moved along much faster than it had. Only a few hours had passed since the demons left his apartment to interrogate Damian.

"What's on your mind, Cal?" Cherry asked, running her fingers over his hand.

"Trying to figure out where this address is, and have to wait for Koth to get here before I can do that."

She held out a hand. "Let me see. Maybe I know it."

He shrugged and handed over the paper. She looked at the address scrawled there, then looked up to him skeptically.

"Why the hell would you want to go there?" she asked.

"Where is 'there'?"

"It's an old hospital near the river. Not exactly a place I'd like to be after dark."

"Draw me a map."

Cherry shrugged. "Your funeral, Cal. If I were you, I'd wait for Koth."

"Map."

"Don't need one," she said and folded her arms across her chest. "It's right around the corner. What's there?"

"Can't tell you, and you're a doll. Thank you," he told her and kissed her on the lips as he jumped to his feet.

"Be careful, Cal," she called after him as he ran out the door and into the approaching hints of morning.

The place really was just around the corner, so close in fact that he had only gotten halfway through his cigarette. He checked the address he had been given and turned a skeptical look to the building. It looked abandoned. In the back of his mind, the angel lurked and watched as Smith grabbed the chainlink gates with their No Trespassing signs and opened them wide enough to slide between, under the padlock and chain. Brushing debris from his jacket, he looked back, grateful to have avoided a tetanus shot and potential shredding while attempting to climb over the rusted razorwire encircling the top of the fence that surrounded the place.

He tried the main entrance doors, and to his surprise, they opened with no hesitation; none of the screeching of rusty metal one would have expected from an abandoned building. He extinguished his cigarette and entered. Overhead, the fluorescent lighting flickered and hummed, the light a sickly yellow-green in some spots and in others more purple-hued as he made his way down the dingy corridor toward what he assumed to be a front desk.

He was shocked to find a nurse sitting behind the counter, her attention focused on a dog-eared paperback with the front cover torn off. Her uniform was almost blindingly white, and though she appeared young, there was an air of no-nonsense about her that could have rivaled a person much older. She glanced up at him over her glasses, arching a skeptical eyebrow as her lips twisted into an amused smirk that told him there was no way in hell he was getting past her.

"Visiting hours start in ten minutes. Please wait over there." She motioned to the far wall and immediately went back to her book, though he felt as if she was somehow still closely watching him.

Smith made his way to a bench upholstered in a green naugahyde that had not been in fashion since the 1960s, and when he sat down, the stuffing spilling from the cracks in the covering was yellow and crumbly. He looked down at the small pile of old cushion and wrinkled his nose. The whole place smelled more like a wet basement than a hospital. Where were the scents of bleach and cleaners, of deliciously aromatic but deceptively bland hospital food?

He fidgeted while he waited for visiting hours to start, constantly checking his watch for the time. At last the nurse peeked up over the counter and motioned for him to approach.

"Who are you here to visit?" she asked.

"Lily."

"Last name?" The nurse gave him the same disapproving look over the rims of her glasses and he felt suddenly like a small boy in grade school trying to go home sick.

"I–I don't know," he confessed. "She's a goth, about this high?"

"Ahh, that one," said the nurse, nodding before saying, "She's not here."

"What? But you just said–"

"I *said* she isn't here. Visiting hours are over."

"Look, Ms.," Smith tried to appear nonchalant while he searched for a name tag, "Stella, I–"

Nurse Stella stood up from her chair and Smith fell back a step.

"Visiting hours. Are. Over. Are we going to have a problem, *sir*?"

"Lily Morgenstern," he blurted.

The nurse pursed her lips, pressing her fingertips onto the Formica counter as she glared at him. "You sure about that?"

"She recently got married; I forgot her last name," Smith said lamely.

Nurse Stella looked skeptical, but motioned toward the elevator bay. "Go on up. Fourth floor."

He started to leave when the nurse stopped him.

"Check in with the nurse up there. She'll help you find Lily. Otherwise you'll get lost, and believe me, no one wants to get lost up on Fourth."

"Okay, thanks."

"And no smoking."

"Okay." And then for reasons he couldn't quite fathom, he added, "Thank you."

"No problem. No wandering."

"Got it."

He hurried toward the elevator before she could give him any more rules to follow, positive that she would kick his ass if he broke one, even by accident. As the doors closed he could see the nurse pick up her desk phone and make a call. Judging from the surreptitious glance his way, he assumed she was talking about him. He strained to hear any of the conversation, but was unable to do so over the whining of the elevator mechanism. With a final hiss and clank, the doors closed and the car lurched upwards, leaving Smith's stomach on the ground floor.

As the car rose, he felt distinctly nervous and couldn't place his finger on why. He tried whistling to calm down, and then it came to him. There was no music in the elevator, just a disgruntled dinging announcing each floor and the growling sound of reluctant machinery. He watched the round numbers above the door light up with each floor and the journey seemed to take forever. Additionally unnerving was the presence of the number "13" as the top floor.

"So much for superstitions," he whispered.

At last the elevator ground to a stuttering halt on the fourth floor, and Smith had the brief but unsettling feeling the elevator would drop the second he tried to set foot on the other side of the doors, crushing him between elevator car and floor like a victim in a horror movie. As soon as the doors began to open he leapt through and almost into the arms of a short, purple-haired nurse.

"Oh, God, I'm so sorry, ma'am," he stammered.

This nurse was as intimidating as the one at the front desk, in spite of the wide grin she gave him. Instead of a white uniform, she wore colorful scrubs that matched her short, dark purple hair. They looked like Picasso and Jackson Pollock had collaborated on a clothing line for hospital staff. Smith couldn't explain why, but he liked her.

"Just call me Sarah, everyone does," she told him.

"Is that your name?"

"No."

"Then what is your name?" he asked, confused by this short, round enigma in modern art uniform.

"Susan."

He opened his mouth to reply and she laughed and shook her head at him.

"Don't worry about it. You're here to see Lily?"

"Yeah."

Sarah pushed a wheelchair up to him and motioned to it. "Sit down."

"OK," he said without questioning, suddenly wary as he did as she told him.

"Give me your arm."

He raised his left arm and she grabbed it in an iron grip. Before he could move she had pulled out a needle, uncapped it, and injected him with something.

"What the hell was that?" he shouted as he moved to get out of the chair.

Sarah smiled at him, and the amusement danced in her brown eyes. "I wouldn't try to get up if I were you. It'll make things harder for both of us."

"I don't unders…tand," Smith said, feeling as if he had floated off from his body. The sensation was wonderful. He fell back into the wheelchair and smiled up at the nurse. "Who are you?"

"I'm Lily's nurse. Now just stop fighting and go to sleep."

CHAPTER XIII

He could feel himself being pulled further and further away from all that he knew himself to be. He came crashing down to a cold stone floor with the force of a meteorite; he moaned as around him male voices spoke in a lulling sing-song rhythm. He pushed himself to a sitting position, his eyes trying to focus on the faces around him.

"Tell me your name, demon!"

Smith looked with confusion directly into the manic stare of his long-dead brother. Billy held aloft a dagger, reading from an ancient book he held open in one hand.

"I'm not a demon," he said and noted the madness in the younger man's eyes. He wondered if it had always been there and he had never noticed, or if Billy had gone insane after he died.

"I command you to tell me your name, demon!"

Anger flooded him and he felt more than just insulted. It was as if his younger sibling had figured out the one and only name he could call him that would drive him into a rage. He climbed to his feet, unsteady and still struggling to focus. His balance was thrown off by something heavy attached to his back and he swayed on his feet. He caught sight of white curves out of the corner of his eye and looked down at the chalk circle drawn around his position on the floor. He began to laugh at the cloaked figures gathered around him, at their hubris, and at their imminent and collective demise.

Billy was the first to die. Smith tore his younger brother to shreds, screaming in his own head to stop but unable or unwilling to comply. He went through the other men gathered in the room, then froze. He stared down at a man who he knew to be himself when his name had been Virgil Calahan, Jr., his glance then moving to the glint coming off the dagger clutched in one trembling hand. He watched Calahan move forward and caught the man in a tight embrace that left him cold as he felt the dagger slide under his ribs and into his heart. He felt the life and the divine spark fade, knowing he was dying and hating the men in the room for their part in his death. How dare they kill the Metatron?

Smith gasped and tried to sit up, but found the effort was too much and fell back. Instead of the overwhelming scent of candles and incense in a lushly appointed room, he smelled mold and dry rot. He took a deep breath to dispel the leftover rage and hatred that had followed him over into the waking world.

"Who are you and why are you here?"

Her voice came through in waves, hollow and far away as the words sank through the layers of medication. When he opened his eyes he saw one of the most beautiful women he had ever seen. She stared at him intently, the green-gold of her eyes flickering in the fluorescent lighting as her raven black hair fell forward in loose curls to frame her porcelain features.

"Are you the angel?" he asked groggily.

She hoisted him to his feet with very little effort and slapped his face lightly. "Who are you?"

"John Smith, private detective to the denizens of Heaven and Hell," he told her with a lopsided grin.

"No, really. Who *are* you?"

"Would you believe I'm the vessel for The Voice of God?" he tried.

She dropped him back to the floor and glanced out the window in the door, her eyes darting up and down the hallway. She turned at last from the door, and, running a hand through her hair, she knelt down next to him and started unbuckling the straps on his straightjacket.

"If you're lying, I'll kill you."

He gazed up into her perfect eyes and smiled again. "I'd like that."

She shook her head and let out a short, quiet laugh. "You're batshit, whoever you are. But you might also be the person who can help us."

"Us?"

"Me and Lily."

Smith struggled toward coherence. "I'm here looking for her. Is she here?"

"Just said that, I think, didn't I?" the woman said impatiently. "Why are you looking for her?"

"I think she's in trouble, and I'm here to save her," Smith said, cringing at how stupid he sounded but not able to censor his words before they came out. The drugs would see to it that he said many more stupid things before his case was through. The woman gave him a skeptical look and shook her head.

As if reading the question in his mind, she said,

"Lily went missing a while ago. We were supposed to meet up at the coffee shop one day, but she never made it. I haven't been able to get hold of her since, and I don't like it." She paused and dragged him behind her, pressing him flat to the wall as they moved along what appeared to be an abandoned corridor. "I like her whatever-the-hell-he-is-to-her even less. Calls himself her husband for chrissakes." She glanced back at him, her expression grave. "Between you and me, the guy gives me the chills, like if we didn't keep a close eye on him he'd happily hit the big red button and launch every nuke out there. End us all."

She peeked around a corner made blurry by crumbling paint and plaster dust then held a finger to her lips as she motioned with her head for him to follow her. Their footsteps crunched over fallen ceiling tiles and debris, and Smith wondered when this portion of the hospital had been entered last. They came to a locked door and she tapped lightly.

Her voice was barely above a whisper as she said, "Lily? Are you in there? It's Scylla."

Smith leaned against the wall and felt his heart lurch. Scylla. A beautiful name for a beautiful woman. In the back of his mind, Metatron laughed at him. He rolled his eyes inwardly.

She is not quite a woman, the angel told him.

"Then what is she?" Smith thought at The Voice of God.

More than human.

It was all the angel would tell him. He wished the angel had its own body so he could punch it in the face just once. He wondered at his strange desire of late to punch everyone and dismissed it. Metatron was the roommate who left dishes in the sink and made a mess all over the apartment, then had perfectly timed work schedules and meetings to get to on cleaning day. Behavior more than deserving of a punch to the face.

From behind the door came a sleepy response and Scylla looked back at Smith to confirm he had also heard it. She tapped again, leaning closer to the door.

"Lily? Is that you?"

"Scy? Yes, it's me," came the reply, more awake now.

"Hang on, we'll get the door open as soon as we can."

Scylla pulled out a keyring and began to test each key in the door's rusted lock.

"Where did you get the keys from?" Smith asked in awe.

Scylla smirked at him. "My father was a patient here one time. When my mother came to get him they took some souvenirs."

"Your father was a patient here?"

"Yeah," she paused and counted on one hand. "It was about twenty years ago."

"Why was he here?" Smith asked, dreading the answer.

She snorted and shook her head. "Some bullshit about him starting a war on humanity." She shoved a key into the lock, moved onto the next. "*He* didn't start it, though, it was just something humans said so they had someone to blame when they started killing each other."

"Oh."

When at last she had found the right one and opened the door, it creaked on its hinges so loudly

Smith was sure it would summon those badass nurses to toss them out. Even Scylla paused, listening to the echoing silence.

From beyond the door, Lily said, "I need a little help, please."

They entered the small, dingy room to find Lily wrapped in a straightjacket and propped on a cot in one corner. Scylla uttered a curse and ran to help her friend, tearing at the straps on the canvas.

"What the hell did they do to you?" she growled.

Lily smiled at her anger, eyes glassy. "I don't even know where I am or what's going on, Scy. Last thing I remember is heading out to meet up for coffee."

Scylla shook her head and pushed her hair out of her face as she unfastened the last of the buckles. Lily stretched her arms, an expression of ecstasy on her face. When she caught sight of Smith her smile widened.

"Howdy, stranger."

"Howdy yourself," he said, returning her grin.

"You guys really do know each other." Scylla shook her head in amused disbelief. "No time for chit-chat, though. We have to get out of here before my father realizes where I went. He'll blow a gasket."

A shadow crossed over Lily's face at the mention of Scylla's father and she said, "Will your mother be coming with him if he shows?"

Scylla appeared worried as she shook her head, and it made Smith's blood run cold. He looked to see the same concern mirrored in Lily's face.

"Damn. She'd have at least kept him in check."

Scylla nodded. "Yeah, I know. He gets a little nuts sometimes. He can't help himself. It's kind of his gig."

"Then let's get out of here while everyone's still alive. I don't want anyone getting hurt because of me."

Scylla's short laugh was humorless. "Shit. If only he stopped at 'hurt.'"

"Who the hell is this guy?" Smith asked with growing alarm.

"Scylla's father," Lily told him, "No need for names. Let's just get the hell out of here."

They got as far as the entrance to the abandoned wing when they were met by the nurse with the purple hair. She stood in the middle of the door and watched them as they approached, an amused glint in her eye.

Lily smiled and hugged the nurse to her when they reached her. Sarah returned the hug, the laughter in her eyes finally escaping from her lips.

"You should have seen the look on his face when I drugged him," she told Lily, still laughing.

Lily looked back at Smith and joined in laughing at him. "I can imagine."

"If you two are done?" the detective said, annoyed.

Nurse Sarah covered her mouth and pretended to try to suppress her mirth, but somehow it was as if she was laughing at him even more. She looked over at Scylla, who had also joined in the laughter, and said, "You're Scylla?"

She nodded.

"Your father wanted me to tell you he's here to make sure you get out okay."

"Where is he?" Scylla asked, her face growing impossibly pale. "And how the hell are you still alive?"

The nurse smirked at her worry and waved a hand. "I knew him when he stayed here the first time. He's not so bad. Not bad on the eyes, either." She was lost in thought, but bounced back quickly. "He's out in the hallway by the desk. I'll take you to him."

Scylla blushed, speechless as they followed the nurse out to the main desk area. Smith froze at the sight of the man.

To say Scylla's father was intimidating was an understatement in the way saying a plane crash can be dangerous. Smith looked nearly straight up at him. The man stood close to seven feet tall, and was powerfully built. He was dressed from head to toe in black, with long black hair and green eyes that mirrored those of his daughter's. Every detail of his bearing was that of a Greco-Roman statue, godlike, and full of wrath. Smith felt all desire for Scylla drain from him when her father turned his gaze toward him, meeting his eyes.

For a moment the detective was sure the man would sense his impure thoughts for his daughter and kill him on the spot. Instead, Scylla's father cocked his head at a slight angle and stared down at Smith in confusion.

"Do I know you?" he asked, and his voice rumbled like thunder in the distance in the empty hallway.

"Hello, Nemesis," said Metatron through Smith's mouth, *"It has been a very long time."*

The man called Nemesis seemed confused. "Refresh my memory; I'm afraid it's gotten a bit damaged over the millennia. Who are you and why are you with my daughter in an abandoned wing of a hospital?"

"Old god, do you not remember The Voice?"

Smith could only stare in horror, effectively paralyzed, as Nemesis approached. The man towered over him, his chalk-white skin luminously yellow beneath the glow of humming fluorescents.

"You are the Vessel of rumor, then?"

Smith's head nodded of its own accord.

Nemesis smiled down at him and said with a laugh, "I thought you'd be taller." And that was that. He turned to the others and said, "Let's get the hell out of this place. I stayed here once, and it was more than enough."

He hugged Sarah on his way out; the vision made almost comical by his extreme height and her lack of it. "It was good to see you again, Sarah," he said quietly and kissed her cheek. "You were always my favorite nurse."

She rolled her eyes at him. "At the rate you've been going, I'll have to start visiting you at your place just to say hello. Stay out of trouble."

As they exited the building, Smith pulled out his pack of cigarettes and lit one almost in one movement. He inhaled deeply, savoring the taste of smoke and freedom.

Nemesis visibly relaxed as the doors closed behind them and Scylla wrapped an arm around him, her head just reaching his chest. Clearly she had not inherited her father's height, and only some of his looks. He looked down at his daughter and squeezed her.

"Don't disappear like that again, Scylla," he told her as he leaned over and kissed the top of her head.

She pulled away and looked up at him. "Dad, I'm not a kid anymore."

His face became serious. "In our family, yes, you are. You'll be a kid for at least a hundred years, and you'll always be my little girl regardless of your age."

"I'll keep her safe," Lily volunteered, interrupting what looked like a parental speech about to commence.

Nemesis was skeptical. "Very kind words, Nazarene, but you have your hands full just keeping yourself out of trouble. If you don't mind, I'll protect my daughter."

"Fair enough." Lily shrugged to show there were no hard feelings.

"If you're all done saving me from myself," Scylla said, "where are we going now that we're out?"

"You're coming home," Nemesis told her.

"Like hell I am," she began and Lily placed a hand on her arm.

"Scy, I'll be okay. Cal and I need to go see some people and you'll be safer at home. Coming to find me wasn't the smartest thing you've ever done."

"But you're glad I did." Scylla's smile was filled with mischief.

"Yes, of course. Just be glad you guys got Nurse Sarah instead of one of the other ones, or you might both have ended up in there with me." Lily shook her head at her friend. "Then who'd save us? This guy?" She pointed to Smith, not without mirth, and he shrugged. Lily turned to smile at Scylla. "We really do have to get going now. It was good seeing you."

They said their goodbyes and Scylla followed Nemesis back into the city. She cast reluctant glances behind, knowing there was trouble ahead and clearly wishing she could be a part of it.

CHAPTER XIV

"Will she be okay?" Smith asked.

Lily smirked. "She'll be fine. She's being dramatic. She's got Nemesis wrapped around her finger. The most she'll get is a stern talking-to before he sends her on her merry way. She'll probably catch more actual hell from Lamia."

"Who is Lamia?"

"Her mother."

"Oh," was all Smith could say. Nemesis didn't seem like the type of man who would stop at words, but if Lily said in this case he was, Smith supposed had to trust her.

"I'm guessing since you're here to get me, that Koth figured out who the bad guy was?" she asked him without actually looking at him. Instead, her gaze was following Nemesis and Scylla into the distance.

"Yeah," Smith said, following her gaze. "At least I think he did."

"You *think*? He did send you here, right?"

Smith shifted uncomfortably. "Well, sort of. I asked him where you were and he slipped me this paper and–"

"And you took it upon yourself to head off without my saying so," Koth said from behind them.

"How bad is it?" Lily asked, whirling around to face the demon.

The case manager laughed as he came closer. "Not as bad as I just made it sound, I promise." He held his hands out at them. "That's not to say it's not bad, however. How about some coffee? I could really use some coffee. It was one hell of a night."

He opened a tear in front of them and they walked through and straight to the back booth at the place Smith had dubbed the Limbo Diner. Pazuzu and Marduk were already waiting for them, both demons looking particularly haggard. Deep scratches etched their faces in crisscross patterns and spatters of something akin to oxidized silver covered their clothes.

"Rough night?" Smith asked, only half joking. Now that the adrenaline and drugs had worn off, he felt drained.

"Yes," Pazuzu said quietly, wrapping his hands around a steaming cup of black coffee and shuddering.

"What's that stuff all over you?" the detective asked.

Marduk didn't look up from his own cup of coffee as he said, "The demon blood?"

"Yeah," Smith said. "Is Damian okay?"

The demons avoided their eyes as they slid into the booth and Lily stared at the demons, a frown curling the corners of her mouth. Marduk shifted farther down the seat with an impatient glance at her which he quickly dropped back to his coffee.

"You killed her?" Lily whispered.

Koth glared at the pair of demons with a look of amazement. "Do you guys play poker professionally?"

he asked, the sarcasm oozing from the words. "Jeez." He turned to Lily, his expression grave. "Before you get all judgey, we kind of had to. She wasn't going to stop until you were dead, and we both know that can't be allowed to happen. Not this time around."

Lily pressed her lips together and gave a single nod, clearly not liking the explanation. "Was she acting alone, or…?" She let the question hang in the air between them.

Koth folded his hands and dropped his head. "We took care of them all last night."

Tears rolled down Lily's cheeks and she placed a hand over Koth's. "I'm so sorry."

The case manager sniffed and clasped her hand in his. "Nothing to be sorry about. You didn't ask for this, and they knew what they were doing and what the consequences would be. Spilled milk, honey."

Smith cleared his throat. "I won't pretend I know a damned thing of what you're talking about," he said, "So you can explain it all to me after I've had some coffee."

He looked up toward the counter and hoped to see Cherry smiling at him, but instead found what appeared to be another nodding drug addict leaning on the counter. With a sigh he got to his feet and looked at the others. "Anyone else need anything while I'm up?"

Pazuzu and Marduk raised empty coffee mugs, and Koth gave a nod. Smith had to wave a hand in front of Lily's face before she snapped out of her thoughts and looked at him.

"Do you want anything while I'm up, Lily?" he asked her.

"Coffee's fine," she told him, her voice distracted and far away.

Inside Smith's head, Metatron was doing something that sounded like humming. The detective mentally poked the angel. *"What are you doing?"*

Communicating.

Smith sighed. *"Who with?"*

The Creator and the Nazarene. Please remain silent.

"Oh, like a conference call?" Smith asked. To his sarcasm, he got a curt nod from the angel, a dismissive one. He shook his head and decided to let it drop. He was too tired to drag answers out of Metatron, the lack of sleep from the previous night catching up with him at last.

He stepped behind the counter, nudging the junkie attendant out of his way as he did so, and reached for the carafe of coffee on the hot plate. He took three coffee mugs from beneath the counter and carried them and the carafe back to the table, setting them down on the scarred Formica. As he poured, he said, "So make with the details, Koth. What the hell's been going on?"

The case manager took his mug of coffee and glanced over at Lily. "I was hired to protect her."

She looked up at him, her reverie broken. "Who hired you?"

"Your husband," Koth said, and his cheeks reddened.

Lily's eyebrows shot up. "My husband?"

"That guy hired you, too?" Smith asked, annoyed. "What the hell?"

"It's complicated," the case manager went on, "He got wind of some demons who were looking to speed some things along in a certain direction instead of letting the cards fall where they would. He believed you both could work on it together and avoid the final battle entirely, so he hired me to get you out of the way for him–"

Lily stood. "Out of the–"

Koth pushed her genly down by the shoulder. "To keep you safe while we figured out who was trying to kill you. I had a hunch who it was, and I knew Cal here would get caught in the middle, so I gave him something to do in the meantime to keep him out of trouble."

Smith glared at the demon and shook his head. "So, to protect us you got her institutionalized and damn near got me killed again is what you did," he muttered into his coffee.

The demon smiled at him and went on, "What I didn't foresee is that your husband would miss you so soon, nor that he would hit up wonderboy here. He had given me pretty express orders not to tell him where you were, so I followed them," he told Lily. "It never occurred to me he'd hire a detective to try to find you. I guess he thought he had everything under control."

Lily let out an angry laugh. "Oh, that's what he though, is it? Just one problem: *I'm not married.*"

The demons stared at her in shock, their faces pale. Koth's mouth fell open, closed, opened again. They all turned as the door to the diner opened, sunlight streaming in, highlighting fire engine red hair and broad shoulders.

Luke Morgenstern, Jr. walked through to their table and Smith noticed for the first time that the diner was empty except for the junkie at the counter. His stomach fluttered with unease as the man approached.

Lily shook her head, one eyebrow raised. "Seriously?"

Luke grinned and nodded at her, planting a kiss on her cheek. "You can't blame a guy for trying," he said with a laugh.

He looked around the table, nodding to the demons, then held a hand out to Smith. "Hi, Luke Morgenstern, Jr. Nice to meet you."

"We've met," Smith said, confused.

An out of place frown flitted across Luke Morgenstern's face and he gave Smith a confused smile. "Afraid not. I've been out dealing with some serious BS for the last few months."

"No…. You came in to my office just a few days ago and hired me to find your wife."

The confused smile faded and Luke looked to Koth, questioning. Koth shrugged and nodded. Luke shook his head. "No, I had this guy here lock my wife in an insane asylum until I was sure she was safe."

"We are NOT married," Lily cut in, crossing her arms and glaring up at him.

"Semantics," Luke said.

Lily coughed in angry disbelief. "Are you kidding me? We are not and never will be married. I can't stand you!"

"You love me and you know it. I know I've loved you since the moment I saw you."

When he moved in close to kiss her, she slapped him. Hard. He stared at her, not quite surprised. "OK, I deserved that one."

"Hate to interrupt the love fest here, but if you aren't the Luke Morgenstern, Jr. who hired me to find

Lily, then who is?"

Koth cleared his throat and rubbed the bridge of his nose. "It was Damian's brother." As Luke opened his mouth to interrupt, the demon raised a hand. "He has been dealt with. Crowley, too."

Luke let out a low whistle. "Crowley? Damn, that's a shame. I really thought he was loyal."

"Yeah, not so much," Koth said. "The good news in this whole mess is it's been cleaned up and everything's right as rain."

Lily slammed her hands on the tabletop and glared around her. "Not quite." She looked at Luke and shook her head, so angry that words failed her. After an extended pause she turned to Smith. "Take me home, Cal."

Luke Morgenstern's face grew white with anger and his jaw clenched, but he said nothing. Lily grabbed the detective by the arm and dragged him out of the diner. When they reached the sidewalk she took out a pack of Djarum Blacks. Smith held out his lighter and she lit the end of the clove cigarette, breathing in deeply. The smoke permeated the air around her with a luxurious incense-like aroma and the detective sniffed ecstatically.

"You got an extra one?" he asked her and she held one, dangerously black cigarette out to him.

He placed the filter between his lips and decided he needed to quit smoking regular cigarettes. At the expression on his face, Lily smiled.

"Honey-dipped filters. Nice, right?"

He nodded and inhaled the heady incense of the cigarette as he lit it. It was official. He would buy a pack of clove cigarettes as soon as he found a shop that sold them.

"You know I have no idea where you live, right?" he asked.

She smiled up at him. "I live a little bit of everywhere. I just needed to get out of there before they had me sold off for a bushel of apples or something equally stupid." At the expression on his face she said, "I'm not married to him. He's just my boyfriend."

"None of my business," Smith told her, holding his hand up. It occurred to him when he looked at the buildings and landscape around them that he was high. The colors seemed brighter, richer somehow, and he felt light-headed. He touched the tip of his tongue and discovered it was numb. "What's in these cigarettes?"

"Tobacco, cloves. Probably a crap-ton of other things that will eat your lungs over time." She shrugged. "The usual."

They reached a staircase leading downward into the sidewalk and Lily stopped. There were no signs designating the stop, and the entryway was blocked by security gates.

"Can't get in there," Smith observed, inhaling his clove.

Lily snorted and looked back at him as she made her way down the stairs and through the bars. From the other side, she called back to him, "Come on, Cal. It's just an illusion."

He followed her and paused at the gates. With a chuckle she grabbed his arm and pulled him through. He felt the metal pass into and through him and he shuddered.

"Why are we here? Do you live here?"

"No, I don't."

She walked into the shadows and Smith had to jog to catch up with her. The only light filtered in from above through subway grates and he squinted to see in the darkness. Up ahead of him he could make out the occasional orange glow of Lily's cigarette, and he followed it farther into the darkness.

Deeper in, he could hear the muffled sound of voices echoing along the damp concrete and tile walls. They passed a sign that told him they had reached the 19th Street subway platform and the hair on the back of his neck prickled to attention. Dust and droppings coated everything, and the rumble of the subways could be heard all around them. The platform was lit in strobed shafts of light as a New Jersey PATH train rumbled past, and in the light from the windows Smith saw the source of the voices.

They were gathered much as he had seen them when last he had visited the station. There were new faces added to the group of dusty-looking individuals, and Smith's breath caught at the sight of red hair in the crowd.

Lily touched his arm. "You should go to her."

Smith felt a lump rising in his throat as he extinguished the clove cigarette. As the last tendrils of smoke rose into the dank air Cherry caught sight of him. He met her halfway across the platform, both of them panting when they embraced.

"Cal! Thank God I get to say goodbye before I go."

"Goodbye?" Smith asked, but in his gut and in his head he had known this day was coming for a long time.

Cherry nodded. "On to the next adventure, I guess.

Wherever that is."

Lily walked over to them and Smith felt a small flare of anger at her intrusion on a private moment. At least the humming in his head had stopped. Lily wrapped her arm around Cherry's waist and hugged her to her in a tight embrace.

"You've paid your debt, Cher. You get to pick where to go next."

"What if I choose to, you know, *go*? Then what? Where will I end up?"

Lily shrugged. "Up to you, hon. Wherever your heart takes you. I just wanted you to know Hell was off the table…unless you actually picked it as a place to go; some do."

Cherry wiped at tears as they fell and looked at Smith. He hung his head, already knowing wherever Cherry went, it wasn't going to be with him.

"I'm sorry, Cal. We never were exclusive, not even in the old days. But you knew that."

He nodded, unable and unwilling to speak lest his voice betray the emotions churning within him. He shoved his hands in his pockets and looked up into the emergency lighting.

"Maybe I'll see you around sometime," she tried, "If you're up for it?"

He cleared his throat. "Yeah, that'd be nice. For old time's sake."

"Right."

"How about we get out of here and say our goodbyes topside?" Lily asked, breaking the beginnings of an awkward moment. The lost souls of the station had begun to gather nearer to them, perhaps sensing someone was about to break free.

They left quickly and walked in silence until they reached the sidewalk above. Cherry looked at Smith and he thought she had never looked more beautiful than she did in the filtered industrialized sunlight of New York. He sighed and leaned toward her, planting a light kiss on her cheek as he hugged her.

"Be safe."

"You too, Cal. And just remember, with you and me, it's never really goodbye. Never was and never will be. Just 'see you later', okay?"

"Right."

He turned and walked away, straining not to turn around to see if Cherry was still there and looking at him. He didn't need to, he could feel her watching him. Lily caught up with him and slid a folded piece of paper into his hand.

"What's this?"

She smirked at him. "I have no idea. Scylla said to give it to you."

He tucked the paper into his pants pocket and sighed. One door closes, he thought wryly. Lily smiled up at him and hugged him to her in a tight embrace.

"I'm sure I'll see you again soon," she said, taking a clove cigarette out of the pack and sticking it between his lips. "Until later, Cal."

As he woke up the next morning, he could just hear the last notes of *Call Again, Mr. Calligan* echoing into his bedroom, the ghost of Crown Heliotrope lingering in the sheets, and the remnants of a dream he could no longer remember dissolving in the sunlight. He sighed as a tear escaped his eye and wiped at it impatiently.

"Good lord, man, you look like hell."

Smith lurched up and stared at the demon sitting on

the edge of his bed smoking his cigarettes and drinking his liquor. Anger replaced sadness and he snapped, "What part of 'don't come visiting without calling first' wasn't clear last time?"

Koth laughed. "Buddy, it's in my blood. Demon, remember? I live to torment." He threw Smith the pack of cigarettes and handed him a glass of Jack Daniel's. "Get up, Cal. You can't wallow in misery when you get dumped."

"How did you know about that?"

The demon arched an eyebrow at him. "Demons and angels love to gossip, and news travels fast. Especially when the Vessel gets dumped by the hottest and most competent waitress to ever grace the Diner."

Smith shook his head as he climbed to his feet and pulled on the pants he had worn the night before. A quick sniff told him they were okay for one more day, and since he was officially single again, he didn't have to worry about offending anyone when he got home. He tapped out a cigarette from his pack and frowned. A Djarum Black rolled in the palm of his hand, its heady aroma already permeating the air around him.

A thought struck him, and he reached into his pocket. Something crumpled beneath his fingers and he pulled out the folded piece of paper. His mouth fell open as he read the brief note written in handwriting that looked almost like spiderwebs in its delicate perfection. It said simply, "Call me. –Scylla" and listed her number.

Koth glanced over his shoulder and whistled. "You work fast, Cal. Is she pretty?"

"A little young…stunning, actually," Smith said, distracted.

The demonic case manager whistled. "So why haven't you called her already?"

"Her father is scary as hell."

"Who's her father?"

"Some guy named Nemesis."

Koth stepped back, then laughed at Smith. "Oh, shit. Good luck with that."

"That bad?" Smith asked, his heart sinking.

The demon placed a sympathetic hand on his shoulder, a wolfish grin spreading across his face. "Oh, no. He's far worse. But that's another story, and we've got work to do. Get dressed."

"What's the new case?" Smith asked as he pulled on his shirt and lit his cigarette.

"A couple hundred years ago about thirty monks went missing at Glastonbury Tor."

"Where's that?"

"England."

"Okay, so what? I'm not a time traveller, Koth, what am I supposed to do about it?"

"Nothing at all," replied the demon, taking a sip of his whiskey.

Smith downed his own drink and took a drag on his clove cigarette as he shrugged his shoulders. "Then what's the mystery? I'd imagine they're long dead by now. Not like I would even know where to start."

"That's the easy part. They all appeared in the 19th Street subway station last night.

"Mystery solved, then. What's the case?"

"The case, Cal, is to find out where the hell they've been all this time. None of them are talking, which is pretty odd for the dead."

Smith rubbed the bridge of his nose. "I'm going to

regret this, I know it." He pulled on his shoes and let out a heavy sigh. "Fine, I'll take the case, but first, I need coffee. A lot of it."

THE END

Also By Suzanne Madron

The Immortal War Series

Metatron Mysteries Books 1-3

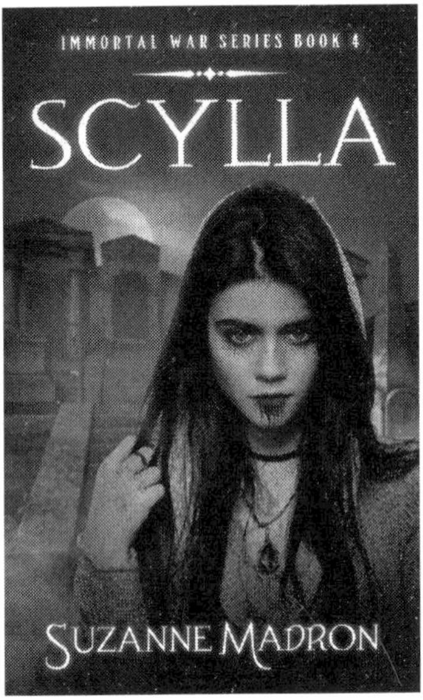
IMMORTAL WAR SERIES BOOK 4
SCYLLA
SUZANNE MADRON

About The Author

For news on upcoming releases please follow Suzanne at:
https://www.facebook.com/SuzanneMadron/

Suzanne Madron was born in New York City and has lived up and down the east coast. Currently she resides on a house built over a Civil War battlefield in the wilds of Pennsylvania where she has been known to host some interesting Halloween parties. She has authored several novels and stories under various names including Suzi M, James Glass, and Xircon

.

Suzanne Madron

ALSO BY DEVILDOG PRESS

www.devildogpress.com

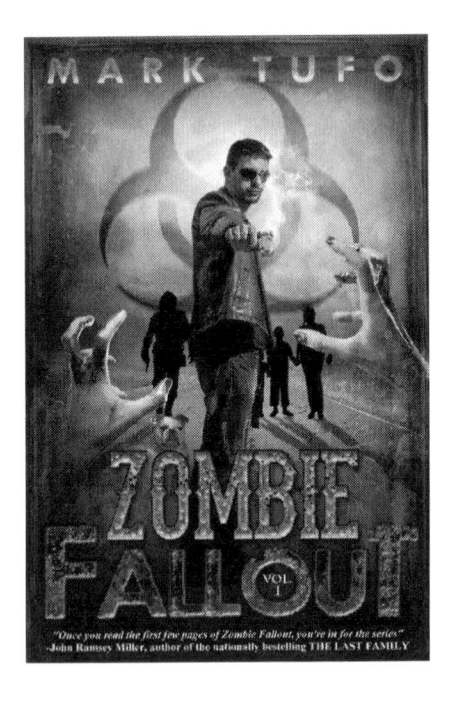

Zombie Fallout by Mark Tufo

Mossy Creek by Jill S. Behe

All That Remain by Travis Tufo

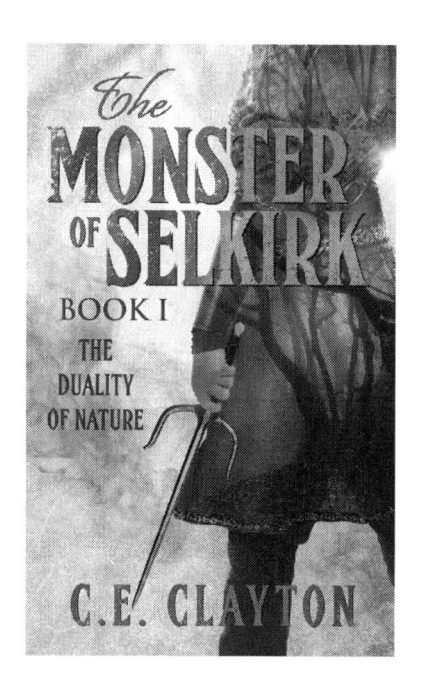

The Monster of Selkirk By C.E. Clayton

Prey: Blood of The Ancients By Tim Majka

Made in the USA
Middletown, DE
22 September 2023